RETURN TO MOONCREST INN

FAERIES OF DOOR COUNTY

TONI CABELL

PROLOGUE – THE PROBLEM WITH MOONCREST

JAKE

Monday, October 15

"There's nothing wrong with Mooncrest!" snaps Rick DeMaris as he follows me onto the hotel's wide front porch. The angry, white-haired, supernatural innkeeper doesn't bother glamouring away his pointy ears or tipped-up eyebrows, which is a violation of several township ordinances. But since he's already furious with me, I let it slide.

I hold up my clipboard as a chilly gust of wind rustles the trees, sending red and gold leaves spiraling down to the still-green lawn. "I'm sorry, Mr. DeMaris, but I have a ten-page checklist covered with *Xs* and notations that tells a different story. Mooncrest Inn is bad enough, but Mooncrest Chapel is one big fire hazard."

Rick snorts. "I don't give a faerie's wing feathers about your checklists! You're still wet behind your furry ears and have no business telling me how to run Mooncrest!"

I draw myself up to my full height, towering over the grouchy man. I don't appreciate his jab about my ears, which become furry only when I shift. "I'm the new fire chief, Mr. DeMaris. It's my job—and my duty—to inspect your property and ensure you're adhering to all the safety codes, which as we both know, you've been skirting for years."

"I always pay the fines," he huffs.

"That's not the point."

"It was good enough for the last fire chief, and the one before that. What makes you so special, huh?"

I rub the back of my neck, wondering how to get through to him. "Your last inspection was two years ago, and that chief cited many of the same violations. He allowed you to pay the fine with the understanding you would address his findings."

"I've been busy... and... and there's no way I can afford everything on that list."

"You can afford to replace expired extinguishers and remove extension cords."

"Yeah? Would I pass the next inspection if that's all I do?" he asks.

"It would be a good start, but you need to address *all* the safety violations. I'm especially concerned about the chapel."

Rick's face turns stony. "There's no way I'm remodeling that building."

It's clear this man has no intention of following through—again. "I'll be back in December for the reinspection," I announce stiffly. "And if you haven't attended to these issues by then, you'll leave me with no choice."

"What's that supposed to mean?"

"It means I'll shut you down." Stepping off the porch, I head toward my parked SUV.

"You can't do that," shouts Rick. "This is Mona Lisa's inheritance!"

Why did he have to bring up Mona? A stab of regret pierces through me at the mention of her name, my breath hitching at the sudden ache lodging in my chest.

How long has it been since she's been home for a visit? Two years? No, almost three.

I pivot back around to face the biggest grump in Riddle Hill. "Then please make the necessary repairs, Mr. DeMaris. It's not fair to saddle Mona with your mistakes."

I turn away, not bothering to see whether my words have the desired effect.

Probably not; Rick DeMaris is a stubborn old fool. There's only one person he's ever listened to, and she's about as far away from Riddle Hill—and me—as she can get.

CHAPTER 1
FUNDRAISER WITH FANGS

JAKE

Monday, December 31

"Tell me why we're doing this again? You know I hate wearing a suit, let alone a tux. I look like Paul Bunyan dressed for a penguin convention." I'm standing in the entrance to the Sage Mage Supper Club, grumbling to Rob Wolferman, who's talked me into something I'm regretting already.

Who wants to auction himself off to some unknown woman for a blind date on New Year's Eve? Even if it's for a good cause?

I turn my wool coat over to the curvy blonde vampire at the coat-check counter. She hands me her phone number along with the ticket for retrieving my coat later. I thank her with a smile, and she grins, showing me a bit of fang. Too bad she's not attending the *Bid on a Bachelor* fundraiser. My date for the night will probably be an old witch with bad breath.

"

"Stop complaining," says Rob, running a hand through his short, sand-colored hair. "You know why we're doing this." He ushers me into the lobby, where a huge statue of a knight clad in bright, silver armor sits on top of his shiny steed. The pair appear ready to charge out the door any minute, and I'd like nothing better than to follow right behind them.

I salute the knight. "Sir Reginald, you're looking spiffy tonight."

Accompanied by the clangs and squeals of ancient armor bending and twisting, the ghost of Sir Reginald slowly swivels and nods his helmeted head in my direction. I try not to wince at the metallic clanking as he returns to his original position.

Rob rolls his eyes at the noise and mutters. "Why do you have to do that every time?"

I shrug. "Because he's family." Sir Reginald is an ancestor on my birth father's side. "I figure he gets lonely, sitting up there all day and night."

Rob and I walk down the dimly lit passageway to the right, our dress shoes clacking against the polished stone floors. Black iron sconces cast a soft glow on the paneled walls and wooden doors as we pass. Laughter, soft music, and silverware clinking against dishes resound from the private rooms on either side of us. I hear something else too, the low purrs, hisses, growls, and giggles of supernaturals out for an evening of entertainment.

Too bad I can't wolf out a bit and let some fur fly. Instead, I'm heading for the auction block to support the Riddle Hill Senior Center. "Who came up with this hare-brained fundraiser anyway?"

Rob scratches his dark blond beard. "My mother."

Ouch. "Alright, I'll try to behave." Trixie Wolferman is the former alpha of our pack and the last woman I'd want to tussle with tonight.

My buddy sighs. "There's another reason we're here, even if you're not going to admit it."

"Don't want to talk about it," I grumble.

"That's fine," says Rob. "But I'm going to help you keep your New Year's resolution, whether you like it or not."

"It was a moment of weakness," I grunt.

"It was a near-death experience!" corrects Rob. And he's right. Rob claps his hand on my shoulder. "Come on, we're early. Let's go find a beer."

We descend the stairs to The Dungeon and head over to a massive teakwood bar with brushed-nickel foot rails. Rob snags us a pair of just-vacated stools covered in fake fur—real fur would be an insult to every shifter present—and orders us two Ghastly Ales.

"Looks like your mom's decorating committee has been working overtime," I say, waving my hand around the room. The bar's scarred plank tables are now draped in ivory linen and topped with antique candlesticks and foil-wrapped chocolate trolls, elves, bats, and wolves. The mounted monster heads hanging on the walls above us have mistletoe and faerie lights dangling from their horns, snouts, and ears.

Rob chuckles. "It's not exactly a Hallmark movie set, but it'll do."

I glance around at the pre-auction crowd; well over half the single ladies present are on the far side of sixty.

Grunting, I take a swig from my mug of ale. It's going to be a long, long night.

People continue filtering into the place until everyone, even those of us with supernatural hearing, have to shout to be understood. Rob taps my shoulder and yells into my ear, "Finally, some women our age." He nods in the direction of the stairs as several of our former schoolmates filter into the room. "Didn't you used to date Gracie Ryerson?"

I shake my head. "I wouldn't call taking her to senior prom 'dating.' Why?"

Rob shrugs. "Just wondering…"

I grin. "If you like Gracie, go say hi." We both know Gracie's ex, a gigantic, green-haired leprechaun, ran off last year to join the circus.

"Really?"

When I nod, Rob says, "Okay… come with me. You have to mingle, not just stand around growling under your breath. You're a regular alpha male wallflower."

I place my mug on the bar and snort, "That's an oxymoron." But I hop off the stool anyway.

We start wending our way over to Gracie when Rob gives a low whistle. "Mona Lisa DeMaris. I'm surprised to see *her* at a local charity event; she's the champagne-and-caviar type."

Mona is wearing a short, black dress, lacy stockings, and leather boots with four-inch spiky heels. Her lustrous, dark curls form loose tendrils around her face and tumble to her waist. I could detect her unique scent anywhere, even with my eyes closed. Sea breeze and citrus.

I stop in my tracks and swallow hard. "You go on without me." My shirt suddenly feels two sizes too small. I slip a finger inside my collar and give the black tie a quick tug, trying to loosen its stranglehold around my throat.

Rob glances my way. "You alright?"

"Yeah. I'll meet up with you in a bit."

Rob continues pushing through the crowd, and I barrel in the opposite direction. I slip down the narrow, darkened hall behind the bar area and dash into the men's room.

Leaning on one of the sinks, I stare at my reflection in the mirror. My forehead glistens with perspiration; beads of sweat are trickling down the sides of my face, and I'm huffing to catch my breath.

Confound it all! I'm having a panic attack at a fundraiser in the basement of a Wisconsin supper club.

I knew I'd be more susceptible tonight, and I even called my sister for some mutual moral support. At least Cassia's doing better managing her anxiety now that her faerie form has finally manifested.

I never struggled to access my werewolf form; I shifted for the first time when I was still a toddler. On the other hand, our supernatural parentage has nothing to do with our anxiety issues, which started twenty years ago this very night. I was twelve at the time, and my sister was nine.

Get a grip, Jake! I mutter into the mirror.

After splashing cold water on my face and beard, I dry off with some paper towels. A few guys come in, give me a head nod, take care of business, and leave again. I take some deep breaths and rake my hands through my thick, brown hair, which is unruly despite my best efforts to control it.

I can do this, I tell myself. Just because I never expected to see Mona here doesn't mean my heart has to strum triple-time. Besides, I spoke with her just last week at the inn, when she needed my help breaking up a fight between my sister's boyfriend and three goblins. We had a normal conversation; well, it was more of a crisis communication. I asked Mona to call security while I wrestled with the stupid goblins.

Mona's presence at this fundraiser tonight shouldn't be triggering me whatsoever. My schoolboy crush is nothing more than a memory now. We never actually dated, because I was a tongue-tied, pimply-faced teen, and Mona was... is... the most beautiful woman I've ever seen. When she returned home to help her dad after his accident two months ago, I figured I'd simply avoid her. I couldn't see the point in starting something when she'd be leaving again.

That's the thing about a mermaid; they never stick around for very long. Just ask Rick DeMaris. His heart was broken decades ago by Mona's mother, and he's been running Mooncrest Inn by himself ever since.

I toss the damp paper towels in the trash bin and head back to the crowd. It's easy to find Rob since his voice carries across the room. He gives me a friendly wave and turns back to ask Gracie a question. Maybe Rob will luck out, and Gracie will bid on him tonight.

Then I wonder whether Mona will bid on me but

immediately dismiss the notion. She's never shown any interest in me, except that one time. I blew it, and she's been distant ever since.

Malaki Acheron hops onto the dais at the opposite end of the room. He smooths down his silver-streaked, black hair and steps up to the mic, looking dapper in a designer tux that probably cost more than my monthly mortgage payment. He smiles and raises his beringed hands to quiet the room. Once he has everyone's attention, he speaks into the mic, his Transylvanian accent as thick as the fog rolling off the bay every spring.

"Velcome to dis first annual *Bid on a Bachelor*. I'm yer host, Malaki Acheron, of Malaki's Mens-vear on Main." He invites all the contestants to come up on the stage behind him.

I follow Rob onto the platform and sigh when I realize there are eighteen men who agreed to put themselves through this humiliating process, all in the name of charity. I just hope I'm among the first and can get this over with. But I quickly realize Malaki has other plans. He sends half of us—the younger half—to wait behind the heavy maroon curtain at the back of the dais. Then he kicks off the bidding process with Balthasar Grimm, a wiry, white-haired, eighty-year-old gnome.

The bidding goes surprisingly fast, and before long Malaki invites the rest of us onto the stage. He changes it up a bit, auctioning guys in random age-order until only Rob and I are left.

Malaki calls up Rob and starts the bidding at a hundred bucks. *Mona raises her hand.* I grit my teeth to stay quiet. Mona and Rob? No way. But then Gracie outbids her girlfriend, and I realize Mona's here to encourage Gracie. Another lady chimes in, and the bidding war continues until Gracie "wins" Rob for seven-hundred-eighty-two dollars, the highest amount yet.

Malaki gives me his flashiest grin, the one he uses when he wants to close a big sale. His upper fangs glint in the dim light cast by the iron chandeliers overhead. *Oh no!* I bite back a groan when I realize what Malaki's up to. Not only is my forehead glistening again, but my palms are sweaty, and my shirt is sticking to my back.

I can feel the moon's pull. It's nearly full, and I want nothing more than to shed my clothes, free my inner werewolf, and run for ten miles along the snow-covered shore. The last thing I need is my "uncle" Malaki—who's not my real uncle but has been interfering in my life for so long he may as well be family—setting me up tonight. But I know him well enough to see that's what the cagey vampire is up to.

"Last but not least, eez our final bachelor—he's also da mayor, da fire chief, an' da alpha of da Bay Howlers wolf pack. Talk about a treeple threat." Malaki softly chuckles, and then he shouts into the mic, "Give eet up for Mister Jake Grayclaw Spellman!"

The crowd breaks into loud applause, probably because they want this over with as much as I do. Malaki starts the bidding at three hundred dollars, which I think is steep.

But what do I know? Balthasar's ex-girlfriend raises her hand. She's quickly outbid by the newest member of our extended family, Tallulah Barker, who drank too much wine and then shifted in front of an unsuspecting human at my cousin Sophie's wedding. If Tallulah Barker winds up as my date tonight, I may never forgive Rob.

I moan under my breath as Malaki keeps raising the ante, and the two sixtyish women continue battling over me. I glance around the room, my eyes finally settling on Mona, who is biting her lower lip, probably to keep from laughing out loud. I send her a pleading look, but she giggles and tosses her head, obviously enjoying my total mortification.

She can't possibly still be holding a grudge, can she? I was a dumb teenager.

There's a small commotion near the stairs, and the blonde vampire from coat-check has joined the party. She raises her hand, outbidding the other two ladies. Balthasar's ex shakes her head; the stakes are too high for her. I'm rooting for the cute vampire to rescue me when someone bumps into her from behind. The blonde loses her balance and crashes into a server, who drops a tray of mostly empty glasses right next to Mona's chair.

Startled, Mona jumps up just as Malaki shouts, "Goin' once, goin' twice, sold to Mona Lisa DeMaris for one-thousand-one-hundred-twelve dollahs!"

Mona turns her large brown eyes on me. Her glossy red lips, shaped like Cupid's bow, are parted in surprise. I raise my shoulders in a half-shrug and grin at her. This night just might turn out alright after all.

Finally, after years of pining, and through absolutely no effort of my own, I'm on an actual date with Mona Lisa DeMaris.

But then Mona folds her arms across her chest,

purses her perfect lips, and glares—leaving little doubt I'm the last man in Riddle Hill she wants to see on New Year's Eve.

CHAPTER 2
BID ON A BACHELOR

MONA

Later, December 31

Jake Grayclaw Spellman is the last man I want to spend the evening with, but now I'm stuck with him until midnight.

He's heading my way, looking absurdly handsome... er, I mean determined... Yes, that's it. In fact, I think Jake might be so determined he's actually scowling, which isn't fair. He's not out eleven hundred dollars.

I can't deny Jake is remarkably good looking; he's tall even for a werewolf, with broad shoulders and a muscular build his black tux only accentuates. And though his dense beard is always well-trimmed, his attempts to regulate his thick, brown hair with gel generally fail. Rather than remaining firmly in place, a chunk of his hair has fallen forward, grazing his right eyebrow. I have a ridiculous urge to brush that errant lock back in place.

Jake is also unfailingly polite—even to my curmudgeonly father—and an overachiever to boot. How many guys do you know who can run a supernatural town, a werewolf pack, and a fire station? I'm still furious with Malaki for setting me up, but he was right when he called Jake a triple threat.

A weaker woman would find Jake's charms irresistible. But I'm not weak, and I already have a boyfriend. More or less.

Emilio and I agreed to take some time to sort out our feelings after our last argument. Although Em supported my decision to take a leave of absence when Dad got hurt, he doesn't believe I should be managing the inn for my father. Em figures I'm prolonging the inevitable and wants me to convince my father to sell the inn. But it's home, and Dad loves Mooncrest Inn, so how can I refuse to keep the place going for a couple months while he recovers?

"Is it safe for me to come any closer?" Jake asks with a sheepish grin. "You look angry enough to bite me."

"I am. But it's not you I want to bite, it's Malaki."

Jake shuffles his highly polished dress shoes. "I feel bad about this. At least let me pay the bid amount on your behalf."

"Why?" I huff. "Do you think I'm so hard up for cash I can't pay for my own bachelor?" Aargh! That came out all wrong.

Jake rolls his eyes. "Of course not. I'm just trying to be a gentleman here. I don't think it's fair for you to be saddled with the bill."

"It's for charity—" I wave my hand dismissively, like

I'm some wealthy princess instead of a hard-working cruise director on unpaid leave "—and I was planning to make a donation anyway. Let's forget it and go find a table."

"Fair enough." Jake guides me over to the last remaining table for two and pulls out my chair.

I hear him snuffling behind my neck and swivel around to ask, "Do you need a tissue? Or a cold tablet or antihistamine? I carry all the above... the perils of my trade."

Jake appears embarrassed but murmurs, "No thanks." I've spent a decade dealing with passengers who board ships with colds, flus, fungal infections, even pneumonia and bubonic plague. I can handle a few sniffles.

I take my seat, unfold the linen napkin, and drape it across my lap. I feel Jake's eyes on me, but when I glance up, he hastily drops his gaze and picks up the menus. Handing me one, he says, "Dover sole, beef tenderloin, or pasta primavera. I'm guessing even ten years of cruising hasn't changed your first love."

"My first love?" I ask, perhaps a bit too sharply.

Jake arches an eyebrow. "Pasta. Or more precisely, macaroni and cheese. That's all you ate, day in and day out, at school."

I shake my head, smiling. "I can't believe you remember that." I'm still a vegetarian, and for obvious reasons, fish of any kind will never cross these lips of mine.

"I remember quite a lot actually," he replies softly.

I feel the slightest stirring, deep down in the pit of

my stomach, and I force myself to ignore it. I'm going to keep things light and easy between us, even if it kills me. "To answer your question... I'll have the pasta primavera."

"I'm glad some things haven't changed." Jake chuckles, his amber eyes sparkling with humor.

I fiddle with my knife. "No, but plenty of other things have." My tone comes out snappier than I intend.

The server arrives to take our food and drink order. After he leaves, Jake asks, "How's your father doing?"

"Much better... thanks for asking." I'm grateful for the change of topic. "The physical therapy is helping; Dad's actually covering for me tonight. I've made him promise to hire someone to clean out the gutters next fall. I don't want him on those tall ladders anymore."

"Tell Rick to call me when he needs those gutters cleaned. If I can't find someone at the fire station to help him, I'll do it myself."

"Thank you, Jake." My eyes prick with gratitude. I decide to cut him some slack. After all, it's not Jake's fault I accidentally bid on him. Nor can I blame him for the weirdly mixed feelings I'm having right now in his presence.

"It's the least I can do, given the size of your donation tonight," he says, grinning.

"Yeah, well, speaking of donations, I heard the fire department raised a lot of money for the families left homeless in the recent fire. I suspect that was your idea."

Jake draws his brows together and murmurs, "We all agreed. Everyone really wanted to help. It... it was a rough fire."

The fire tore through a vintage apartment building a couple weeks before Christmas; four families lost everything. "But you managed to get everyone out—you should be proud of that!"

He clears his throat. "It was touch and go. Like I said, it was a very difficult fire... a tough day for all concerned."

Jake glances away and starts toying with the foil-wrapped chocolates on the table. He's clearly uncomfortable talking about it, which makes no sense. He's the fire chief, after all. He must have filled out all kinds of reports and answered all sorts of questions.

"What happened?" I'm surprised to discover I really want to know the answer.

"Why are you so curious?"

"Because you're acting all mysterious and moody—" I wave my hands in the air— "not at all like the old Jake. You know. Star quarterback. Homecoming King. Voted most likely to succeed—which you've achieved at the ripe old age of thirty-two."

"Yeah." Jake snorts. "So I guess it's all downhill from here, eh?"

I shake my head. "What's gotten into you?"

He runs a hand through his hair, forcing even more of it to topple onto his forehead, and sighs. "If you really must know... we almost lost two firefighters that day when the roof caved in."

"Oh, Jake, I'm sorry. I had no idea." I'm horrified that I've pushed him so hard to talk about something he'd clearly like to forget.

But then I get a sudden flash of insight, and I think I know why Jake is so reluctant to discuss it. This guy has a major hero complex; he's always the first to volunteer for anything that smacks of danger. "You were on that roof when it collapsed, weren't you?"

"Yep." He ducks his head in a sort of half nod.

I can't think of anything more to say, other than to murmur something inane, like I'm thankful he wasn't injured. But the truth is I'm flustered because *he could have died.* I can't imagine Riddle Hill without Jake Spellman, or vice versa. The two are practically synonymous. In fact, I don't think Jake's been gone from my hometown for longer than a weekend since he finished college.

The server delivers our drinks and salads. After he leaves, Jake swirls his wine around, finally taking a sip. Then he blurts out, "I guess you'll be heading back to your ship before long?"

I could swear Jake sounds *almost hopeful* that I'll be leaving town soon. He's even more aggravating at times than Emilio, and that's saying a lot. "I'm undecided."

"What's there to decide?"

I really don't want to talk about my current inertia, because I'm usually a take-charge kind of gal. You have to be in my line of work. The truth is I'm in a muddle about a lot of things, including Emilio, my dad's health, what to do about Mooncrest Inn, and my job, which I used to love.

My eyebrows pull downward as I struggle to keep the defensiveness out of my voice. "Why do you ask?"

Jake shrugs. "Just trying to understand, I guess. I always figured you'd found the perfect career."

"Because I inherited my mom's wanderlust and love of the sea?" I humph.

"Something like that." His voice is mild, like he's trying not to offend me.

I'm not even sure why his question riles me. Jake is only stating aloud what everyone else in this town has always believed. *She's a mermaid, and merfolk always leave in the end. Look at poor Rick DeMaris; he's stuck raising that wild merchild all by himself.*

I take a sip of my wine, a crisp Riesling, and blow out a puff of air. "My job's great, and in many ways, it has been the perfect career for me…"

"But?" Prompts Jake gently. He sounds as if he's actually interested in what I'm about to say, rather than merely making polite conversation.

"But I miss the company of other supernaturals," I say, tracing a pattern on the tablecloth as I try to explain. "The passengers and crew on my cruise line are nearly always human. They're great and all, but they can't understand what it's like to be different—really, really different. Sometimes I think that's why Em and I got so close. We're the only two officers who are also supers."

"At least you have one good friend you can rely on."

I snort. "Em's not particularly reliable."

Our main course arrives, and I ask Jake to catch me up on some of the highlights of the past few years. His mood improves somewhat as he tells a couple of humorous anecdotes about our wacky town. But I spot him tugging on his collar several times, like it's too tight, and his forehead is moist with perspiration. Something's definitely wrong, but he's buttoned up tighter than barnacles on a boat.

While we're waiting for dessert, Jake brings the

conversation back around to me. "Tell me about Em," he says. "What's she like?"

"Em is almost as tall as you, with an olive complexion, brown-black hair, and a beard to match." I notice a line forming between Jake's brows, so I add with a chuckle, "Em is short for Emilio."

"Emilio?" Jake sits back, picks up his water glass, and downs the contents. Then he grasps his wine glass by its skinny stem and twirls it before taking a few sips. "What's *he* like?"

"Em is the ship's captain, so we naturally work closely together. He's Spanish, speaks five languages, and is half merfolk, like me."

"He's your boyfriend, then," says Jake flatly. His amber eyes take on a golden hue, a reminder of the wolf within.

I scowl at Jake, irritated by his tone. "We've been dating on and off for the past few months." I refrain from telling him that Emilio and I are "off" at the moment, because it's none of his business. "What's it to you?"

"Nothing." Jake swirls his wine again before finishing it off. "Nothing at all."

I'm wondering how to lighten the mood when the server brings out two slices of red velvet cake with white frosting and rainbow sprinkles on top. My mouth starts to water, but Jake has turned deathly white. He's gripping his empty wine glass so hard the stem snaps in two, cutting his hand. Several drops of blood spill onto the tablecloth, and every vampire in the room swivels their heads to look at us. Even though they drink tart cherry juice to manage their cravings, it's still disconcerting to feel so many eyes on us.

"Jake—here let me get you a bandage!" I reach into my handbag, but Jake lurches to his feet, clutching the napkin to his hand.

"I'm so sorry Mona," Jake grunts. "I need some air."

"It's five degrees outside!"

But he just shakes his head, mouths, *I'm sorry*, and dashes up the stairs. I frown, debating my next move. I really, really want a bite of that cake, but Jake seems actually distressed. He may be a big boy, but right now, he needs someone to check up on him, and I guess that someone is me.

I grab my purse and race after him. When I reach the top of the stairs, I pause, trying to figure out which direction he took. Front lobby, probably. I hurry down the dark hall, past the statue of Sir Reggie, and spot the blonde vampire who checked my coat. "Did you see...?"

She nods and points outside. "He was in such a hurry he left without his coat." She sorts through all the outerwear in the closet, finally returning with Jake's coat and mine, which I quickly button up before dashing outside.

Using my loudest cruise-director voice, I shout, "Jake Spellman, where are you? I have your coat!"

I jog toward the woodsy area adjacent to the parking lot, because I sense Jake wants privacy, and that's where wolves head when they want to be alone—the forest. But I'm not leaving Jake until he gets his coat, and I'm sure he doesn't need medical care.

"Jake! It's freezing out here!" I stand near the edge of the woods, trying to gaze through the snow-laden branches. I'm not dressed for traipsing through the trees, and I won't be much better off than Jake if I stay outside much longer. I cup my hands and shout, "Jake—please answer me!"

"No need to holler," grumbles Jake, emerging from the shadows. His teeth are chattering, his arms are wrapped around himself, and he's still clutching the bloody napkin in his right hand.

I find myself feeling sorry for this great, big, hulking man, despite my earlier irritation. "Get over here, you oaf!" I say gruffly, holding open his coat for him.

Jake slips his arms into the sleeves, but his fingers are so cold he's fumbling with the buttons, so I help him. He apologizes, but I shush him and hurry him toward the restaurant. As we near the entrance, he resists.

"Can't. Go back," he says through frozen lips. "Going. Home." He pivots toward a row of cars and SUVs.

"Jake!" I yell. He gazes at me over his shoulder, but his body language tells me he's on the verge of sprinting. "Why are you ditching me?"

"Not. Ditching. You." Jake's voice is quivering; whether from the frigid temperatures or something else, I can't tell. As he turns and jogs to his SUV, I think I hear him whisper my name.

Why is the most successful man from my high-school class falling apart like this on New Year's Eve? And more to the point, why has he left me alone out here in the cold?

"Mona! What's going on?" Gracie is standing in the open doorway to the supper club. She beckons to me with one hand. Shivering inside my coat, I hurry back inside.

Rob is pacing around the statue of Sir Reggie atop his horse. "Where's Jake?"

"He just left."

"What? Why?" asks Gracie, her blue eyes round in sympathy. She's probably thinking the same thing I'm thinking.

What woman wants to be dumped on New Year's Eve by her hot date? Especially when she overpaid for said hot date in the first place?

"This is all my fault." Rob throws his hands in the air. "I was hoping to distract Jake tonight, but my plan has obviously backfired."

"Distract him from what?" I ask, wondering what I've missed since I've been gone.

But then Rob reminds me. "The car accident on New Year's Eve—"

"Oh no!" I murmur, bringing my hand to my mouth. Now I feel like such a heel, accusing Jake of ditching me when he's obviously in pain—the emotional kind that's the hardest to overcome. I know better than most what that's like.

"I remember it now," says Gracie softly. "Jake's mom and stepdad both died that night."

I sigh. "So I take it Jake doesn't like to go out on New Year's Eve?"

"He prefers to spend a quiet night at home. But he's not been this upset since we were kids," says Rob. He turns to Gracie. "Can I meet you back downstairs? I'm going to try calling Jake now. I doubt he'll answer, but I want to try."

"Of course, take your time," says Gracie.

I give my friend a quick hug, tell her to enjoy the rest of the evening, and slip back outside. The bitter temperature practically freezes the air in my lungs, so different from the balmy nights in the Mediterranean, when I walk the deck and stare out at sea.

I glance up. The moon is nearly full; perhaps a good run tomorrow night will help Jake feel better.

But why is he still struggling two decades after the accident?

And why, after all this time, do I still care?

CHAPTER 3
WORST DATE EVER

JAKE

Midnight, December 31

Confound it all! I barely manage to get behind the wheel and start my SUV when a fat tear rolls down my cheek into my beard. Then another one comes, and before long my vision is blurry. I sniffle, reverse out of my spot, and force myself to slow down. I drive at the speed limit rather than gunning the engine all the way home, which I'm raring to do.

I'm so frustrated and sorrowful I could howl. In fact, that's a very good idea. But it's cold, even for a wolf, and I don't want to run into anyone—super or non-super—so I pull into my garage and turn off the headlights. I sit in my vehicle, taking deep, calming breaths until the tears dry on my face, until the cold seeps into my bones, propelling me inside for warmth.

I don't bother turning on the lights; I can see just fine by the moonlight shining through the floor-to-ceiling windows that face the frozen bay. I slump down onto the floor and lean against the wall, still gripping the soiled napkin, grateful to be home.

But my small, snug cottage, built with my own two hands, offers me no comfort tonight. I left that behind when I bailed on Mona, who will probably never speak to me again. And who could blame her?

Mona, who's even more beautiful today than fifteen years ago, when nearly every boy at school crushed on the exotic mermaid with the sun-kissed complexion, long, dark, spiraling curls, and chocolate brown eyes.

Mona, whose heady scent leaves me feeling intoxicated, and whose red lips draw me like iron to a lodestone.

Mona, whose boyfriend speaks five languages and shares her love of travel and merfolk heritage.

Mona, who's been invading my sleep since the apartment fire.

That last thought stops me cold, because I don't know why I've been dreaming of Mona every night for the past two weeks.

And each time, it's the same dream.

We're sitting at a table across from each other. It's obvious we're on a date; we've finished dinner and are waiting for dessert. Mona is laughing about something, and I can sense—in my dream that is—that she wouldn't mind if I kissed her just then. So I reach across the table, bring my hands up to her halo of dark curls, and pull her face gently toward me. She smiles and leans closer. Our lips are nearly touching, when I hear sirens blasting, feel the scorch of hot flames, and suddenly I'm tumbling backward into an inferno.

As I'm falling toward my certain demise, I spot the dessert that's just been delivered to our table: two slices of red velvet cake, slathered with white icing and rainbow sprinkles.

Now I'm not the nervous, angsty type; I can't be in my line of work. But when that red cake showed up on the table in front of me, I panicked.

I'd been imagining myself reaching across the table toward Mona, who didn't appear nearly as accommodating in real life as she was in my dream state. Anyway, I sort of snapped—I definitely snapped the wine glass—and knew if I didn't get outside fast, I'd either confess my true feelings to Mona and beg for a kiss, or I'd shift on the spot, destroying my new tux and my reputation as a calm, cool alpha.

So I instead scarpered.

I never expected Mona to run after me in her spiky-heeled boots, clutching my coat, and hollering my name. While I'd like to think it was because she cares about me (as an old classmate, of course), I won't delude myself. Mona's training as a cruise director obviously kicked in when I bolted outside without either a jacket or reasonable explanation.

By the time I picked up Mona's scent in the parking lot, I could barely speak through my chattering teeth. She saw my helplessness and wordlessly buttoned up my coat. That simple, tender act nearly brought me to my knees, and I had no choice. I had to leave before I started blubbering in front of her.

I don't know what's happening to me, but whatever it is, I need to get myself sorted out before Trixie Wolferman gets a whiff. Not only is she alpha emeritus, she also represents the werewolf community on Riddle Hill's elder council. Trixie wouldn't hesitate to issue a call for challengers; her top priority is pack stability, regardless of the fact she still bakes killer brownies for my birthday.

My phone is vibrating again. Growling, I pull it from my pocket; three texts from Rob and a voicemail I don't bother listening to. Even Rob doesn't know about my dream, and I'm not about to confide in him now. Rob is my best friend and a firefighter like me. When he's not on duty, he's also the best supernatural realtor in the county. Most important of all, Rob is my pack beta, which means I trust him with my life. Even so, his inability to keep a secret is legendary. My buddy is a blabbermouth.

After I send Rob a quick text, letting him know I'm alright and to enjoy his evening, I decide it's time for me to figure out what's going on with these dreams and Mona.

Looks like I'm having breakfast in the morning at the Sit for a Spell Café. I need advice from the most powerful faerie in Riddle Hill—my aunt Phoebe.

CHAPTER 4
A HOWLING NEW YEAR

JAKE

TUESDAY, JANUARY 1

Every time I closed my eyes last night, I woke up in a cold sweat, my heart pounding in my chest. I kept dreaming of almost kissing Mona and tumbling backward into the inferno. About four in the morning, I finally gave up and ran on my treadmill for half an hour. Then I stood in the shower for a while, berating myself for behaving like such an idiot last night with Mona. Eventually I toweled off and pulled on my jeans and plaid flannel shirt.

It's still dark when I leave for the cafe; the place doesn't open for another forty minutes. I enter through the restaurant's back door, inhaling the scent of freshly baked bread and frying potatoes. Poking my head into the kitchen, filled with enough stainless-steel appliances to equip two restaurants, I say hello to my uncle. Nash's enormous, copper-colored wings are furled tightly

31

against his back as he cooks; otherwise he'd be knocking over pots or setting his feathers on fire.

My uncle is a big, burly, baldheaded Irish kitchen faerie, often referred to as a brownie, with a bushy beard he tucks into a hairnet while working. He's also the man who raised me after I lost my folks. Nash gives me a friendly nod. "Happy New Year! Phoebe's waiting for you."

Now how did my aunt and uncle know I'd be swinging by for a visit in the wee hours of the morning? That's faeries for you; they're practically mind readers.

I head out front to the dining area, half-expecting to see my sister, but Cassia and her daughter are in Nash-ville visiting her boyfriend's family. I'd be very surprised if she doesn't come home engaged—and this time to the right guy, even if he is a human rock star with goblin paparazzi trailing after him.

Meanwhile, Aunt Phoebe is attempting to train two of Nash's young cousins to be back-up servers. Vick and Wick have chin-length black hair and wide, blue eyes that make them seem perpetually dazed. I'm not surprised it takes two male kitchen faeries to do my sister's job. Cassia is pretty amazing.

All three faeries have their wings partially extended while they work, but once the cafe opens, everyone will use a glamour to mask their wings, tipped-up eyebrows, and pointy ears. Even though Riddle Hill is a supernat-ural community, we rely heavily on tourism from supers and non-supers alike. The fewer humans who know about us, the safer for all concerned. In fact, it's against the law to reveal ourselves without prior authorization from the elder council.

Vick, the taller of the two, is attempting to get the coffee started behind the counter, but it looks like he's botched it, because Phoebe is shaking her head. Wick is dusting the paintings on the walls. Inside each picture frame resides one of our ancestors, all of whom are just waking up. Most are cheerful when they rise; they smile and give a little wave. But a few, like Captain Killian, grumble at being disturbed. He shakes his hook in the air and huffs.

I glance under the long, stone countertop that runs along the back wall. Five gargoyles, one per corbel, wrinkle their large noses as if they don't like the way I smell. Some nerve; I huff like Captain Killian and look away. Even the smallest encouragement gets them overly excited, which inevitably leads to trouble.

Phoebe spots me and smiles. "Jake! I've been expecting you. Go on and grab a seat. I'll get us some coffee." She pauses and cocks her head. "And you're going to need the daily special. I'll tell Nash to get it started."

My aunt is a special class of faerie known as a gate-keeper, which is the most powerful kind anywhere. Phoebe's magic includes the ability to suss out what food and beverages will help each of her customers feel better. She's also pretty fierce when riled up, which is how those five gargoyles wound up here, supporting her counter-top. No one knows exactly what they did to earn a hundred years of servitude, but it must've been pretty bad, because my aunt is scrupulously fair.

I grab one of the booths in the front of the cafe so I can look out the picture window as the sun comes up. It's funny, but I never tire of the view of Main Street, with the Rhyme 'N Riddle Bakeshop across the street, Malaki's Menswear two doors down, and the fire station a couple blocks away. I love this town, and the supers who live here... even the grumpy ones like Mona's father.

Phoebe hands me a steaming mug of coffee and sits down across from me. "You look terrible."

"Wow. So much for hello and happy New Year," I grunt, inhaling the rich java aroma before taking a swallow.

My aunt flaps her hand. "I heard about your unfortunate date with Mona from Trixie Wolferman. She texted me last night."

I roll my eyes. Of course Rob would've told his mother about my dramatic departure, along with a lot of conjecture and speculation as to the reasons why. I'll have to be extra careful around Trixie for the time being.

"It wasn't Mona's fault," I mumble. "It just wasn't a good night for me... too many bad memories."

Phoebe's gray eyes soften. "Yes, I know." She reaches across the table and squeezes my arm. "Twenty years can seem like yesterday when you've suffered a loss... and then there was that awful fire a few weeks ago. You're not alone in this, Jake. You don't need to keep it all bottled up inside."

I sniff and look away. My aunt waits patiently, even though I know she's a very busy woman, with a business to run and two incompetent faeries to manage in my sister's absence. Slowly, haltingly, I tell her about my recurring dream and my disastrous date with Mona.

Phoebe shakes her head. "Well that's a truly weird set of coincidences, isn't it?" Then my aunt pins me with a hard stare. "But I get the sense there's more. If you're looking for my insights, I can't help if you're not completely transparent with me."

I swallow some more coffee and nod. It's time to tell Phoebe about my deepest fear of all. "When that roof caved in, I didn't see my life pass before my eyes like you hear about."

Phoebe tilts her head, her auburn bob swaying slightly. "What did you see?"

"I saw what could've been... what should've been... but wasn't, because I never bothered to try."

"Go on."

I take a deep breath and exhale slowly. "I realized there's no one at home to mourn me—" my aunt is pursing her lips and frowning now, so I hastily add "—of course I know you, Nash, and our family would miss me, but I have no one else in my life."

Pausing, I search for the right words. "What I'm trying to say in my clumsy way is that I want to leave something meaningful behind when it's my time to go... I guess you'd call it a legacy of sorts... In other words, I'm finally ready to settle down with the right woman and start a family of my own."

Phoebe arches her reddish-brown, faerie eyebrows. "Then perhaps you ought to start dating someone you might actually want a relationship with, instead of your usual bimbos."

"Whoa. You're not pulling any punches today, are you?"

Worry lines mar my aunt's brow. "Not when my beloved nephew tells me about his near-death experience." Then she adds more softly, "So what are you going to do about Mona?"

I sit up straight. "What do you mean?"

"Oh please. We both know how much you liked Mona when you were too young to do anything about it... and I think, if your dream is any indicator, you still like her. Why don't you apologize and then ask her out on a real date?"

I shake my head. "Mona has a boyfriend."

"She does, eh?" Phoebe scratches her chin. "That's funny, because in the two months since Mona's been home, I don't recall her mentioning his name once to me, and she's in here two or three times a week."

"His name's Emilio, and he's the ship's captain."

"Hmm. Did she actually say Emilio is her 'boyfriend,' or did you make an assumption?"

"Well of course..." I start to reply, but then I rewind the conversation we had in my head and realize Phoebe is right. Maybe Emilio is more of a friend than a love interest. "Mona said they'd been seeing each other on and off."

"There, see what I mean? That's her way of telling you she's open to the possibility of dating you."

"Huh? How do you figure that?"

My aunt chuckles. "Trust me on this."

"But what's the point?" I grumble. "Mona's only in

town until Rick recovers and can manage the inn on his own, and then she'll be leaving again."

"For such an accomplished man, you really are hopeless sometimes." Phoebe shakes her head at me. "So what if Mona is leaving again? She won't be gone forever. If you like her... and she likes you... things have a way of working out."

I sigh and run a hand through my hair. "First things first. I can't even think about asking Mona out until I apologize for ruining her evening."

"That's true. What do you have in mind?"

I shrug. "I figured I'd send her a text message and say I'm sorry about last night."

"No," says Phoebe firmly. "That's totally unromantic."

"Who said anything about romance? This is an apology we're talking about!"

Phoebe folds her arms across her chest just as Vick drops off my breakfast. "If you want to date a woman like Mona, you're going to have to do a whole lot better than a text message." She drums her fingers on the table while I tuck into my western omelet, filled with bits of country ham, little green onions, diced tomatoes, and three kinds of cheese. Nash piled on a double helping of hash browns, deep-fried the way I like it.

Phoebe snaps her fingers. "Mona started the Jane Austen Book Club when she was in high school; I remember because Cassia and Sophie joined their freshman year, when you and Mona were seniors."

I stop eating long enough to ask, "What's that got to do with saying I'm sorry?"

"You need to write Mona an old-fashioned letter of apology, like Darcy composed for Elizabeth."

"What?" I have no idea what my aunt is talking about.

"Read *Pride and Prejudice*, it'll give you an idea."

"Can I watch the movie, instead?"

"Yes, if you're talking about the BBC miniseries starring Colin Firth and Jennifer Ehle."

"A miniseries!" I grunt. "How long will that take?"

"About as long as reading the book."

"Fine." I throw my hands in the air. "I'm off today... I'll do one or the other, read the book or watch the series." I finish my breakfast, feeling marginally better that I have a plan for my apology. I'm still not sure I have the nerve to ask Mona out, but I figure that can wait until I see how she reacts to this letter I need to write.

As I'm zipping up my parka, Phoebe says, "Aren't you watering Cassia's plants while she's out of town?"

Nodding, I say, "I'm heading there now."

"Then you can borrow *Pride and Prejudice* from her. She owns both the book and the miniseries."

"I just hope none of the guys at the fire station find out about this," I grumble.

I'M BACK at the cottage after watering Cassia's plants and picking up the BBC miniseries. I pocket my keys and step into my all-white, soaring great room. The sun is shining through the skylights overhead; at night I can count the stars and watch the moon as it rises. A wall of floor-to-ceiling windows faces the frosty, frozen bay on my left, with a galley kitchen and quarter-sawn oak table across the room on my right.

Straight ahead are a navy, *U*-shaped sofa, smart TV mounted above the wood-burning fireplace, and a couple of side tables with lamps. Since I sometimes entertain non-supers here, in my official capacity as mayor of Riddle Hill, there's nothing that would indicate my werewolf heritage. However, I've had a few people ask about my extensive collection of Native American paintings and sculptures, all of which depict wolves.

I sprawl on the sofa, a bowl of popcorn on the low table in front of me, and start the show. I take an immediate dislike to that arrogant twerp, Darcy, until I learn he lost his parents at an early age and has been on his own for quite some time. Turns out he's actually a standup guy with a lot on his plate. He even looks out for his younger sister, protecting her from Wickham, who unfortunately reminds me of my sister's ex.

When Darcy proposes to Lizzie Bennet, it's pretty obvious he's gotten ahead of his own paws. After all, he insulted her looks when they first met, and then he interfered in her sister's love life. Lizzie's also been taken in by Wickham's lies, but Darcy has mostly himself to blame for the initial damage to his reputation. Lizzie can't see past the tarnished image to the real man beneath.

Somehow, I've become totally vested in the outcome, and I think I can see why Aunt Phoebe recommended this story. Darcy spends a sleepless night brooding over loving and losing Lizzie, and then he sits down to write a letter. I can't imagine using one of those quills, but he manages to scratch out several long pages.

Now here's the part that really gets me. *Darcy hand delivers his letter of apology to the woman who just rejected him.* Wow. That takes gumption. I rewind that scene and watch it again. I figure if Mona likes this story, maybe I can pick up some pointers from Darcy.

It's dusk by the time I finish watching the show. I flip on the lights, pick up the empty popcorn bowl, and carry it to the kitchen sink. The full moon will be rising soon, and I'm getting pretty antsy. While I can control my shifting to a point, I'll be one hundred percent werewolf in a few more hours. That gives me very little time to compose my letter and deliver it to Mona.

I reheat a pot of leftover stew while I go in search of pen and paper. While I'm eating, I jot down a few notes about what I want to say to Mona. Some of my phrasing sounds a bit old-fashioned, but I figure that's the point, isn't it?

After dinner, I spread out my notes and start writing… and rewriting… and rewriting some more. Aargh! What a mess! I have six pages of rambling hogwash. Growling low in my throat, I start over again.

It's after nine by the time I'm reasonably satisfied, stuff my letter into an envelope, and address it to "Mona Lisa DeMaris." I'm starting to itch all over; it's going to be a struggle to keep my wolf inside for another half hour.

I race around my bedroom, yipping as I stub a toe on my dresser, and hastily change into loose-fitting sweats.

Grabbing my keys, I dash out to my SUV, Mona's apology in my hand. I stuff my wallet in my glove compartment and lock it for safekeeping; once I shift, I won't be driving anywhere until dawn.

I roll down the windows as I drive, letting the cold air slap me in the face while I focus on maintaining my human form. As I grip the steering wheel, patches of sleek, gray fur break out on the backs of my hands.

"No-o!" I yowl. "Not yet!"

I'm really straining to remain human, and I'm starting to wonder whether driving to Mona's in my current state is such a good idea. But I don't want to let any more time pass before I apologize. Now I'm second-guessing the whole letter-writing idea; if I'd just texted her my apology like I'd planned, I wouldn't be fighting against my inner werewolf right now.

I throw my Suburban into park and grab Mona's letter, tearing it slightly with my sharp claws. "No!" I yelp, smoothing the envelope against my thigh.

I concentrate on maintaining my human form, my claws reforming into fingernails once more. I glance in the mirror and shriek in horror, like little Red Riding Hood when she pulls back the covers on Grandma.

A set of long, razor-sharp incisors gleam where my front teeth used to be, and my large tail has formed a lump beneath my butt. Soon my face will morph into a furry snout, followed by my forearms, torso, and legs.

"Five more minutes, that's all I need!" I shout at my alternate self. My incisors recede, but I can feel the wolf hovering just beneath my skin.

I hide my keys under the front mat and race over to the private apartment Mona shares with her dad, which is tucked at the back of Mooncrest Inn. The large, rambling white inn glistens in the moonlight as I dash around to the rear.

I pound on the door, probably with more force than necessary, but I'm getting desperate. When I hear footsteps approaching, I bound down the steps and pace in front of the stoop. Suddenly Mona is standing in the spill of light from the open doorway. She brushes back one long, curly lock and glances around. Why can't she see me? I'm standing right under her nose.

"Mona," I start to say, but it sounds more like a bark.

Holy conflagration, I'm shifting—in front of Mona!

I never lose track of who I am, but sometimes I wish I could, like right now. It hurts more than usual because I've resisted for so long, and I throw back my head, howling at the moon.

"Jake..." whispers Mona shakily. "Are you okay?"

I hear my sweatshirt tearing as my chest and forearms expand. I know my pants are next, and I definitely don't want Mona to see that spectacle. I'm clutching the letter in my right paw, but now it's wrinkled and two edges are torn.

"Am. Ok-ay." Scurrying forward to drop the letter at Mona's feet, I yip, "Do. Me. Honor?"

That's the best Darcy impression I can muster now that I'm shifting. At least Mona appears to understand me. But when she bends down to retrieve the crumpled envelope, the sound of fabric ripping apart pierces the cold night air.

My pants are hanging by a thread!

Whimpering, I turn and flee toward the beach, my furry gray tail swishing in the wind as I run.

CHAPTER 5
IF DARCY WERE A WEREWOLF

MONA

Almost Midnight, January 1

I thought Jake's behavior last night was strange, but tonight? I can't figure him out. Of course I know he's a werewolf, and his body *has* to respond to the pull of the moon. But what prompted Jake to compose and deliver a formal apology and then shift right in front of me?

And when his pants ripped... well, I looked away.

Naturally I'm curious, but it just didn't seem right to stare.

And then there's the letter itself, which I had to carefully withdraw from the envelope so it wouldn't tear any further. The ink is smudged in a number of places, and there's a bit of food, beef stew I think, stuck to the last page.

But when I get past all that... Jake's apology is really very sweet, if a bit old fashioned. It's almost as if he spent the day immersed in Jane Austen and then composed this letter, which I know sounds silly.

Dear Mona,

I doubt it's possible for me to fully express how sorry I am about my rude behavior last night. Let me begin by saying the fault is all mine. You were charming and lovely and tried to make the best of an awkward situation.

On the other hand, I was anxious and jittery and impossible. The reasons are several, which I will share now—not because I'm seeking your sympathy but because you deserve a rational explanation.

I don't expect you to recall this, but yesterday was the twentieth anniversary of my parents' accident, which weighed heavily on my mind. Another drag on my spirits was the apartment fire several weeks ago, when the roof collapsed with me and another firefighter nearly going down with it. I have suffered recurring nightmares since then, which only added to my edginess last night.

It was for these reasons that I almost turned down Rob's invitation to the fundraiser, but he is a very convincing salesman and good friend. And although you were a reluctant participant in the auction, getting to spend time with you was a singular highlight for me.

I know you won't like what I'm about to reveal (I believe you are scowling as you read this), but I covered your bid with Malaki. He will be voiding your check for the fundraiser. There... I'm sure you're angry with me, but I could not, in good conscience, allow you to pay for a bachelor who bolted before the first dance!

At the risk of repeating myself, I'll say again how sorry I am about all of this, especially missing out on that dance, which seems to be a pattern with us.

How so? You may ask. Let me explain.

I have always deeply regretted not being able to accept your invitation to the turnabout dance our senior year. However, I had just agreed to accompany Katie Wolferman, Rob's sister. I didn't feel it was appropriate to renege on my word, despite my strong desire to attend the dance with you. In fact, I was so frustrated after I turned you down that I punched a hole in the drywall in the boy's locker room. My uncle paid to repair the damage, and I spent several months cleaning pots and pans in Nash's kitchen to compensate him.

Since I'm on the topic of regrets, let me set the record straight on one other point. I always intended to ask you to senior prom. But every time I tried speaking with you after the turnabout dance debacle, you walked away. Finally, in a fit of pique, I asked your best friend instead.

I'm truly sorry about using Gracie to get at you, but there you have it. My only excuse is that I was seventeen. I hope you can forgive me (and perhaps not mention this to Gracie?).

I'll stop now, as the hour is late, the moon is full, and I want to deliver this before I lose my nerve.

Your friend,

Jake Grayclaw Spellman

Wow… just wow!

Hands down, this is the best apology ever.

Emilio could learn a thing or two from Jake, who said I was "charming and lovely," and that spending time with me was a "singular highlight."

Jake has never struck me as the romantic type. But for a werewolf alpha who's never shown the least inclination to read or write flowery prose, this letter is proof he has a soul after all. Only a hard-hearted merwitch wouldn't feel some sympathy for the guy after reading it.

I still don't understand why Jake got so twitchy and scarpered during dessert, but at least I have a better idea of what was going through his head. Even more surprising are Jake's revelations about our senior year. I had no idea he wanted to ask me to prom... or that he punched a hole in the boys locker room over that turnabout dance.

After all this time, it's almost as if Jake is trying to tell me he likes me. Or at least that he used to like me when we were kids. Too bad he didn't tell me this fifteen years ago, when it really mattered. My teenaged self would have benefited from a boost of self-esteem.

I don't know what to think or how to react the next time I see Jake.

One thing's for sure... try as I might, I can no longer ignore him... or the way my stomach knots up every time he draws near.

CHAPTER 6

THE FIRE CHIEF

MONA

Thursday, January 3

"That inspector should be here in a few minutes. Do you mind dealing with him?" asks my dad. He's manning the front desk in our Victorian-style lobby, which has a dramatically curved staircase, massive wood-burning fireplace, and white marble flooring.

The only outward evidence we're a supernatural inn are the elves on staff, who do a marvelous job of appearing human to our non-super guests, and the painting above the fireplace of a plump, white-haired woman, fashionably garbed in nineteenth century attire. Auntie Imogen, who was Queen Victoria's faerie godmother and my dad's great aunt, nods regally and flutters her silvery-white wings whenever a super walks past. Otherwise she stares down disdainfully at our non-super guests, wrinkling her nose behind their backs.

Apparently Auntie Imogen still holds a grudge for what happened in Salem.

It's after eleven and blissfully quiet at the moment, since every guest leaving today has already checked out. However, Dad is "busy" reading a romance novel, a new habit he picked up while in the hospital.

I find it kind of cute, and perhaps a bit sad, because I know he still misses my mother.

"Is the inspector a super or non-super?" I assume this is a food safety inspection, which means the inspector could be from the Wisconsin Department of Agriculture, Trade, and Consumer Protection, or the International Food, Potions, Magic, and Monsters Authority. Since we serve both populations at our inn, we're subject to both sets of regulations.

"He's a super."

"But they inspected the kitchen last month, and we passed."

My father puts down the novel long enough to peer at me over his reading glasses. "It's that jock who broke your heart in high school. You know, the fire chief slash mayor."

My mouth drops open. "Jake Spellman is going to be here in a few minutes, and you're just telling me *now*?"

The inn is more short-staffed than usual due to the holiday, which means I've been doing laundry, changing beds, and cleaning bathrooms since six this morning. I'm wearing faded jeans, a tatty flannel shirt, and zero makeup. I tried corralling my wild hair beneath a red paisley bandanna, but my curls refuse to be constrained. I look like Medusa of the Midwest.

"Yeah, what's the big deal?" says my oblivious father. "Technically, it's a reinspection."

"*A reinspection*? That means some things needed to be fixed... but I don't remember talking about it. Unless you've already taken care of things?" That last part is wishful thinking, because I know Dad's been struggling—financially and physically—with the inn's upkeep.

"I've been kinda busy," Dad huffs. "Besides, there wasn't anything dangerous, just the usual picky items."

"Such as?" I prompt.

"He doesn't like extension cords, for one thing. How can you operate an inn anymore without 'em? Our guests carry so many electronics these days—laptops, tablets, phones, smartwatches—and they all need to be charged."

"Oh Dad," I groan, knowing full well this is a definite code violation. We never, ever use extension cords in the cabins onboard our ships, for the same reason. Now I'm mad at myself; I should've noticed them and done something sooner. But ever since Dad's injury, I've been running around like a madwoman just trying to keep the inn afloat.

"Hello?" calls a deep, male voice from somewhere behind me. I didn't hear him come in, the sneaky werewolf.

I stiffen slightly, push back the twirly curls that escaped from my scarf, and turn around to face Jake. He's in uniform: white button-down shirt, black tie, navy pants, tactical-style jacket with his name badge and gold bars showing his rank, and a navy ball cap with the department's insignia on it.

Jake gives me a businesslike nod, like he's trying to convey he's here in his official capacity, unlike the other night. But his amber eyes are sparkling with humor, probably because I'm dressed like a resale shop runaway.

On the other hand, Jake is so smoking hot he could start a fire.

I start to fan myself, realize what I'm doing a moment too late, and wave my hand nonchalantly in the air.

"Chief Spellman," my voice squeaks, so I clear my throat. "Could we... perhaps... reschedule this inspection?"

Jake purses his lips, drawing his brows downward. "I'm afraid not, Miss DeMaris. This reinspection is already overdue, given your father's injury and then the holidays."

"Just one more week, Chief Spellman, that's all I'm asking."

"Unfortunately, I'm not able to bend the rules any further, even for you, Miss DeMaris." Jake manages to sound apologetic, but now I'm scowling.

What does he mean by that last part, *even for you, Miss DeMaris*? It's not like we're dating or anything. Well, technically, we had half a date. But I'm beginning to fume, nonetheless. If only he didn't *look so danged good*, just standing here, waiting for my reply.

"Fine," I toss my head, which makes a spiral of hair topple into my eyes. I push my curly lock back from my face. "Where would you like to begin?"

"Let's use the checklist and tick off the items as we

go." He's holding a clipboard and looking at me expectantly, as if I should know what he's talking about.

"Um… I seem to have misplaced my copy of the checklist."

"No problem. I always bring extras." Jake hands me a document covered with *Xs* and notations, front and back.

I quickly scan it, my heart sinking fast. It's worse than I thought, and everything noted appears to be a legitimate concern. Despite my dad's protests, there's nothing "picky" listed here.

Jake must notice I'm growing more anxious by the minute, because he says, "Look, let's do a walkthrough together, and I'll make some suggestions as we go. Why don't we start with one of the guest rooms?"

"Fine," I mumble, leading him up two flights of stairs to the largest guest room. The honeymoon suite has a king-sized bed, pink floral wallpaper, and fluffy, red and pink heart pillows scattered across the ivory sofa and matching chairs. An oil reproduction of "A Mermaid" by John William Waterhouse hangs on the wall above the bed. The mermaid looks contemplative as she combs out her hair… like maybe she's thinking about her lover… and she's not as modest as I recall. Her long hair doesn't quite cover everything.

Jake's eyes flick toward the painting; I'm suddenly flustered standing there beside him, so I walk over to the sofa. A cute statue of a naked, male cherub perches on the coffee table, which I've just now noticed is anatomically accurate. All his teensy boy parts are on full display.

Gah! I'm such an idiot. There are five other vacant

rooms in the inn at the moment. Why did I pick this one to show Jake?

I'm growing warm inside my vintage flannel shirt. I run a hand through my hair, forgetting the red paisley scarf holding back my springy curls. The bandana flies off, and my wild, twirly locks bounce all over my head.

Blowing out a puff of air, I pick up the raggedy head-scarf, stuff it down my jeans pocket, and fold my arms. "Other than the extension cord issue, is there anything else to note in here?"

Jake sucks on the insides of his cheeks; I think he's trying not to laugh at my unkempt, char-lady appearance.

Today is, without a doubt, my worst-dressed day ever. Then again, I don't usually spend my mornings scrubbing toilets and then playing tour guide to the best-looking fire chief in Wisconsin. As a cruise director, I'm one of a handful of senior officers aboard our ship. I don't leave my cabin without ensuring my uniform is pressed, my curls are tamed, and I'm wearing makeup.

Once Jake gets himself under control, he points out an electrical outlet missing a cover next to the bed. Then we head back into the hallway, and he shows me the fire extinguisher; according to the tag, it expired two years ago.

Jake patiently takes me through every notation on the checklist. I can tell he's trying to be helpful, reminding me that most of the issues can be rectified without too much expense.

By the time we've inspected the main building and basement, which has two dozen cans of old paint stored near the boiler, exposed wiring, and another expired fire extinguisher, I'm clutching fistfuls of hair. How in the seven seas am I going to get this place shipshape before Jake returns for his "final" inspection?

Our last stop is Mooncrest Chapel, which connects to the rest of the inn via a covered walkway. We've hosted countless weddings here through the years, and it's vital to our ongoing business operation. One of the oldest buildings in Riddle Hill, the picturesque chapel needs major refurbishing, which Dad has been putting off for years due to the cost.

Jake waits for me to unlock the heavy door, painted a cheery lake blue. As we enter, the sun emerges from behind a cloud and streams through the stained-glass windows, casting a rainbow of bright colors across the white-washed walls and wooden pews.

This is such a pretty, peaceful spot.

Some kids have treehouses; others use backyards or basements as their own special hideaway. This was mine.

After Mama left, I used to retreat here all the time to read my books, write in my journal, and plot ways to lure her back home. She never did come back. Sniffling, I shake my head, determined to stuff those memories back where they belong, firmly in the past.

Then I flip on the overhead lights, one of which pops, fizzles, and blows out. I manage not to wince in front of Jake, who's rubbing the back of his neck. I get the sense he's about to drop a bombshell on me.

"Everything we've talked about so far can be remedied fairly easily," says Jake with a frown. "But the chapel? It's one big fire hazard."

I put my hands on my hips and huff. "Those are thick, plaster walls—and the exterior is solid limestone. Nothing's going to burn through them!"

Jake points to the paneled ceiling, polished doors, hand-carved trim, and rows of pews. "Nearly everything else is made of wood, which has been lovingly maintained by your father, and your grandparents before him. But it's still old, brittle wood. One little spark—" he snaps his fingers, causing me to flinch "—and this entire interior will catch fire."

Jake starts ticking off all the violations to drive home his point. Missing smoke detectors, broken circuit breakers, two expired fire extinguishers, exposed wires, and lastly, an exit that's been blocked for so long I didn't even know it existed.

I'm not about to debate the other stuff, which obviously needs to be corrected. However, requiring us to break through the plaster to open up an extra exit seems excessive. "But we already have two other exits. Why do we need a third?"

"A building this size requires three accessible exits to accommodate the number of occupants," replies Jake.

"If it's so important," I stammer, "why didn't any of your predecessors point it out?"

"They did. And each time your father paid the fine, promised to look into it, and then left everything as is."

"Well then, I guess we'll have to pay the fine again!" I throw my hands in the air. "I wouldn't want to deprive the fire department of their income!"

Jake's amber eyes take on a yellow glint. He practically growls at me. "I resent that implication, Mona! A blocked exit is a serious code violation and a safety hazard for all your guests."

"Phooey," I say, glowering at him. "We've hosted weddings and special events here for generations of supernaturals! And we've never had a serious incident."

Jake draws himself up to his full height—six feet, two inches of angry alpha male. He's obviously furious with me, and I *almost* take a step backward, stopping myself just in time. I refuse to be intimidated by Jake Grayclaw Spellman, who told me on our first day of kindergarten that he was going to marry me "when we were grown up."

He was a nervy, overachieving twerp back then—and he still is. That wolf managed to dog my footsteps until graduation, and now he's hounding me again, in his official capacity as Chief Spellman.

Jake marches outside, waits for me to follow, and slams the blue door shut behind us. Then he removes a big red sticker from his clipboard—which tells me he's been planning this all along—and slaps it across the door.

In bold, black letters it reads: "Closed Until Further Notice," and in smaller font, "By order of Jake Spellman, Fire Chief, Riddle Hill."

I stomp around him, flailing my arms. "But... but you can't do this!"

"Not only *can* I do this...I *have* to do it. Rick has been skirting violations long enough." Jake squares his jaw.

"There will be no more weddings or special events until this building is brought up to code."

"But the inn can't survive without Mooncrest Chapel." A tear slides down my cheek, which I quickly swipe away. I refuse to cry in front of him. "You'll put us out of business for good."

"Not if you get the repairs done quickly enough." Jake makes it sound so simple, but he's not the one who has to do all the work.

"You're a sorry excuse for a fire chief," I hiss at him. "And a mayor... all that power has gone to your head."

He nods curtly, walks to the parking lot, and climbs into his black SUV.

I have no idea how I'm going to fix the chapel and save the inn, but there's no way I'm letting Jake Spellman destroy my father's dream.

Half in shock, I stand there numbly as the arrogant, self-important wolf of a man drives away.

CHAPTER 7
JUST A BIG, BAD WOLF

JAKE

Later, January 3

I'm watching Mona in my rearview mirror as I pull away. She's standing there in front of the chapel, her hands fisted at her sides, looking forlorn despite her fury, all of it directed at me. I'm sorely tempted to slam on my brakes, rush back, and tell her to just pay the fine for one more year. But I can't do that and continue to be this town's fire chief. My conscience won't allow me.

Instead I press down on the accelerator to put some distance between me and Mona, which is the very last thing I want to do.

Some people think fighting fires is the worst part of the job, but near-death experiences aside, nothing could be further from the truth. When you're in your gear battling the flames, your training kicks in, and you're running on pure adrenaline; all your senses are on high

58

alert. You feel truly alive and one hundred percent focused on your mission.

That's when I love my job the most.

But what I did just now—closing down Mooncrest Chapel because Rick DeMaris has consistently refused to correct safety issues—that's the worst. I wish I could look the other way, but I can't disregard how Rick's just not following through anymore.

Mona may not believe this, but I feel horrible about the whole thing. The worst part is I finally worked up the nerve to ask her out. I figured I might have a chance after penning that flowery apology, despite the fact it didn't go down as smoothly as I'd hoped. Shredding one's pants in front of the woman you're trying to woo is not what I'd call a class act... and that's Mona in a nutshell. She's classy, through and through.

Well, most of the time. It took all my self-control to not chuckle out loud when I spotted her getup today: red bandana jammed onto her flyaway curls, flannel shirt two sizes too big, and a pair of Wrangler jeans that were probably from high school. She was entirely unprepared for my inspection and adorably embarrassed.

I had half a mind to toss aside the checklist and ask her out on the spot. I think she might have said yes if I'd asked her right then, before we started the inspection.

And then when we were standing in front of the king-sized bed with the half-naked mermaid painting hanging above it... Let's just say I had a difficult time staying focused on my job. I think Mona felt the same, because she seemed fluttery and nervous. She managed to lose her headscarf, freeing her gorgeous, dark locks

I had to suck in my cheeks and grip my clipboard with both hands to keep myself from declaring how much I ardently admire her.

Wait a minute!

What's happening to me? Now I'm sounding like Fitzwilliam Darcy in my own head.

At least Darcy's letter had some positive effects on how Elizabeth Bennet thought of him afterward. But in real life, my letter to Mona has made no difference.

And instead of Darcy and Elizabeth, all I can think of is Little Red Riding Hood and the big, bad wolf.

Yup, that's me, Jake Grayclaw Spellman. One big, bad, and incredibly lonely werewolf.

I'M SITTING in my vehicle in the parking lot of Howling Shores Pub. It's past nine; after conducting two additional fire inspections today and then presiding over a village council meeting, I'm bushed—but I don't want to go home to my empty cottage. My chest feels heavy, and I can't shake the memory of Mona close to tears because I was doing my job.

I check my messages to be sure there's nothing urgent, and that's when I spot a text sent by Cassia about half an hour ago. Sweet moonglow—my sister's engaged! I'm thrilled for her and happy to welcome Will Rossi, her rock star fiancé, into our quirky, supernatural family.

"Congratulations!" I text her. "Tell Will 'hey' from me and to look out for paparazzi."

"Ha-ha," writes Cassia. "Very funny." Cassia and Will had their hands full dealing with a nasty, smelly drove of goblin paparazzi just before the holidays.

"Have you picked a date yet?"

"Valentine's Day!" Cassia adds a few pink and purple hearts.

"That gives you plenty of time to plan your own perfect wedding," I text her, figuring she has thirteen months or so to nail down the details. In addition to working at our aunt's café, Cassia is also a supernatural wedding planner.

"It's in six weeks! Not much time at all... but we don't want to wait." Cassia adds a smiley face and a couple more hearts.

"Wow," I write. "That's really soon. But can you find a venue in time?" I'm getting a sinking feeling in the pit of my stomach, because I'm pretty sure I know *where* my sister wants to get married... and I just shut it down.

"Valentine's Day falls on a weekday this year, so we should be fine. Besides, last I checked, Mooncrest Chapel is still available."

I groan under my breath and write, "That tiny, cramped, old place? Why there?"

"You're such a grump! It's where Will and I first met, and it's a lovely spot." Cassia adds, "I texted Mona and asked her to reserve the chapel."

I bang my head against my seat back. After everything my sister's been through, I hate the thought of her hopes being dashed again. I'm almost afraid to ask, "What did Mona say?"

"Mona sent me a thumbs up and said we can plan it when I'm back in town."

Now why did Mona say that? What's that woman up to?

Mona would never intentionally mislead my sister, so she's definitely cooking up a plan. Given the extent of the repairs needed, it's going to take a lot more than elbow grease and faerie dust to get Mooncrest Chapel ready to pass inspection before Valentine's Day.

"Cool!" I write back. "Give my niece a hug for me."

Cassia likes my message and says goodnight.

I climb out of my Suburban and head toward Howling Shores for a brew, a burger, and two ibuprofens for my pounding head—courtesy of the wiliest, wittiest, and prettiest mermaid I know—Mona Lisa DeMaris, who's just outsmarted me.

Fishnets overflowing with starfish and shells hang from the corners of the pub; nautical-themed artwork covers everything in between, and a scarred oak bar with brass foot rails stretches across the back wall. My eyes sweep the room, and I wave at a handful of packmates clustered around a few tables, the single ones who have no one at home waiting for them. They haven't found their mates yet, same as me. That last thought causes me to glower as I plunk down on a stool and lean my elbows against the bar.

"Hey, Wes," I grumble. The pub owner is another pack member, a family man with a lovely mate and three wolf cubs of his own.

"Alpha," says the huge man cautiously, probably because my brows are drawn downward in a mighty scowl. Normally Wes addresses me by my first name.

I attempt to school my features, but it's no use; I'm in a foul state of mind, which is patently obvious to everyone in the room. My wolves are staring intently into their beer mugs and not at me. No one is willing to make eye contact, not even Wes. I heave a loud sigh.

"The usual?" Wes rubs his scruffy black beard.

"Yeah, and a glass of water please. I've got a killer headache."

He gives me a quick, sympathetic glance before turning away to pour my water. "Word on the street is you shut down Mooncrest Chapel today—one too many violations. Old Ricky must have been screaming your ears off."

I wash down the ibuprofen before replying. "Rick was nowhere in sight. He left the dirty work to his daughter; I had to deliver the bad news to her."

Wes whistles. "No wonder you have a headache. Mona Lisa is a spitfire."

I feel the need to defend Mona for some reason. Misplaced gallantry, perhaps? I think of my Darcy letter-writing endeavor, shake my head, and practically growl, "It's not her fault the chapel failed inspection."

Wes cocks his head to the side. "Hey, you'll get no argument from me. We both know Ricky has been skating by for years."

I harrumph at Wes, who hands me a Ghastly Ale from a local brewery and scurries off to place my order. Holy conflagration! I've got to get myself under control. This is no way for a pack alpha to behave.

I need a distraction, something to shake off my black mood. I spot a dartboard in the corner, presently deserted, and wander over. Extracting the darts from the cork, I retreat ten paces, narrow my eyes, and start flinging the small missiles. Each one hits the bullseye. I repeat the action, over and over, until Wes approaches me. "Food's ready. How 'bout a booth?"

I let the last dart fly and snarl low in my throat. "Countertop's fine. It's not like I'm with anyone."

"O-o... ka-ay," he says, backing away.

I spin around. "Sorry, Wes. It's just—"

Wes raises his hands, palms outward. "No need to apologize. You've had a bad day."

"Yeah, but I shouldn't take it out on you. It's *my* bad day."

"We're a pack—we're family. We've got you, Jake."

I give him a rueful smile. "Thanks, Wes. I appreciate it."

As Wes grins and turns back toward the bar, he doesn't see me wince and rub my chest, my heart stumbling over that one word: *family*.

I may be the mayor, fire chief, and pack alpha, but a family of my own is the one thing I don't have. And unless I can find my true mate, I never will.

For starters, my fixation on Mona is part of the problem. Putting all my energy into a woman who lives and works overseas makes no sense; it's time for me to face reality.

Somehow, I need to stop obsessing about the pretty, prickly mermaid who occupies too many of my waking thoughts—and who, after today, will never consider dating me anyway.

No, if anything, Mona probably hates me more today

than she ever did in high school. Unfortunately, the opposite is true for me; my attraction to Mona grows with every encounter.

Growling under my breath, I stuff a curly fry in my mouth and wonder what it will take for me to forget Mona Lisa DeMaris once and for all.

Probably nothing short of total amnesia.

CHAPTER 8
CLUELESS CURMUDGEON

MONA

Later, January 3

When Jake slapped that ugly red sticker on the chapel's lovely blue door and then drove away, it took all my self-control not to chase after his SUV, shaking my fist and shouting, "You're nothing but a big, bad wolf dressed like a hot, hunky man!"

At least my years of training as a cruise director came in handy for something other than corralling passengers, conducting safety drills, and directing musical revues. I managed to restrain my wilder impulses by slowly counting to ten... once, twice, three times. By then Jake's vehicle was out of sight.

I'm incredibly sad and outrageously mad at the same time, and the two powerful emotions are warring inside me for dominance. I wipe my damp cheek with the back of my hand, deciding that anger is a more useful emotion at the moment.

I'm going to find a way to make Jake pay for this.

And I don't mean the code violations that obviously need to be addressed. I'm talking about shutting down a Riddle Hill landmark, Mooncrest Chapel, for a closed-off exit that we never even missed. If every other fire inspector could live with it, why can't he?

I'll tell you why: Jake Grayclaw Spellman is a hidebound rule-follower who sees everything as black and white.

Once, in third grade, Jake confessed to the whole class his eyes had wandered during a spelling test. Apparently he'd copied down someone else's answer for one word and scored a perfect hundred on the exam. And you know what happened? The teacher was so moved by Jake's humble confession she let him keep his *A+*.

In sixth grade, Jake tried to break up a playground fight between two members of his pack by wrestling one of the kids to the ground. The teacher assumed Jake was the instigator and gave him detention for a week. Jake didn't object or point out he'd been trying to stop the other boys. When Rob Wolferman asked him about it later, Jake said the punishment was just, since he *had* been tussling when the teacher stopped the fight.

See what I mean? Jake holds himself to a ridiculously high standard and then is surprised when everyone else either can't or won't do the same.

I pause in my mental rant against Jake because my teeth are starting to chatter; I haven't budged from the chapel's front door. Sniffling, I turn around, lock up, and then trudge around to our apartment behind the inn. I need to get cleaned up and then find my dad, the clueless curmudgeon.

I stop in my tracks. Wait a minute. Dad's not clueless at all; *he knew we would fail the reinspection.* My father set me up, letting me undergo utter humiliation with Jake.

While I'm still outraged at Jake for closing down the chapel, my not-so-innocent father has been ignoring code violations for quite some time. Although Dad may be getting up in years, and his recent injury is a reminder he can't continue running Mooncrest Inn by himself, Dad's mind is as sharp as Dracula's fangs. I stomp back to the apartment, mulling over my father's motivations.

Once I've showered, tamed my hair, applied makeup, and slipped into clean jeans and a turtleneck sweater, I return to the inn's lobby. I can hear Auntie Imogen's soft snores as she dozes above the fireplace. A short elf with large, pointy ears and a long, brown beard is sweeping out the ashes as quietly as possible beneath Auntie's frame. Cosmo Peppertail knows better than to incur her wrath—or one of her curses.

Cosmo's shoes curl up at the toes; his red cap has a little bell on top, and his blue overalls are always neatly pressed. He's the eldest of two brothers who live in a small cottage at the back of our property and work at the inn for their room and board. Since Cosmo and Elmo prefer to cook their meals over a hob and read by candle-light, they can't help me upgrade the electrical panels or do any rewiring. They are handy with a hammer, a box of nails, and a paint brush though, so that's something. And if we needed to rethatch the roof, which is covered in gray asphalt shingles instead of straw, they'd be all over it.

Dad is where I left him, sitting behind the antique mahogany desk. He must've finished his latest romance; now he's busy typing on his laptop.

"Dad, we need to talk," I say bluntly.

My father holds up his hand. "Hang on a minute. Let me finish this post."

Along with his newfound fondness for romance novels, Dad has discovered social media. I was hopeful at first, assuming he was using online marketing to promote the inn. But when I peeked over his shoulder, I was dismayed to find my father posting *cat memes*. No wonder the inn is failing inspections!

My father closes the laptop, removes his reading glasses, and glances up, his eyes as clear and blue as a summer sky. His ancestry is a bit of a mish-mash (and consequently so is mine). Dad is part house faerie, part garden gnome, and part shoemaking elf; his ears are pointy and his eyebrows tip upward. However, he has no faerie wings; his shoes don't curl up at the toes, and he doesn't wear little top hats or beanies with bells.

Dad's magical abilities consist of opening locked doors, coaxing flowers to bloom, and repairing shoes. And like all house faeries, my father is great at greeting guests and making them feel at home in our inn.

All I inherited from his family tree is the faerie knack for hospitality and the ability to keep cut flowers looking fresh for up to two weeks. Although not a particularly useful skill at sea, I have rescued a few sad-looking bouquets for some of our guests when no one was looking. I'm very thankful my mother's side is one hundred percent merfolk; otherwise, the ability to extend and retract my tail fin may have passed me by.

Like all supers in Riddle Hill, Dad casts a glamour whenever he could be observed by non-supers, such as now, seated at the front desk in our lobby. Stroking his trim white beard, he asks, "I guess we failed Spellman's reinspection, huh?"

"Of course we failed!" I throw my hands in the air. Auntie Imogen snorts and mumbles in her sleep, so I lower my voice. "Why didn't you give me a heads up so we could be better prepared? Most of the code violations are easy to remedy."

"But some of 'em are not," replies Dad. "Like the issues with the chapel."

"Which Jake Spellman closed today!" I'm expecting my father to react with indignation and outrage.

Instead, he shrugs. "It was bound to happen, sooner or later. I could only pay the fines for so many years before someone shut the place down."

I don't understand why my dad is so nonchalant. Has he looked at our books lately? "But we need the chapel! We'll lose all our wedding business without it."

I start pacing around the inn's lobby, which is empty now that Cosmo has carted off the ashes and restacked the wood in the grate. Normally, I'd be worried about the lack of guests, but January is our slow month. It's also the ideal time to roll up our sleeves and get started on the much-needed repairs.

Dad comes out from behind the desk and perches on

the sofa facing the fireplace. "Is this really about the inn... or is something else bothering you?"

I sit in an adjacent wing-backed chair. "Of course this is about the inn."

"Are you sure? Because I saw how you lit up when Spellman entered the lobby. If I didn't know better, I'd say you still like him."

I fold my arms and snort. "That's ridiculous... I haven't thought about Jake Spellman since high school." That's a little white lie, but my dad is on a need-to-know basis. Besides, there's nothing going on between me and Jake. I scowl at my dad. "I know what you're doing. You're trying to distract me."

"Maybe a little," Dad admits. "But you've been so anxious since you got back home, worrying about the inn and how to keep it afloat, and also fretting over me. You work too hard as it is; the last thing I want is for you to have to carry my load too."

"Then why did you let me handle the inspection on my own, since you knew we were going to fail?"

"Ah, well," my dad gives me an impish grin. "I was sort of hoping Spellman would give us another extension if you asked him."

"Now why would he do that?"

"Because you're so charming, and I figured if you asked him sweetly enough, he might agree."

I roll my eyes. "You don't know Jake Spellman if you think he'd cut us any slack whatsoever. If we don't get our act together before Jake returns, he's going to be shutting down more than the chapel."

Dad speaks so softly I have to ask him to repeat himself. "Would that be so bad, Mona?"

My mouth drops open. Dad loves Mooncrest Inn; it's been his whole life. I'm starting to worry something else is going on, like maybe he's got some incurable illness. I'm not known for my subtlety, so I blurt out, "Oh Daddy, what's wrong? If the doctors here can't help you, I'll talk to Catbeam Spellman—she's got international connections—we'll find you a cure."

"A cure for what?"

"For whatever ails you."

My dad leans forward and pats my hand. "Honey, the only thing ailing me is my bad back, which is improving." He straightens and says firmly, "Look, let's go over that checklist right now and decide how we're going to tackle it."

I feel better after we review the list and come up with a plan. Dad calls some of his cronies, a couple of gnomes he plays poker with, and before long he's negotiated the repairs for both the inn and the chapel, at a price we can actually afford. I don't know why he's waited so long to schedule this work, but at least he's finally taking these code violations seriously.

I'm going to pull Cosmo off his regular duties—cleaning the kitchen, bussing luggage, and valeting cars—and have him help me inside the chapel. We're going to break through the plaster wall and open up that blocked exit. Once we've removed the wall, Dad's gnomes can help us figure out what sort of a door to install, and then we'll have to put the whole thing back together. I used to help my father with basic repairs around the inn, and I know how to swing a sledgehammer, so I figure the demolition work should be doable for a competent house elf and a mermaid cruise director.

At least I hope so.

I've been so preoccupied with the code violations and getting my dad motivated enough to help me that I've neglected my phone. When I finally check my messages, I find a text from Cassia Spellman, who's sweet as pie and nothing like her wolfish half-brother.

Her handsome, human, rock star boyfriend has proposed to her! I'm thrilled for her—for both of them, actually. He's a nice guy who's had a run of really bad luck.

I send her a "Congrats" message with some sparkles and balloons, and then she writes back. "We want to get married in Mooncrest Chapel this coming Valentine's Day—please tell me it's still available!!"

Wow. This is awkward. Cassia's big brother just shut down the chapel, and now she wants to use it. Hmm... I guess I should tell her the truth. But then I realize this is the perfect opportunity for some Jake Spellman payback.

So I reply to Cassia, "The chapel's available—and it's yours! We can talk more when you're back in town. This is so exciting!"

Of course I'll open up that blocked exit inside the chapel, and I'll make sure the electrical work is finished in time to pass our next inspection; I'd never do anything to hurt Cassia or derail her wedding plans.

But in the meantime, why not let Jake squirm a bit?

CHAPTER 9
THIS IS NOT A DRILL

JAKE

Thursday, January 10

It's been a solid week since I closed down the chapel —and almost three months since I conducted my initial inspection of Mooncrest with Rick DeMaris.

I'm sitting behind the dark oak desk in my office, staring at the photos of previous fire chiefs hanging on the opposite wall, and wondering if I went too far this time. Perhaps letting Rick pay the fine for another year would've been the prudent thing to do. Mona might still be speaking to me, and my gut wouldn't twist with remorse every time I think of her.

I keep replaying my last conversation with Mona in front of Mooncrest Chapel. She was so hurt and angry I don't see how I can ever make it up to her. Honestly, I expected Mona to petition for another extension by now, or at the very least, to ask for some advice on how to prioritize and manage so many repairs. Instead, she's been silent... and conspicuously absent.

Mona hasn't even popped into the Sit for a Spell Café, which is pretty unusual. Aunt Phoebe asked me about it. When I told her Rick DeMaris forced my hand, and I had no choice but to close Mooncrest Chapel until the code violations were rectified, my aunt's face turned as stony as one of her gargoyles. She actually *growled* at me.

I guess Mona and Cassia must have discussed it, because my sister knows the chapel is temporarily out of commission. Let's face it; in a town this size, word travels faster than a bat can fly. However, Mona has obviously reassured Cassia the chapel will be ready by Valentine's Day. Cassia says she's confident everything will work out. I wish I shared her confidence, because the last thing I want is to burst my sister's happiness bubble and further alienate Mona.

I stand, stretch, and run a hand through my hair, wondering whether I should cruise past the chapel again before it gets too dark to see anything. I've been driving by Mooncrest on my way home every day—although technically it's in the opposite direction—but I can't determine if anyone's working on repairs.

Maybe I should call Rick DeMaris, who's barely civil to me on a good day, and see if there's anything I can do to help him and his daughter. I'd feel better just talking to the man, and it might assuage some of the guilt I'm feeling about shutting down the chapel.

I'm just reaching for my mobile on the desk when a fire text alarm flashes on the screen. I snatch it up and start jogging toward the garage as a general alert sounds throughout the station.

Communication alerts light up my mobile app, providing me with a stream of updates on the whereabouts of every firefighter, whether they're staff or volunteer, on duty or off. My crew is comprised of mostly werewolves and a handful of vampires, and they're all responding at once, so it takes a few moments for me to register the location of the fire.

I wish I could say I'm surprised, but I'm not.

Mooncrest Chapel.

My throat tightens as the bottom falls out of my stomach.

Blast and blazes! Where's Mona? Is she safe?

I'm joined in the garage by my three on-duty firefighters, including Teddy Barker, back from his honeymoon, plus Rob Wolferman, who apparently dropped into the station to say hello. We pull on our protective suits, which have an extra feature developed just for werewolves; our gear is pliable and can stretch to accommodate our larger body frames when we shift. There's even extra room in the seats for our bushy tails. The only exception is our face masks, which can't expand, so we always wear the extra-long, snout-sized models.

Rob's behind the wheel of the fire engine as we race toward the chapel. Rick DeMaris is standing outside, shouting as two neighbors struggle to hold him back. He clearly wants to run inside.

I never really understood that old phrase, "my heart's in my throat," until this moment, but as I take in the scene, I'm terrified Mona's inside that building.

Before we've come to a complete stop, I'm opening the door and jumping out to assess the situation. I don't see flames, but there's an acrid, smokey odor in the air; I'm pretty sure something electrical started this fire, which means we can't use water to put it out.

"Likely Class C Fire!" I bark at my crew.

Rob hands me a specialized extinguisher as Rick hollers, "Mona's in there, and Cosmo!"

"Get the civilians out of the way!" I shout as a couple of police officers arrive in the yard. They kindly but firmly guide Rick and his friends away from the chapel.

Rick's voice is hoarse from the smoke and stress as he screams at me, "Hurry up, you crazy werewolf! She needs you!"

If it's the last thing I do, I'm rescuing Mona and Cosmo. "Where'd you see her last?" I yell.

Rick's face hardens. "Downstairs, working on that exit."

I'm shouting orders as a second truck pulls up, spilling out more firefighters. I send three of my most experienced professionals, including Teddy, through the front door. Since this is an active fire, everyone's shifted by now, except me; I can't transform until the last possible moment, because I need to be able to transmit clear, verbal commands through my headset as I manage the scene.

Rob and I run around to the side door. Once inside, Rob yips to signal he's picked up something with his wolfish senses; I can only pray it's Mona and Cosmo, and we're not too late. I nod for him to take the lead.

I still don't see flames, but the haze of smoke grows

denser as we race to the rear of the chapel and descend a half-flight of steps to a wide landing. If we continue all the way down, we'll reach the basement and furnace. To our left is an unoccupied bathroom, and on the right is the inaccessible third exit, which is now blocked by a mound of rubble.

Whining, Rob lopes over to Cosmo, lying amid the broken chunks of plaster on the floor. But where's Mona?

"You take Cosmo; I'll find Mona!" I holler at Rob, who's already anticipated me.

He's more wolf than man at this point, but he's not completely shifted, which is standard practice for were-wolf firefighters. We still need to retain the use of our hands and arms, which grow more muscular and furry in our interim-wolf state. The only time we're unable to control our transformation is during a full moon, which is when our vampire crew members are on call.

Rob scoops up the elf and lopes back up the steps, heading for the side door.

"Maayne. Floorr. Clearr." A werewolf's throaty voice rumbles inside my earpiece, carefully enunciating each syllable through his snout. It's hard to understand wolf-speak, which is why I'm still in my human form.

"No-oo. Flaames." It's Teddy. His team has checked the chapel's sanctuary, office, and restrooms, confirming no one's trapped inside—and he's also signaling the fire hasn't reached the main floor yet.

I give the order for everyone else to clear out of the building until I've inspected the basement. Then I partially shift, stopping before I transform completely, and dash down the stairs with a Class C extinguisher in my fur-covered hands. The haze of smoke is thicker here, and the source of the fire is plain to see; small arcs of electricity sputter and fizzle from a faulty circuit inside the blackened electrical panel, which is so damaged I can't switch off the main circuit breaker.

It's obvious someone's already been down here, because the back wall and panel are sprayed with repellent from an extinguisher. But while they've managed to mostly douse the flames, it's clear the basement quickly filled with smoke and fumes, the fire spreading too fast for a civilian to try putting out.

I'm feeling panicky now, because I don't see Mona anywhere, and this air is dangerous to breathe without apparatus.

Then I spot something so out of context I wonder if I'm hallucinating: a very large fish tail on the floor behind the furnace.

My blood freezes in my veins despite the heavy suit I'm wearing. It's Mona!

She's lying crumpled on the concrete, a fire extinguisher nearby—but her shapely legs are gone, replaced by a pearlescent green tail fin. Her jeans are split open and hang in loose strips from her waist.

I have no idea why Mona's in mermaid form; all I know is I've found her, and I need to get her outside fast. I drop my extinguisher on the floor and then sweep her into my arms, but her head lolls to the side. She's unconscious.

I cry out, "Mona, my love!" but it sounds more like a muffled growl.

I hurtle toward the stairs, promising myself that if

Mona survives, I'll confess to her my true feelings. My right foot's on the bottom step when I hear a loud crack, and one of the old support beams gives way behind me. I hunch over Mona to protect her body from any further harm, yelping as wood and debris rain down on us, piercing my back and cracking several ribs.

I howl in pain and drag myself up each step on shaking legs, holding Mona as steadily as possible against my chest as I climb. Gritting my teeth from the sharp stabs in my back, I pray for some sign of life from Mona. I stumble toward the side door, panting heavily, as Rob and Teddy barrel inside; they must've heard me cry out and realized I'm injured.

I gingerly hand Mona over to Teddy, who dashes outside with her. My legs give way beneath me, and I fall to my knees with a loud moan. Rob hauls me up by my armpits and pulls me out the side door, where another firefighter catches me.

"Mownna?" I rumble deep in my throat and drop down on all fours. My back is killing me; my breath's coming in short, wheezy gasps, and I'm nauseous, probably from the pain, my anxiety over Mona, and the adrenaline still pumping through my veins.

"She's alive," says Marv, who kneels beside me. A massive wolf of a man, he's a pack member and one of the best cops I know. "We're not sure how much toxic smoke she inhaled before she transformed, so we're taking her to the hospital."

Then it dawns on me that Mona intentionally shifted into her mermaid form to protect her human lungs from the smoke. Since merfolk can breathe underwater, their respiratory systems are not dependent on inhaling oxygen from the air. Brilliant, stubborn Mona, who figured she could handle an electrical fire on her own.

Two vampires who work at Malaki's Menswear descend on me—they're also part-time paramedics—and help me onto a stretcher. One of them lays a hand on my shoulder and says, "A piece of debris pierced through your gear, Chief. You're bleeding heavily. You'll need an X-ray, stitches, and possibly surgery."

I nod and close my eyes. I simply don't have the strength to keep them open any longer.

CHAPTER 10
RIDDLE HILL HOSPITAL

MONA

Friday, January 11

I'm lying on something softer than the basement floor, and I can wriggle my toes, so I'm back in my human form. But my head throbs; my throat feels sandpapery, and my lungs are achy. I'm too weary to open my eyes just yet, but the pungent scent of ammonia mixed with lemon oil, the mild beeping near my head, and the oxygen mask on my face are clues to my whereabouts: the hospital.

But wait... how did I get here?

I recall the flames arcing out of the electrical panel, and one of the old wooden beams catching fire. I grabbed the new extinguisher I'd just purchased (I suppose I ought to thank Jake for that bit of luck) and yelled for Cosmo to get help. I remember the basement quickly filling with smoke, spraying the flames, and then I was falling, choking, not able to breathe. I transformed, praying my mermaid lungs would help me survive.

Where's Cosmo now? Is he safe? And what about my dad? He didn't do anything foolish, did he? I force my eyes open and glance around anxiously. The lighting is dim, and the blinds are drawn. It's obviously dark outside.... How long have I been lying here?

I pull the oxygen mask off my face. "Dad?" I croak through parched lips.

"Mona!" cries my dad, who's sitting on a stiff chair near the bed. "Oh sweet moonglow, you're awake!" He rushes over and grasps my hand, tears streaming down his lined face. "I was so worried... and so was your mother."

Frowning, I rasp. "Mama? How did *she* find out."

"I told her you were in the hospital. Your mother loves you deeply, Mona—never, ever doubt that."

I scowl at my father. "I haven't had a mother since I was ten. I certainly don't need her worrying about me *now*."

My father flinches, and I realize I've hurt him, which is the last thing I want to do. Mama walked out the door twenty-two years ago and never came back. I moved on after she deserted us; why can't Dad?

I clear my throat and ask, "How's Cosmo doing?"

"He broke his leg, but otherwise he's fine. He's been worried about you—along with the rest of the neighborhood." My dad hesitates, and then his voice cracks. "I'm so sorry Mona! This is all my fault. I should've found a way to fix the chapel before now, but it was cheaper to pay the fines than take out another bank loan. It's been hard enough making payments on the existing loan... I was trying to avoid adding more debt."

My head and throat are killing me, and I feel scraped raw inside, but I can't allow my dad to take all the blame for this. "I've been chasing after my dreams for the past decade. I'm partly responsible for the sorry state of the chapel too," I whisper.

Dad shakes his head. "No you're not. You have every right to your own life and career. Besides, you can't ignore the call of the sea... you're a mermaid."

"I'm half mermaid... and that's not an excuse for abandoning my duties here," I rasp. Dad drops his gaze; he must realize I'm referring to my mother.

We're interrupted by the nurse coming to check my vitals. She gives me some water, which stings as it goes down my throat, and with a stern flap of her blue wing feathers, she reminds me to use my oxygen mask.

After the nurse leaves, I murmur, "How did I get out of the basement? I don't remember anything."

"Spellman found you—and just in time too. The fire weakened one of the wooden support beams, which cracked, causing part of the basement wall to collapse. I'm thankful Spellman managed to carry you up those stairs despite his injuries."

My heart clenches inside my chest. "Jake got hurt... rescuing me? How... how is he now?"

"I don't know, honey. I've been in here with you."

"Dad, please go find out—I need to know." My eyes well up, and my dad pats my arm.

"Alright, just take it easy. I'll go ask around." He waits until I put my mask back on before leaving the room.

I'm not a patient person; I hate just lying here, waiting for my father to bring me news of Jake. But I'm hooked up to an IV and a heart monitor and feel weak as a kitten. I remind myself Jake is an experienced firefighter and a werewolf.

He's fine; I'm sure of it.

He has to be.

I must've dozed off, because the next time I open my eyes, my father is sipping coffee out of a paper cup and reading on his tablet. The weak light peeking around the edges of the window blind tells me it's early morning. Dad hears me moving in the bed and glances up.

I pull off my oxygen mask. "How's Jake?"

My dad puts down his cup with a small frown, and suddenly, I'm very, very worried. "Dad, tell me... please."

"Spellman is out of the woods. The emergency surgery went fine, and Phoebe said they'll be moving him to a private room shortly."

Out of the woods... emergency surgery... *Jake almost died, again*? But this time, it was my fault... mine and my dad's. That wiring should've been replaced years ago. All I can think of is how furious I was when Jake closed down the chapel and how much I yelled at him.

"Falling debris cracked a few of his ribs," Dad continues. "And a hunk of wood pierced his right lung and, ah, nicked his heart, so the doctors had to operate immediately."

Now I'm crying, and my father is reassuring me Jake

is going to be alright because he's a big tough werewolf, but that makes the tears fall even faster and harder.

I don't think I've cried this much since Mama left.

I'm so guilty about Jake and so conflicted about my own feelings.

Jake might have liked me when we were teens, but I'm certain he must hate me now.

And who could blame him?

CHAPTER 11
VISITING HOURS

JAKE

Friday to Sunday, January 11-13

I hear the low murmur of female voices nearby and soft weeping. I sure hope I'm not dead, because this seems pretty anticlimactic.

But I hurt all over; each breath brings a fresh stab of pain, which seems contrary to my idea of heaven. Then I hear my cousin Sophie, back from her honeymoon with Teddy, whisper something about *Mona DeMaris*.

Now I'm straining to sit up. "Mona!" I croak. "Where's Mona!"

Aunt Phoebe, Sophie, and Cassia rush over to my bed. My sister leans her tear-streaked face over mine and says, "Mona is very lucky. Her father said she suffered minor damage to her lungs; it could've been much, much worse. Without a doubt you saved her life, Jake."

"So she's truly safe?" I murmur.

"Yes," Cassia whispers. "Totally safe."

I nod, close my eyes, and for the first time since the apartment fire last month, I fall into a deep sleep entirely devoid of nightmares.

When I wake up again, I'm in a different room, and the sun is shining through the window. I hear Phoebe and Cassia conversing softly. Olivia, my young niece, stands on her tiptoes to kiss my cheek, her delicate wing feathers brushing across my arm. I manage to mumble, "Thanks, Liv," before falling back asleep.

Uncle Nash and Malaki stop by at some point, and so do Rob, Teddy, and Marv. Flowers and cards start arriving, so many that someone snags a cart to hold them all. The room is brimming with tails, wings, fangs and flowers; it's cheerful, and a bit raucous, but I keep dozing off.

I guess the matronly nurse with the blue wings has finally had enough, though. She enters, puts her hands on her hips, and insists on only two visitors at a time. Malaki, that cunning vampire, reminds her I'm the mayor, and they're here on official business, but she shoos him right out the door.

Through the haze of pain and the meds that keep me drifting in and out of wakefulness, I continue to watch and wait.

Because there's one face above all I'm dying to see; it belongs to the beautiful mermaid whose rescue nearly killed me. But Mona's not here.

How is she really doing?

Has she been discharged yet?

Does she know about my injuries... and does she care?

IT'S DARK OUTSIDE, and the lights in my room are turned down low. Visiting hours are over; Phoebe and Nash just left, and Cassia stopped by earlier with Olivia, who gave me a handmade get-well card that's covered in pink and purple hearts and butterflies. I told her it was my favorite card of all, which brought a huge smile to her sweet face.

I'm relieved my pain level is more manageable, and I can finally take a breath without wincing. But I've been sleeping for most of the past two days, so now I'm lying here wide awake, wondering how I'm going to survive convalescence. I won't be able to run, climb ladders, or lift anything heavy for weeks on end. It's going to be pure torture for an active werewolf like me.

There's a soft knock at my door. "Come in," I mumble, wondering why the nurse with the blue wings is knocking when she hasn't before.

Then I detect a hint of sea breeze and citrus in the air, and my breath catches in my throat.

Sweet moonglow, Mona's just slipped inside and closed the door.

She's across the room, standing still as a statue. Her slender figure and halo of dark curls cast an alluring silhouette on the wall. I fight the urge to jump off the bed and rush over to her; not only would the nurse have a conniption fit, but I don't think I could make it without falling on my face. I can't recall the last time I felt this weak and helpless.

"Jake?" whispers Mona. "Are you... can I... it's after hours but..."

"Mona," I rumble low in my throat. "Please come closer. It's fine; I'm awake."

I need to see your face, Mona... I want to touch the soft curve of your cheek and kiss your perfect bow lips and declare my true feelings... and my intentions, which I assure you are entirely honorable.

Gah! I'm channeling Fitzwilliam Darcy again.

Why did Aunt Phoebe have to recommend Pride and Prejudice *in the first place? Now I can't get that flowery prose out of my head.*

Mona takes a tentative step toward the bed, and then another, but her lovely face is still in shadow. She's jammed her hands into the pockets of her jacket and seems hesitant to come any closer.

"I don't bite," I say softly.

Mona snorts and moves forward another couple steps; at least I can see her clearly now. There's a bandage above her right eye. "Did you need any stitches?"

"Just a couple. I don't even remember getting cut... Everything happened so fast."

I nod. "It's a lesson every firefighter learns early in their career."

"Oh Jake," Mona bites her lower lip. "I'm ashamed of how I behaved during the inspection. I said some things I shouldn't have. And I feel terrible about your injuries. My dad and I are responsible. For—" she waves her hand at me, propped up in bed wearing a flimsy gray hospital gown "—for all of this."

"Please stop beating yourself up over the fire, which,

by the way, you should never have attempted to put out yourself."

"I was hoping I wouldn't have to call 911. I didn't want you to say, 'I told you so.' " Mona hangs her head. "But I never thought you'd wind up getting hurt because of my stubborn streak."

I'm not about to tell Mona that I adore her stubborn streak, except when it places her in danger. Instead I say, "Let's not forget fighting fires is my job—a job I happen to love—but one that also comes with inherent risk. This isn't the first time I've been injured in the line of duty."

"But you were injured because of the chapel's antiquated wiring, which you've been warning us about." Mona's dark curls bounce as she shakes her head. "I'm so, so sorry. I hope you can forgive me."

"Done."

"I don't deserve to be forgiven so easily," Mona objects.

I arch an eyebrow. "Do you *want* me to hold a grudge?"

"Nah." Mona chortles. "But I want to find a way to make it up to you."

"That's not necessary." I flap my hand, briefly considering whether to ask her on a date, but the timing's all wrong. Besides, I'm pretty beat up at the moment; there's no way I could possibly compete with Captain Emilio, the multi-lingual merman, for Mona's affections.

I decide to change the subject. "What are you doing about the chapel?"

Mona pulls up a chair and sits down... so close and

yet so far away. I can't even reach for her hand without yanking out my IV. *Patience, Jake,* I tell myself. *You're in this for the long haul. Fifteen years and counting since you blew it with Mona senior year. I'll bet Captain Emilio has the staying power of a minnow by comparison.*

"Dad and I are committed to fixing the chapel—but I don't see how we'll ever get it finished in time for your sister's wedding." Mona draws her eyebrows together. "It seems I'm letting everyone down."

"Cassia will understand," I say, but then I'm struck by a sudden inspiration. I sit up straighter in bed, grimacing at the pain shooting down my back.

"What's wrong?" Mona's eyes widen in alarm. "Can I get you something?"

"I'll be fine; it's momentary." That's not entirely true, but I plow ahead. "Look, I'm not going to be able to return to my job at the fire station for a while, which means I'll have extra time on my hands. Why don't I help you with the chapel repairs?"

Mona's mouth drops open. "How?" She probably thinks my idea is looney given my current physical limitations. "I'm sure your doctors want you to take it easy and rest up."

"I will take it easy—I won't get on any ladders or carry anything heavier than a hammer. But I can help supervise the repairs, see that everything's handled according to code, and maybe drive a few nails into a wooden beam while I'm there."

Mona purses her full lips, which I find a monstrous distraction, as she ponders my offer of help. I'm afraid she's going to say no because she doesn't want to put me out, so I hastily add, "Look, you'd be helping me. I'm already bored out of my mind, and it's only been two days. I'll be an overgrown, growly wolf in another week if I can't do something."

Mona snorts and then covers it with a cough. "Well, if it's something you really want to do... then absolutely. That would be incredibly helpful."

I grin, although inside my head I'm high-fiving every get-well balloon in the room. "It's settled then. Once I'm discharged, I'll text you, and we can get started in earnest. Depending on the extent of the damage, maybe we can get the chapel ready by Valentine's Day."

Mona smiles as she stands to leave. "Now that would be nothing short of miraculous."

That's probably true.

But here's the real miracle: I've just finagled my way into spending the rest of the month with Mona Lisa DeMaris.

So there, Captain Emilio.

AFTER HOURS

MONA

Sunday, January 13

When the hospital discharged me this morning, I debated visiting Jake on my way home. But I didn't want to walk into a room filled with his buddies from the fire department, and I certainly didn't want my dad tagging along. I waited until the end of the day and returned when visiting hours were over.

I know that sounds a bit sketchy, but I went to school with half the security guards and nurses at the hospital. I knew I could skate by without any questions being asked.

So I let myself into Jake's room tonight, not at all prepared to see him laid up in that hospital bed, weak as a newborn lamb and clearly still in pain. Sure, I knew he had emergency surgery, but the stark contrast between hot, hunky Jake and weary, hurting Jake just about did me in. It took all my self-control not to burst into tears and rush to his side. My hand itched to brush that stray lock of hair back from his forehead, so I stuffed both hands inside my jacket and just stood there, uncertain what to say or do.

Here's the thing about Jake: he's always been larger than life. He's a big guy, even for a shifter, and he's constantly on the move. Even when he's sitting still, Jake is like a tightly wound coil, primed and ready to spring into action wherever he's needed next.

And when I worked up the nerve to ask for forgiveness, and all Jake said was "Done"—I had to swallow down a lump in my throat the size of my fist. Because knowing Jake, he actually means it. He doesn't hold grudges.

Unlike me. Honestly, if there were a contest to select the person who holds on to their resentment the longest, I'd win the gold medal.

Now that I'm back home, lying on the old twin bed inside my room, I can't fall asleep. I'm staring up at the glow-in-the-dark constellations stuck to the ceiling, thinking about my conversation with Jake. While I'm totally drained by all the emotions running through me and the events of the past few days, I'm also thrilled by Jake's offer of help. And I'm a little bit unnerved by how intensely Jake was gazing at me tonight—which, come to think of it, was probably due to his heavy-duty meds —and not because he still harbors any feelings for me.

I sigh deeply and then cough, which is a side effect of inhaling those toxic fumes. The doctors say my lungs will eventually heal, but in the meantime, I'm going to be coughing whenever I take a deep breath.

I manage to stop myself from sighing again as I ponder how to convince Dad to allow Jake to help us with the chapel repairs.

Dad is naturally grateful to Jake for getting me out of the basement before the wall collapsed, but he's also a proud man who doesn't accept help easily. Besides, Dad still remembers my tears when Jake turned down my invitation to the turnabout dance and when he took Gracie to senior prom; Dad's probably worried my schoolgirl crush is in danger of reasserting itself, and he doesn't want to see me get hurt.

Yawning, I decide to let tomorrow worry about itself, and drift off to sleep, counting the stars on my ceiling.

CHAPTER 13
REALITY CHECK

MONA

Monday, January 14

The nutty aroma of freshly brewed coffee draws me from my bedroom, down the hall, and into Dad's cozy blue-and-white kitchen. All the appliances date from the late nineties and are somehow still functioning, thanks mostly to Auntie Imogen's faerie magic, which she still sprinkles on occasion. Dad is the chef in our family; I'm quite content to eat the meals he prepares, praise his amazing cooking, and clean up afterward. I figure it's a fair trade. Of course, since Dad injured his back, we've been eating mostly leftovers from the inn's kitchen, carryout from Vlad's Victuals, or grilled cheese sandwiches that I inevitably burn.

My father has obviously let me sleep in this morning, because it's after ten when I stumble into the kitchen; any departing guests have already left the inn. Dad

97

hands me a steaming mug and gives me one of his "we need to talk" looks.

A nagging sense of worry settles in the pit of my stomach. I carry the cup over to the window seat behind the old maple table, positioning myself so I can look outside while at the same time listening to my dad; we've had all our serious conversations here, in the tidy kitchen tucked inside our private apartment at the back of the inn.

I was sitting in this same spot when my dad broke the news that Mama had left while I was in school. That was by far the worst of our conversations to occur in this kitchen, but something tells me I won't like what my father has to say this morning. He's been more contemplative lately, and I overheard him in his study, speaking in dulcet tones with the family lawyer a few times in the past month.

Dad pulls out a chair at the table and sits down facing me. His blue eyes, normally bright and twinkly, are solemn. "There's no easy way to say this, so I'll come right out with it. I've been struggling these last couple years, Mona; I'm not referring to my health, which is fine other than my bad back, and I don't mean the inn's finances, which are in the black, though not by much.

"The truth is I'm tired of innkeeping; tired of spending all my days and nights in Riddle Hill; tired of never having a day off. Other than my stint in the Navy, which was how I met your mother, I've never had the chance to travel." My dad glances out the window with a sigh and then turns back at me. "I need to make some changes, and that fire in the chapel confirmed I need to make them now."

My father has never spoken this frankly to me about either his weariness or his desire to travel. He's always seemed content to stay in Riddle Hill. "What sort of changes?" I ask uneasily.

"I'm planning to retire, but first I need to find a buyer for the inn."

"You're not serious... are you?" I've noticed my father has slowed down considerably since my last trip home, which was a few years ago, but I'm still shocked he's talking about selling the inn. Dad's received several purchase offers over the years, and he's always said he'd never sell the inn to opportunists looking to make a quick buck. I remind him of what he used to say.

He nods. "I know what I used to say, and that still holds. I'm seeking a serious buyer who'll appreciate Mooncrest Inn and our rich history. I've asked our lawyer to make a few discreet inquiries within the supernatural community."

"So *that's* the real reason..." My voice trails off.

"What do you mean?"

"That's why you asked me to take a leave of absence and come home to help you at the inn. So you could get it ready to sell."

Dad shakes head. "I asked you to come home because I needed your help. And I've missed you, Mona. But I also wanted to see how you felt about the inn, about working here day in and day out. Having you here has been wonderful, and it's also given me clarity."

"What kind of clarity?"

"About how talented you are, which I've always known, of course." Dad smiles. "But seeing how well you manage the details of a wedding one minute, and the needs of even the crankiest overnight guest the next, it's clear to me why you've excelled as a cruise director all these years. You get to combine your remarkable people skills with the ability to travel; it's the perfect job for you."

I knit my brows together and look at my dad. "So are you trying to tell me that I belong on board a ship, and not here in Riddle Hill with you? That I should let the mermaid side of my nature dominate?"

"Not at all. I'm just saying your faerie knack for hospitality and your merfolk love of the sea are perfectly suited to the cruise industry." Dad blows out a puff of air and rubs his short white beard. "Look, I didn't mean to overhear your phone conversation the other day, but I did. I'm trying to tell you I understand why you're thinking of leaving next month."

I sit up straighter. "Oh. I wasn't going to say anything until I'd made a decision. I'm still not sure what I want to do."

Emilio called me the day before the chapel fire to tell me he's accepted a new position on a larger, more luxurious ship—and to let me know the cruise director job is also available. He's recommended me for the role, which would be a step up in pay and rank. Em made it sound like it's mine for the asking, but I'll need to go into the company's online system to formally apply. I'm still undecided about what I really want, but I guess I'd be crazy not to complete the application.

"It's alright, honey. You belong at sea, not stuck here in some quirky small town in the Midwest."

"I love Riddle Hill," I say softly. "And it's not like we're landlocked or anything. We live on a peninsula surrounded by water!"

Dad arches one silver eyebrow. "If I didn't know better, I'd say you're trying to talk yourself—or me—into staying put."

"No, it's not that. It's just... Riddle Hill is a special place. And I'm really surprised you're going to sell the inn Auntie Imogen founded. Are you sure you won't miss it? I mean, you've been working here forever."

My father laughs. "Forever is right! I've been working here since I started bussing tables for my pop when I was eight years old. Sixty years. I think I've earned my retirement."

"Oh, Dad, of course you have. I don't know anyone who's worked harder than you... it's just... I never thought this day would come."

Dad reaches over and grips my hand. "You know I'm not leaving *you*, right?"

I sniffle and nod. "Sure, I know that."

"This has to remain our little secret," says Dad. "We can't breathe a word of it to anyone before we've found the right buyer; otherwise we may lose business we can't afford to lose." He sighs. "In the meantime we have more work than ever, including fixing up that chapel."

"I think I may have found a way to accelerate things," I say, hoping my father agrees. "I went to see Jake Spellman last night at the hospital—to personally thank him—and he's offered to help us with the chapel."

My heart speeds up as I explain about Jake's offer, figuring any minute now Dad is going to tell me to forget it. Somehow I've got to convince my father this is a good idea, without revealing the truth: I want to spend the next few weeks working alongside Jake so I can figure out if what he's stirring up inside me is real or imaginary.

I need to know if the siren call of Riddle Hill, which draws me home whenever I've been away too long, has anything to do with the one man I can't seem to shake loose—from my life, my head, or my heart.

I'm preparing all sorts of arguments for why we could use Jake's help with the chapel, but Dad surprises me. "You know, that's actually not a bad idea. I mean... if the fire chief is supervising the repairs we're making, that's got to hasten the process and save us some headaches in the end." Dad scratches his beard. "And you say Spellman wants to try and get it all done in time for his sister's wedding?"

When I nod, Dad shrugs. "Seems like a long shot to me, but let's see what we can do. The sooner we can get that chapel up and running again, the easier it'll be to sell this inn."

I feel a little stab in my chest at the thought of selling Mooncrest, but I also don't want to run this inn by myself. I need more downtime than a typical innkeeper can afford to take, and I do love to travel. Rising, I go to the sink to rinse out my mug. It's time to shower, dress, and start my day. Suddenly I remember something and turn to my dad. "While we've been sitting here chatting for the past half hour, who's manning the front desk?"

"Don't worry, I've got it covered," says Dad. "Cosmo

can't very well valet cars or bus luggage with his broken leg. So I've been training him on front desk duties, such as how to make a reservation, how to accept a credit card payment, that sort of thing."

My mouth hangs open. "But that requires basic computer skills. Just last week Cosmo asked me what an eBook is. And what if he forgets to use a glamour in the lobby to mask his pointy ears, little red hat, and curled up shoes?"

"Stop worrying so much. Cosmo will be fine. But now Elmo needs help; you're overworked, and my back is still healing... so I hired Twila Peppertail to help us out."

I narrow my eyes at my dad. "You hired Cosmo and Elmo's younger sister? Wouldn't we be better off hiring someone with relevant work experience?"

"Twila needs a job, and I figure you can train her. She can be your assistant."

I realize there's no point in debating Dad's hiring decisions, because the deed is already done. Besides I have other things on my mind, like updating my char-lady wardrobe.

There'll be no more tatty flannels and ripped-up jeans when Jake starts working with me inside the chapel.

I'm determined to look confident, competent, and above all, cute.

CHAPTER 14
PAID TIME OFF

JAKE

Thursday, January 17

I'm sitting at my kitchen table waiting for Rob to give me a lift because I'm not allowed to drive yet. Today's the first day I'm leaving my cottage since the fire; I texted Mona yesterday to let her know when I'd be coming over. She responded with a thumbs up. Period. I know Mona uses lots of sparkly hearts and emojis in her texts with Cassia.

Should I be concerned about receiving one yellow thumb?

Scratch that question; it's stupid.

Confident, healthy, successful Jake would never have given it a second thought. But I'm feeling a bit low at the moment and way too antsy. It would help if I could exercise, but I'm not allowed to lift weights or use my treadmill or run anywhere for the time being. And I'm definitely not allowed to go back to work.

Doc Demetrius won't clear me to return to the fire station until three weeks after surgery, and I'll be on a restricted schedule for another couple weeks after that. If you know Doc, you may be wondering why a vampire veterinarian is also the fire department's staff physician.

Doc is board certified in internal medicine (for both supers and non-supers) as well as veterinary medicine, which means he's medically qualified to judge my fitness as both a man and a shifter. Plus, like nearly everyone else in Riddle Hill, Doc needs the extra income. It's not easy living in a small supernatural town in Door County that relies heavily on tourism. Our winters can be mighty fierce even for the residents.

Like Doc, I'm perfectly content working two jobs to make ends meet. Which makes it really hard for me to sit still while I'm recovering. At least I'll be going over to Mooncrest Inn soon with Rob. We'll be touring the chapel with Mona and Rick, examining the damage together. Rob is going to help me assess the repair work needed and make recommendations; I figure two trained firefighters are better than one where Rick DeMaris is concerned.

After today, I expect I'll be spending a great deal of time working with Mona, which is exactly what I want... but the prospect also makes me anxious. For one thing, I tire easily these days and need to take frequent breaks. For another, I'm not allowed to lift anything heavier than a textbook. I'm not exactly helpless, but I may as well be compared to old Jake.

Of course I'll be fine once I'm fully healed, and I'm very lucky there wasn't more damage to my heart or lungs. But having two wake-up calls in the span of a month does get a man thinking about the future... and the woman he let get away... the woman with dark, curly hair and delightful curves and full Cupid's bow lips.

Rob honks his horn, and with a low sigh that sounds almost like a growl, I slip on my parka. Time to head back to the scene of my near demise.

"Hey, you're looking a little better," says my pack beta as I struggle to climb into his SUV. I have fresh appreciation for the elderly as I grunt and manage to pull the door shut, grimacing at the twinges in my back and chest. "At least your eyes are open."

"Ha-ha," I grumble good-naturedly. "Yeah... now I can stay awake for a couple hours at a time!" We both chuckle at my pathetic little joke, which is far truer than I care to admit. I'm afraid to sit down for too long when I'm in the chapel with Mona; I'm liable to fall asleep. At least Rob will be with me today and can poke me if I start yawning.

We drive through downtown, and Rob slows down, staring out the window at some guy in a black parka and jeans. I lean around Rob to get a better look, but the man lopes around a corner. Although he's in human form, there's no doubt in my mind he's a werewolf. "I didn't get a look at his face. Did you?"

"Briefly." The corners of Rob's mouth turn down. "I can't be certain, but he looked an awful lot like Rafe."

My heart races at the mention of that name. "I hope for everyone's sake you're mistaken." No decent alpha wants the likes of Rafaellus MacTire hanging around his territory. That creep once challenged me for pack leadership, and he created huge problems for Sophie and Teddy.

"Yeah, he was probably a tourist just passing through."

Rob parks in front of the chapel's blue door with my bright red "Closed" sticker smack dab in the middle. I'm no longer second-guessing my decision to close down the chapel, and in light of everything that's occurred since, it was the right call. Still... I feel bad about how it went down. At least now Rick DeMaris realizes the danger of skirting safety regulations.

My goal is to help Mona and her father restore the chapel as soon as possible for two reasons: the inn needs a functioning chapel for their wedding business, and my sister's heart is set on getting married there. Although Cassia and Mona have come up with an alternate plan—holding the ceremony in the inn's main lobby instead of the chapel—it won't be the same. I want to give my sister the wedding she really wants.

And I'll be getting what I want too... more time with Mona.

Rick opens the chapel door and invites us inside, where it's slightly warmer but not by much. I inhale a whiff of ashes and sooty dust; the place has obviously been closed up for the past week. I let Rob walk in ahead of me so I can pause and gulp some fresh air before entering the building.

Rick gives me a once over and purses his lips. "Glad you could make it." I guess that's as close as he'll get to apologizing for the code violations that nearly took his daughter's life and mine.

I may stand a head taller than Mona's father, but I've always found the man intimidating. With his pointy ears, trim white beard, and icy blue eyes, all Rick needs is a spiky hat and pitchfork to look like a menacing gnome intent on protecting his daughter from lovelorn werewolves.

I give Rick a nod and then glance over at Mona, who looks so amazing my pulse immediately ramps up, my heart jackhammering beneath my flannel shirt. She's wearing a crimson sweater the same color as her lip gloss, form-fitting jeans, and leather boots. Her gorgeous curls are partially tamed beneath a colorful headwrap. Despite her close call a week ago, Mona is practically glowing with good health.

I start to say hello, but the fetid air catches in the back of my throat. Suddenly my body's wracked by a painful coughing fit that makes me wince and brings tears to my eyes. Rob waits patiently for my wheezing to subside and then hands me a bottle of water. I take several slow sips, willing the tickle in my throat to settle back down as I try to catch my breath.

Mona draws her brows together; she's probably concerned about my fitness to help her. Rick rubs his beard and glances away. Eventually I manage to stop coughing long enough to mumble, "Let's start on the main floor and work our way down to the basement."

As Mona leads us slowly around the perimeter of the chapel's sanctuary, we examine the ceiling, walls, windows, and outlets for any signs of fire damage and find none. "Well that's some good news, eh?" asks Rick.

"It's encouraging," Rob agrees, before reminding Rick about the checklist on the clipboard he's carrying. "But it doesn't change the fact the chapel needs to be rewired and that exit made functional."

"I know that," grumbles Rick. "I hired Gnome Sweet Gnome after we failed our last inspection. They've just wrapped up their work inside the inn and can start on the chapel whenever the chief here gives the word."

"Gnome Sweet Gnome are general contractors," I point out. "I'd like to know who they've hired to do your electrical work."

Rick folds his arms across his chest, clearly miffed I'm questioning his judgment. I don't care; Mona and I nearly died, and Cosmo broke his leg due to Rick's cost-cutting ways. I'm going to ensure he's doing everything by the book this time.

Mona places a hand on her father's arm, and his face immediately softens. Rick DeMaris may be a crank, but he adores his daughter. At least we agree on something.

Rick juts out his jaw and mutters, "The electrical subcontractor is Lamps, Amps, and Vamps."

"Excellent; they're a good firm," I reply.

"Humph," Rick grunts.

Mona leads us through the rest of the first floor, which has a lingering smoky odor but no lasting damage. Then she takes a deep breath and heads downstairs to the landing where Rob discovered Cosmo lying in the rubble by the partially blocked exit.

Rob glances down at his clipboard. "You've made a

good start opening up this exit. Of course, you'll still need to finish the work before the chief can sign off, but this looks promising."

Mona glances up at me, her large brown eyes clouded. "But it's the middle of winter; even if we finish the interior, we're not going to be able to pour concrete to provide a base for a new staircase outside. And we can't afford to have the chapel closed until summer— we'll lose the peak wedding season if we do."

"I understand you need to reopen the chapel as soon as possible," I tell her. "And you don't need to pour concrete; the landing for the base of the stairs can be any material that provides a level surface, including gravel. So long as you have an exit with a doorway and steps leading down to the ground, and the other violations are corrected, I can issue a permit to reopen."

"You sure we don't need a concrete base?" snaps Rick.

"I'm sure." I nod without taking my eyes off Mona.

She frowns. "Why didn't you explain this a few weeks ago, when you closed us down?"

I give her a half-smile. "Because you didn't give me the chance."

She purses her incredibly kissable lips, and I have a hard time recalling why I'm standing in a stinky building getting plaster dust all over my work boots. I notice her father glaring at me but ignore him.

"Oh," she says. "I see."

I suck on the insides of my cheeks to keep from chuckling out loud and stuff my hands into my pockets so they don't stray over to Mona's gorgeous face. She has a smudge of soot on the tip of her nose I'm dying to wipe off with my thumb.

Rob clears his throat and suggests we move downstairs to the basement to catalogue the damage. My heart speeds up as we descend, and I falter as we reach the bottom step, where the jagged edge of a wooden beam blocks our way. Rob must realize I'm suffering from a bout of post-traumatic stress, because he hands me the clipboard and carefully drags the beam away from the stairs so we can all fan out on the basement floor.

I nod at Rob to take the lead. He points out the scorch marks from the electrical arcs and reminds Rick he'll need his general contractor to examine the basement wall for structural integrity. Rick grunts his assent. We run through the rest of the items on the checklist, make a few notations, and head back upstairs.

As we near the front door I turn to Mona, who looks paler now than when we'd arrived. I suspect she's suffering from some post-traumatic stress of her own. "If the electrical work on the inn is finished, I can come back tomorrow to reinspect it."

Mona nods. "That would be great. Tell me what time, and we'll be ready for you."

"Ah, about that... I can't drive for another week. Any chance you could give me a lift? You can choose the time." I'm embarrassed and feel like a teenager again, begging for a ride.

Before Mona can respond, her father interjects, "I can pick you up at ten a.m. Does that work?"

"Sure." I plaster a smile on my face. Rick is the last

super in Riddle Hill I want to share a ride with. And he's glaring at me again. What's with this guy?

Mona gives me a small wave. "See you tomorrow then."

If your father doesn't kill me first for the way I'm obviously pining over you.

"Sounds good," I say, following Rob out the door.

CHAPTER 15

CRAFTY, CRANKY, AND INCORRIGIBLE

MONA

Later, January 17

I wait until Jake pulls the chapel door firmly closed before I round on my dad. "Why on earth did you offer to drive Jake tomorrow?"

Dad sniffs. "Because I want to have a little chat with him."

I narrow my eyes at my father. "Jake was just here; you could've had a chat with him anytime. Instead you spent the past forty minutes grumping and growling at the man who saved my life! And you never once smiled."

My father rolls his eyes. "I did not grump and growl."

"Yes you did!" I try hard not to raise my voice.

Tears spring to my eyes as I recall Jake's coughing fit; I feel terrible knowing I was the cause of it. Jake seemed embarrassed and probably thinks any illness on his part is a sign of weakness. I wish I could tell him he doesn't always have to be the biggest, strongest alpha in the room. If anything, Jake's vulnerability makes him even more endearing because he resists it so much.

If we'd been alone, I might have told him that... and then given him a hug because that big guy really needs one.

I swipe my damp eyes, which Dad must notice because he immediately backpedals. "Fine," he replies. "I'll try to smile once in a while. And you can drive Spellman the rest of the week."

I fold my arms and glower at my dad. He's up to something; I just know it. "Why can't I drive Jake tomorrow?"

"You can give him a lift back home when he's finished here."

I throw my hands in the air. "Just please... try to be nice."

"I'm always nice."

Yeah, right. Except to the one guy who makes me forget why I'm considering that new cruise director role. I started the job application but haven't submitted anything yet.

My dad puts an arm around my shoulders. "How about I make spinach souffle for dinner tonight? Hmm?"

"Are you trying to buy me off with a good meal?" I try to sound stern, but Dad knows my weak spot is his incredible cooking.

"Wouldn't dream of it!" he says with a wink.

I shake my head and chuckle.

He's a crafty, cranky, incorrigible curmudgeon. But I love him.

I'M DRYING the last pot in our blue-and-white kitchen when my phone buzzes on the table. I toss the towel over the oven door handle, scoop up my phone, and check the caller: it's Twila Peppertail, who's covering the front desk.

"Hey, Twila. Everything alright?"

She's whispering into the phone, but I can't make out a single word due to the background noise. It sounds like she's standing in a wind tunnel. When I ask her to repeat herself, she hisses, "Auntie Imogen... is—" There's a crash and a shriek.

"Stay put. I'm coming!" I shout into the phone.

Dad glances up from the romance novel he's reading at the table. "Don't tell me Auntie's throwing another tantrum."

"Fine... I won't!" I call over my shoulder as I speed down the hall past our bedrooms, sprinting toward the last door at the end that connects directly to the inn. I step onto the thick carpeting, run past the library, Dad's office, and several meeting rooms, and dash into the main lobby.

Pausing, I wonder whether I've made a wrong turn, which is plain ridiculous. I grew up at Mooncrest, and even though I've spent nearly all of the past decade living on ships, I could walk this place blindfolded and not crash into a door or wall or even a piece of furniture. Other than repairs and routine maintenance—new carpeting five years ago, and a fresh coat of paint three years later—my dad's not made any changes here since

Mama left. It's a good thing Auntie Imogen occasionally sprinkles her faerie dust to freshen the place up.

Except now... I can't walk to the antique mahogany desk without tripping over a crumpled, overturned sofa and stepping on crushed glass. Every stick of furniture has been tossed about; two of the tables have broken legs. Downy feathers are drifting around the room like tiny white clouds. In a moment of clarity, I realize those feathers used to reside inside the upholstered chairs and couch, which Auntie has shredded in her rage.

I put my hands on my hips and holler up at my white-haired, pleasantly plump, and mostly deceased faerie ancestor. "Toss down your hat, Auntie!"

That gets her attention. She swivels her head one full rotation and stares down at me with stony gray eyes. "Why do you want it now? You have never listened to my fashion advice before, young lady!" She waves one lace-gloved hand at my jeans and shudders. I suppose my twenty-first-century style is a bit jarring to her nine-teenth-century sensibilities.

I fold my arms crossly and shout, "Because there's a bee in your bonnet!"

"A bee!" Imogen screeches, pulls out her hat pins, and flings away her frumpy headpiece, which is piled high with fake fruit and taxidermized blackbirds. "I am deathly allergic to bee stings!"

Which, of course, I already knew. Dad and I both learned a long time ago the best way to stop Auntie in her tracks is to tell her a bee's flying around her head. We've probably pulled the same stunt at least twenty times through the years; fortunately, Imogen's memory has some convenient gaps. Too bad she hasn't forgotten how to break furniture.

Dad arrives and goes over to the desk, where he speaks in soothing tones with Twila. She nods and scurries down the hall to the private room where she's staying. I feel sorry for her; she's a sweet elf who's probably never had to deal with a cantankerous faerie godmother. Imogen is ninety percent ghost, but she can raise a mighty magical ruckus with that last ten percent when she's mad.

"Alright, Auntie," calls out my dad. "You've certainly got our attention. Now tell us what's upset you to this extent." He spreads out his hands to indicate the destruction. A downy feather lands on his shoulder, which he ignores.

"How could you, Richard Mayflower DeMaris?" pouts Auntie.

My dad heaves a heavy sigh; I think we're both surprised she's remembered his full name. "What have I done to offend you?"

Auntie glowers down at him over the pince-nez perched on the end of her nose. Now I'm scratching my head, because Imogen rarely wears spectacles in public; she's terribly vain. I have a sneaking suspicion she's been reading in the library again... or perhaps snooping in Dad's office.

Imogen is able to navigate her way around the inn by moving from one picture frame to another, but she rarely bothers because she believes it's her duty to oversee the main lobby. I suspect she also doesn't want to leave her canvas unoccupied for very long, in case another mostly ghostly faerie takes up residence.

Her lower lip trembling, she whines, "You are attempting to sell Mooncrest out from under me!"

That's a surprisingly accurate statement, and I'm stunned she's found out about Dad's plans, because he's been very close-lipped since our discussion. My father's shoulders slump, and all of a sudden he looks much older. I'm struck by the realization my dad will join the ancestors one day... and then I'll be all alone.

Nodding, he says softly, "I'm sorry Auntie, but I'm so weary... and... and sad much of the time. I can't do it anymore." His voice drops to a whisper. "I miss her too much."

Now I'm staring at my dad, because he's never admitted to actually missing my mother... or struggling with depression. Perhaps he figures that at thirty-two years of age, I'm finally able to handle the truth.

Auntie Imogen's face softens, and she removes her pince-nez. "Oh, Ricky, my boy, so do I. But how can you sell our family's home? Watching a bunch of strangers manage my inn shall be the death of me."

"Auntie, I'd never leave you behind! Wherever I go, you'll come with me!"

Imogen shakes her head. "No, dear boy, that simply won't do. This is my home; I'll not abandon it." She compresses her lips and is silent for a full minute. Then she murmurs, "You're planning on seeing her again, aren't you?"

I'm shocked for the second time this evening when

Dad nods. "Karyn has invited me to stay with her for a while in Palermo—after I sell the place of course."

I whip my head around, my mouth agape. "You're going to stay with Mama? In her apartment in Sicily?"

Dad turns to me with a shy grin. "Yes... Your mother's doing better, Mona, much better. And she wants to see me again too."

I'm stunned and speechless and maybe a bit scared. This is a huge change that I can't handle in the midst of my own issues and up-in-the-air plans. I need to talk to Dad about Mama, but now's not the time. I force my attention back to Auntie, who's clearly more in charge than I ever realized. She's truly a faerie force to be reckoned with, and I can imagine her giving even Queen Victoria a run for her money.

"Well," replies Auntie Imogen in her high-pitched voice. "No one can ever accuse me of standing in the way of true love. But that does *not* mean you can sell Mooncrest to the first Troll, Drake, or Harpy who comes along." She takes a deep breath and continues. "I must have the final say on who will be permitted to purchase my inn."

Dad nods. "If that's what you want, Auntie, then of course. I'll let the lawyers know to include you in all negotiations."

Imogen smiles. "You're a good boy, Ricky. I wish you and Karyn all the happiness in this world and the next."

My dad gives Auntie a sheepish smile. "Thank you, Auntie... although we have a lot of work to do before I can see Karyn again. It could take a year or more to find the right buyer for Mooncrest."

"Posh and nonsense," says Imogen with a flutter of her hands. "Not when I'm involved." Auntie glances around at the smashed-up lobby and shakes her head. "I made quite a mess this time, didn't I?"

"Afraid so," Dad replies.

Auntie spreads open her arms, her palms facing the tin ceiling overhead, and says, "Go on back to your apartment and let me get to work. I'll make this lobby spic and span in no time."

Dad and I mumble our thanks and head back down the hallway toward our apartment door. Placing his hand on the knob he says, "I guess you're kinda surprised, huh?"

I snort. "That's an understatement."

My dad is a handsome faerie-gnome-elf in his late sixties with many good years ahead of him. Why does he insist on living in the past, longing for a woman who's caused him nothing but heartache and pain?

"Why don't you take a bath while I'll put on some tea," he replies. "I'm sure you have questions, which I'll do my best to answer."

Dad knows all the merfolk remedies for calming the jitters, the simplest one being an ordinary bath. I nod my head wordlessly because he's right; I need to stretch out my tail fin and decompress before we attempt to talk about Karyn DeMaris, the mermaid who abandoned me without a backward glance.

CHAPTER 16
RIDE ALONG

JAKE

Friday, January 18

I'm pacing in front of the floor-to-ceiling windows in my great room, anxious as a wolf cub before my first full-moon pack run, when I managed to make it a third of the way before losing my supper. One of the older pack members waited patiently for me as I slurped up some cool water from a stream, and then we ran off to join the others.

Although I've outgrown the tendency to puke during every run, my stomach still twists up when I'm nervous, like right now. I don't relish the thought of riding along with Rick DeMaris, even if it's only a few miles.

I hear tires turning into the driveway, slip on my fire chief's tactical jacket, and step outside. I'm in uniform today since this is a reinspection. I'm hoping it lends me an extra air of authority and helps level the playing field with cranky Rick DeMaris, but I doubt it.

Rick pulls up in the inn's ancient van, an old hearse he purchased for next to nothing and repainted white. The paint is so chipped the vehicle looks covered in Dalmatian spots, and the Mooncrest logo on the passenger door is missing one of the *O*s.

Fortunately the inn's supernatural guests aren't put off by the sight of a spotty hearse parked on the property, and the human guests think it's part of the charm of the place. Mooncrest Inn is a popular stop on every ghost hunter's tour. With stories of vases flying through the air and talking pictures—courtesy of Rick's Auntie Imogen—Mooncrest's reputation as a haunted inn is secure.

Rick gives me a curt nod; he's wearing reflective aviator sunglasses, a red ball cap, and an unreadable expression on his lined face. He leans over to unlock the passenger door.

"Good morning, Rick," I say, lowering myself stiffly into the seat. I begin searching for the two halves of the frayed seat belt. (As mayor I'm particularly vigilant about following all the laws and ordinances.) After I buckle up, I glance over at Mona's dad. "Thanks for the lift."

Rick grunts and then does the strangest thing: he grimaces at me, baring all his teeth. I leap back against the door with a small yelp of surprise. If he were a were-wolf I'd assume the man just challenged me.

But Rick frowns and then grimaces again with his front teeth on full display. "No problem."

Holy conflagration! I think Rick DeMaris is attempting to smile at me.

I'm not sure whether this is a good sign or a lead-up

to something else, so I remain silent. Rick backs out of the driveway and turns in the opposite direction of the inn. Now I'm really nervous, and my stomach forms a hard knot.

"Where are we going?"

"One of our guests left his sword behind. He's Malaki's cousin, so I'm dropping it off at the shop. I'll let Malaki worry about shipping the sword back to Romania."

At least a dozen questions revolve in my brain after that statement, but I ask the most obvious one. "Any idea why a Romanian vampire is traveling around here with a sword?"

"It's none of your business, Mister Mayor, nor mine for that matter," grunts Rick. He glances at me, but I can't see his eyes through his shades. "As a supernatural innkeeper, it's my job to protect my guests' privacy, so I don't poke around unless I suspect criminal behavior. However, I can put your mind at ease about this guy; he was traveling with a group of LARPers re-enacting Transylvanian history."

"In Wisconsin in the dead of winter?

Rick snorts. "What can I say? It takes all kinds."

I let the matter drop, since the vampire's already left town, and his sword will be on its way shortly. I fidget in my seat, wondering how to have a normal conversation with Mona's father. The man always seems edgy around me... and I don't know why. I've never said a cross word to him.

Rick and I both sigh at the same time and then swivel our heads in surprise. He pulls into a parking spot on

Main Street about a block from Malaki's Menswear, turns off the engine, and rests his gloved hands on the steering wheel. "You go first, Mister Mayor. You obviously have something to say to me."

Before I lose my nerve, I blurt out, "I know you don't like me... and I'm sorry if I've done something to offend you. Whatever it is, I hope we can put the past behind us."

Rick shakes his head, pulls off his sunglasses, and tosses them on the dashboard. "Why do you think I don't like you?"

"Because you struggle to be civil in my presence."

Rick chuckles softly. "Finally I get an entirely frank answer from the mayor."

"There you go again. Why do you keep poking fun at my role as the mayor or fire chief?"

"I've never teased you about being the fire chief, and I never will. You saved my daughter's life, and I'll be grateful to you until my dying day." Rick rubs his eyes and then peers at me. "That's why I wanted to drive you today—I wanted to say thank you—and to tell you your parents would have been so proud of you."

I draw my brows together. "My parents? I know Riddle Hill's a small town, but I never got the impression you knew them very well."

"Your stepfather and I were on the same bowling team for years," says Rick. "And we used to play cards with your uncle Nash, Malaki, and Bay Wolferman, your friend Rob's dad. Don't you remember?"

I shake my head. "Not really. I know Dad used to go out with his buddies, but that's all I remember."

Rick nods. "Everything changed after the accident. I can only imagine how devastating it was for you and Cassia. And for the rest of us... well, your parents were very popular. The whole community took it hard."

I close my eyes to keep them from tearing up and suddenly, I'm struggling to breathe. "I'm sorry Rick, but I need some fresh air!" I fumble with my seat belt, throw open the door of the hearse, and stumble outside onto the sidewalk.

Rick flings open his door and runs around to me. Placing a firm hand on my shoulder, he says, "Breathe slowly, but be careful. You're still healing."

I nod as I gulp down the cold air, slowly filling my lungs and then exhaling. I'm feeling kind of exposed standing on Main Street with Rick DeMaris hovering nearby, so I say, "Why don't you grab that sword and take it to Malaki. I'll wait inside the van."

Rick agrees and before long he's back behind the wheel. "I didn't mean to get you upset, Jake."

"I know... I'm a lot more sensitive these days." Then I add, "But since we're on the topic, I'd still like to know why you tease me about being the mayor."

Shrugging, Rick puts on his shades. "I'm not a fan of politicians, period. Honestly, it's nothing personal."

"Well you could've fooled me," I grump.

Rick snorts. "Yeah, I'll try to work on my lousy attitude." He turns the hearse around and heads in the direction of the inn. "There's one more thing I wanted to discuss with you."

"Go on, I'm listening," I reply warily.

"Mona Lisa belongs at sea and not stuck in some

supernatural town in northern Wisconsin. But ever since the fire, she seems unsure about what she wants, and I think it's partly your fault."

"My fault? How so?" I ask, hoping Rick will drop some hint about Mona's true feelings. Has she said anything to her father about me?

"There's obviously some hero worship going on," grumbles Rick, "which I suppose is only natural if a handsome fella rushes into a smoky building to rescue you."

I try to process what Rick is saying, ignoring the backhanded compliment about my appearance. "So you think Mona may be... ah... confused in her attitude toward me because I'm the one that carried her from the building?"

"Yup, I do. And it would sure be a shame if Mona doesn't apply for that new cruise director job on a big new ship. I gather it would be a real feather in her cap; she'd get a nice bump in rank and salary too." Rick sniffs. "That Emilio fella keeps asking her to apply, but she's dragging her feet."

I feel myself deflate faster than a balloon someone's just stomped to bits.

I guess it shouldn't bother me Emilio and Mona are in touch, but it does. Even worse, Captain Emilio wants her to apply for some big promotion on a brand new ship. And the only thing holding Mona back appears to be me... or more precisely, her confusion over how she feels about me.

Could Rick be right? The only reason Mona may be softening toward me... is because I saved her life?

If so, that would be the worst possible reason for starting a relationship.

Now I'm totally conflicted. Do I tell Mona how I truly feel... or keep my mouth shut and not risk confusing her further?

Rick pulls around to the back of the inn and parks the hearse. As I push open the door and lumber out, I remind myself I'm here to help Rick and Mona get the chapel back up to code so they can have a functioning business —and my sister can have the wedding of her dreams.

I've waited fifteen years to tell Mona how I really feel, and I guess I'll keep on waiting... because the last thing I'd want is to stand between Mona and her dream job.

CHAPTER 17
PUPPY DOG EYES

MONA

Friday, January 18

"Good morning, Mona," says Jake, entering the lobby alone; my father has probably slunk away to our apartment. Dad obviously wants me to deal with Jake's reinspection, although at least this time I'm ready.

Jake pauses by the door, swiveling his head as he scans the room. "Um... it sure looks different around here... what happened?"

Jake's right; the inn's reception area has had a makeover courtesy of Auntie Imogen's rant. She must've been up all night magicking the lobby back into shape. However, she also managed to turn all the upholstery inside-out when she reassembled the sofa and chairs. Oddly enough, they actually look better this way. Auntie didn't stop there; our coffee table now has a green marble top that matches the mantel over the fireplace, and we have a lovely Persian rug tying the whole room together.

Jake moves more stiffly than before his surgery, which tells me he's still in pain, and he's paler than usual. But he's wearing his navy blue fire chief's uniform, which makes him look positively swoony. My pulse speeds up just looking at him, so I glance away.

That's when I notice Auntie Imogen, who's been snoring all morning long; now she's wearing her spectacles again and leaning partly out of the frame.

Barnacles!

She's checking out Jake's butt! My ridiculous faerie ancestor is ogling him like a debutante at her first ball.

I wave my hand in the opposite direction of Auntie's picture frame, hoping to distract Jake. "Oh, you know how elderly aunties can be. Mine went into a tizzy last night, and this is the result."

"I heard that, young lady," calls out Auntie Imogen from the wall. "I did not have a 'tizzy' as you call it. I merely decided this lobby needed a facelift."

Jake smiles up at my ancestor, who's glaring down at me. "Good morning, Miss Imogen. I like what you did in here."

Auntie's pouty mouth turns up at the corners. "Why hello there." She flaps one of her snowy wings at Jake, managing to knock her silly hat askew. "This cannot be little Jake Grayclaw Spellman, all grown up!"

"Yes, ma'am," he replies, grinning.

"My goodness, you have filled out nicely." She giggles like a schoolgirl. "Did you know my second husband was a werewolf?"

"No, ma'am, I did not," says Jake with a low chuckle that rumbles deep in his throat and leaves me feeling weak in the knees... and also a teensy bit envious of my white-haired ancestor. Jake is aiming his large amber eyes at Auntie and ignoring me, despite the amount of time I invested in my hair and makeup this morning. Plus, I'm standing three feet from him and *clearly very much alive.*

"Oh my, yes," Imogen titters. "Martel and I created quite a stir in London at the Crystal Palace Exhibition back in '51."

Imogen is referring to the World's Fair of *1851.* Since the nineteenth century is her favorite time period, and Martel her favorite husband, I'm concerned we're heading down storybook lane with my flirty faerie auntie. At this rate Jake and I may never get the inspection completed.

"Well, I think it's time we get down to work," I say, casting Auntie a frowny look.

Imogen rolls her eyes at me and then waves her lace-gloved hand at Jake. "Please do come by and see me again, dearie. I enjoy entertaining male callers."

Jake's mouth quirks; he's obviously attempting to retain his composure. He nods solemnly. "Yes, ma'am. I'll do that."

Auntie giggles again, and then just like that, she's back to snoring in her frame.

I put a finger to my lips as we tiptoe past Auntie and descend the back staircase to the basement, where I show Jake our newly installed electrical panel and the new wiring that's safely encased in conduit. I also point out the empty space where the paint cans used to be stored.

Jake says, "Hmm…" a few times and makes a couple of notations on his clipboard.

He's spending quite a lot of time looking at his clipboard or at the improvements we've made, but he's not made eye contact with me since he stepped into our lobby. And he's only cracked a smile once, when Auntie Imogen flirted with him.

Is this just Jake doing his job… a job that almost got him killed not that long ago? Or did Dad say something to Jake on their drive over here? Something that's made him stiff and standoffish?

Jake stares at my shoulder and then gives me a businesslike nod. "You've accomplished a lot here in very short order. Good job, Mona."

Good job, Mona?

My dad definitely said something. I take a deep breath and then stomp all the way up the stairs to the third-floor guest rooms. Jake's panting by the time we reach the top floor, and now I feel guilty all over again. Before he was injured rescuing me, Jake could run miles without breaking a sweat. Now climbing a few flights gets him huffing.

I remind myself the most important thing at the moment is getting through the reinspection, so I square my shoulders and take Jake into several of the unoccupied rooms. I don't step into the honeymoon suite with the provocative mermaid painting this time, but I open the door so he can have a look. "As you can see, we've removed all the extension cords and replaced the fire extinguishers on each floor."

"Uh huh," says Jake matter-of-factly, marking down something on his checklist.

Now I'm just plain irritated.

I stalk down the steps, and we repeat the same routine on the lower levels, with Jake nodding at the improvements we've made and avoiding eye contact. The last room to be inspected is the library on the main floor, and it's getting harder and harder for me to keep silent. No matter what, I need to keep my tongue on a short leash until Jake has finished his inspection.

But if that man grunts one more time I think I just may lose it.

I open the door to the library to show Jake the new outlets we installed. He steps in first, glances at the improvements we made, and then he mumbles like he's discovered something wrong.

"Did we miss anything?" I ask, worrying we're failing yet another inspection. I notice Jake staring at the top of my head, so I reach up to pat my hair, wondering if one of my curls has sprung loose from the hair gel I applied.

Jake clears his throat and looks back down at his clipboard. "Oh no; you've done a great job bringing this place up to code." He signs his name on the document he's been carrying and hands it to me. "Congratulations."

Then he turns to leave.

"Wait," I say. "Please."

Jake turns back, but his eyes are downcast.

"What did my father say to you in the car?"

Shrugging, Jake glances up at the top of my head again. "He thanked me... which I appreciated."

I narrow my eyes. "That's all?"

Jake blinks at the far wall. "He said my parents would've been proud."

"Oh... that was nice of him." I'm watching Jake, who's starting to fidget. He's showing all the signs of a wolf about to bolt. "What else did my father say?"

Jake shakes his head a second time and turns to leave, but I run around to block his exit. Finally, he raises his eyes to meet mine, and what I see there stops me cold.

He's lost his twinkle or sparkle or whatever you want to call it.

Jake looks so wretched I take a step toward him, reaching out my hand, but he pulls back with a small frown. "I'm sorry, Mona, really I am... but I've got to go."

He strides out to the lobby, pulls open the front door, and is gone.

For the second time in as many weeks, I dash outside into the freezing cold, running after a gorgeous werewolf with the saddest puppy-dog eyes I've ever seen.

But I'm too late—Jake is climbing into the sidecar of someone's motorcycle! Who is wacky enough to drive a motorcycle in Door County in January?

The driver is slender and obviously female, and I'm instantly jealous, until I catch a glimpse of long white hair flowing beneath the driver's helmet. At least I have the answer to one of my questions.

There's only one woman I know who thinks nothing of driving a cycle in winter, wearing three layers of flannel in summer, and knows more about comic books and Manga than any spotty-faced teenager on the planet: Catbeam Spellman, Jake's adopted faerie grandmother.

I figure Jake must've texted his granny while I stepped away for a moment to answer a question for Twila, which means he wanted to get away from me as soon as he finished his official business at the inn. Jake's entire demeanor is so different that I have no doubt my father said something to set him off—and I'm determined to get to the bottom of it right now.

I march up to our apartment, but Dad's not here. I yank open the outer door and check the parking spots out back. The hearse is gone; Dad's done a runner. No matter. He'll be back, and when he is, I'll find out what happened today between him and Jake.

I enter my red-and-black, moody teenager bedroom and glare at the laptop on my desk. Em texted me yesterday, reminding me the deadline for submitting my application is today. It's all filled out; I just haven't pressed *submit* yet.

I'm not ready to commit to anything... and I was kind of waiting until I saw Jake again today. I was hoping the little spark I felt between us lately was not a figment of my overactive imagination.

But we're back to Jake acting flaky around me again, which is not a sustainable basis for any kind of relationship. Even if Dad said something dumb to him, which he probably did, it's still no excuse for Jake to address the wall behind my head instead of me.

Sighing, I flip open my laptop, navigate to the open

tab with the application sitting in draft mode, and stare at it.

What have I got to lose? I tap *submit*, close my laptop, and head back down to the lobby.

Auntie is snoring softly... but instead of bothering me, I find it kind of soothing.

Drat it all; once this place is sold I'll have no reason whatsoever to come back to Riddle Hill. Dad is unsure about where he's going to live after he sells the place, but it seems unlikely he's going to stay here in town.

I'm going to miss him of course, and Auntie and the Peppertail elves, as well as the Sit for a Spell Café, Cassia Spellman... and her confounding but courageous brother.

Now I want to claw back that application I just submitted, but it's too late. I text Em to let him know it's done. He sends me a bunch of smiley faces.

Meanwhile, I still need to address the repairs to the chapel; Lamps, Amps, and Vamps are coming in an hour to get started. Guess I'll have to walk them through Jake's list of to-dos without him.

I wonder what he and Catbeam Spellman are doing right about now.

I'll tell you one thing he's *not* doing... he's definitely not thinking about me.

CHAPTER 18

GARGOYLES ON PARADE

JAKE

Lunchtime, January 18

"Granny, please take me home!" I holler as I slip her spare black helmet onto my head. She doesn't reply but revs the engine and takes off so fast I give a yip of surprise. This is one time I don't mind Granny Catbeam's speed-demon ways, because I'm itching to get away from Mooncrest... and beautiful Mona.

I seem to be making a point of acting like a hormonal teenager whenever Mona is around—the complete opposite of how an alpha should behave—and if this continues Trixie Wolferman is definitely going to have my hide. Although even Trixie would have the decency to wait until I'm sufficiently recovered before issuing a call for challengers. My status as pack alpha is safe for the moment.

But I'm more concerned about Mona right now; I just abandoned her again without an explanation. I'm afraid whatever goodwill I may have generated from my hand-written apology has evaporated by now.

Forget about goodwill; I'm just hoping she doesn't hate my guts when I turn up at the chapel tomorrow.

I'm contemplating how badly I've handled everything with Mona—who looked so hot today I struggled not to sweep her into my arms and plant a kiss on her full red lips that would make even Elizabeth Bennet swoon—so it takes me a few moments to realize Granny's stopped the motorcycle. But we're not in my driveway. She's parked in front of the Sit for a Spell Café.

I fold my arms across my frozen chest and shake my head. "Nope. I want to go home."

"Don't give me any of yer guff, sonny. Yer lookin' hollowed out, and I'm hankering after some o' Nash's good cookin'. So get yer butt outta that seat and come inside."

"Fine," I mutter as I remove my helmet. She may be bossy and annoying, but I adore this stubborn faerie woman who's shown me nothing but love from the moment Mom married Zeke Spellman, my stepdad and Catbeam's son. Granny never treated me like a step-grandchild; if anything, she doted on me even more than she doted on Cassia and Sophie, and to tell the truth, I ate it up.

I peer into the café's plate glass windows as I approach the entrance; the place is hopping, so Granny and I will need to wait for a spot to open up before we can snag something to eat. I hold open the door for my grandmother and follow her inside.

The buzz of conversation immediately stops as every

patron in the restaurant rises to their feet. I wonder if there's something wrong... until I realize everyone is looking at me... and smiling. Then Sophie, who should be in the bakery across the street but is standing next to Cassia and Aunt Phoebe, starts to clap. My sister and aunt join in, and then Uncle Nash and his young faerie cousins step out of the kitchen in back, grinning and slapping their hands together.

I notice Rob and Teddy sitting at a pair of tables along with most of the fire department. Teddy yells, "Hail to the Chief!" and soon the whole place is applauding, stomping their boots, and shouting my name.

"What's happening?" I ask under my breath.

Catbeam chortles and drapes her skinny arm across my shoulders. "You're a hero, Jakey, my boy. And the folks want to acknowledge yer service."

I feel my eyes well up and blink fast; I will *not cry* in public. After all, I'm the mayor and fire chief and pack alpha. I have a certain standard to uphold. Granny must notice because she gives my arm a squeeze, and then she cocks her head to the side. "Well lookee at those little stone fiends!"

She points at the five gargoyles attached to the corbels beneath my aunt's countertop; they're marching in place and saluting me as if they're leading a military parade. I burst out laughing, which helps me overcome my awkwardness at so much unwanted attention.

Eventually the cheering dies down, and I'm saved from having to give a thank-you speech by my aunt Phoebe, who waves me and Granny over to the counter in back. My sister pours coffee for me and Granny as we drop onto a pair of stools.

"Thanks," I mumble, still feeling pretty emotional and wrung out.

Cassia winks. "We surprised you, didn't we?"

I roll my eyes. "Yeah. Who's to blame for cooking up this little scheme?"

"The Spellman ladies," says Uncle Nash with a chuckle. "They're dangerous when they put their lovely faerie heads together."

Phoebe orders the daily special for Granny and me, and the two of them start chatting about their latest book club read. I'm content to sip my coffee and listen to the murmur of voices around me, incredibly thankful for my extended family and friends in this zany community. I can't imagine being happy living anywhere else.

I tuck into my bacon, turkey, cheddar, and maple butter panini, relishing the blend of flavors. I guess Granny was right as usual; I haven't been eating well lately. After I finish my sandwich and top it off with a slice of Door County cherry pie, Cassia warms up my coffee and says, "Do you want to talk about it?"

I snort, because I said pretty much the exact same thing to her last month, when she and her fiancé briefly split up. Funny how quickly the tables can turn. I give her the same answer she gave me. "Not really."

"Well that's too bad, because you obviously need some sisterly advice. Grab your coffee and follow me."

"Where are we going?"

"Phoebe's office."

"Aren't you still working?"

"My shift ended five minutes ago. Now no more excuses."

Groaning, I rise from the stool with my steaming mug and follow my sister into Phoebe's tiny office around back. My aunt has managed to cram a polished teakwood desk, two sleek gray chairs, floor-to-ceiling bookshelves, and a comfy three-cushion sofa into a space smaller than my pantry. I strongly suspect faerie magic is involved.

"What's going on Jake?" blurts out my sister. "You're hiding something from me; I just know it."

"What are you talking about?"

"Is there something wrong with your heart?" asks Cassia, her brow furrowed.

"What gives you that idea?" I mumble.

Actually my sister is spot on; there is something very wrong with my heart.

For the second time around, I'm falling for a woman who craves the open sea. And while Door County is surrounded on three sides by water, and I could take Mona out in my sailboat six months of the year... it would never be the same as cruising the Mediterranean all year long.

"Because you seem more emotional than usual. Definitely more angsty."

I shake my head. "I'm fine... or will be when I can start running again... I'm not used to feeling so weak, I guess."

"Humph!"

"Don't humph me... that's my line."

Cassia snorts and then asks the one question I don't want to answer. "How are you and Mona getting along?"

I fiddle with the fringe on Phoebe's throw pillow, which says, *Today is Here. Live in the Moment.* What exactly is that supposed to mean? I realize Cassia is waiting for an answer. "Fine I guess."

Cassia throws her hands in the air. "You're hopeless. And clueless."

"Gee thanks."

"Have you told her how you really feel?"

I draw my brows together. "Aunt Phoebe snitched about my non-date with Mona and my weird dream, didn't she?"

"I wouldn't call it snitching. When we were in the hospital, waiting for you to come out of *emergency surgery*, Phoebe told me and Sophie. She was worried sick about you—we all were."

"Sophie knows too?" When Cassia nods, I lean my head back against the upholstery. "Gah! That girl can't keep a secret for longer than five minutes."

"But why does it have to be a secret? Why can't you just tell Mona how you feel?"

I debate confiding in Cassia about my conversation with Rick this morning, and figure I may as well; she's the one woman in my life who actually can keep a secret. When I tell her the gist of it, Cassia shrugs. "So Rick DeMaris is convinced he knows what's best for Mona— but he could also be mistaken. In fact, I'm just as convinced he doesn't know what his daughter really wants."

"How do you figure that?"

"Mona and I spent a lot of time together last month, when I was planning three weddings in a row at Mooncrest. We had some late-night chats. Girl talk."

"Girl talk?" I sit up straighter. "Did I figure in any of that girl talk?"

Cassia rolls her eyes. "Not in so many words."

"Oh." I lean back, deflated.

"But every time your name came up in conversation, Mona's eyes twinkled."

"Her eyes twinkled? That's not much to go on."

"And sometimes her mouth turned up a teensy bit at the corners."

"Wow. I'm entirely underwhelmed."

"Stop being so obtuse," says Cassia. "These are all signs of a woman in love… or at least, heading in that direction. It's up to you to encourage her."

"And how do I do that?"

"For starters, stop leaving every time you're feeling tense around her!"

"Point taken. What else?"

"Make eye contact."

I stare up at the ceiling. "It's hard for me sometimes, especially when a lot's at stake."

"I know," says my sister softly. "But it's important because otherwise she's going to think you don't like her."

I nod and mumble. "Any other tips?"

"Smile, share a joke, and sweet moonglow, ask the woman out!"

"What about her father?"

"What about him?"

"He's going to be mighty irritated if I ask Mona out on a date."

"So what?" Cassia lifts her shoulders. "It's not his life —it's yours and Mona's. You and Mona get to decide how you feel and what you want."

"You know what..." I chuckle. "You've gotten pretty good at handing out advice."

Cassia gets up from the desk chair and grins. "Well, it's sort of a naturally occurring phenomenon. You become a parent, and suddenly you're spouting advice all over the place."

"Speaking of being a parent... I'm feeling like a kid every morning, waiting around for a ride to school, or in this case, to the inn. Is there any way you can get away from the café for twenty minutes to give me a ride the next few days? I really don't want to ride along with Rick again."

"I'm sure Phoebe won't mind. How about if I swing by around ten, which is between the breakfast rush and the lunch rush?"

"Perfect... and thanks."

"What about the afternoons? Don't you need a ride back?"

"Mona said she'd give me a ride."

Cassia winks. "Good thinking." She turns to leave. "You coming?"

"In a minute," I reply. "I need to call Mona."

"Make it good."

I wave her out the door, pull my phone out of my pocket, and try to compose my thoughts before calling. I soon give up and send Mona a short text instead. "I'm sorry I ran out, Mona. I wasn't feeling well. I'll see you in the morning a little after ten."

Mona's reply comes almost immediately. "Do you need a ride?"

"Cassia can drop me off in the morning. But I'll need a ride back home."

Mona gives me a thumbs up. I'm hoping she'll say something more, like: "See you tomorrow," or "I'll be happy to give you a ride."

But after waiting for several long minutes, I realize Mona doesn't have anything else to say to me.

CHAPTER 19
SUCH SMOLDER

MONA

Saturday, January 19

When Dad finally returned to the inn last night, I confronted him about Jake and their conversation in the hearse. His story syncs up with Jake's, but I'm convinced he's holding out on me. I'm frustrated with both men, but I'm determined to ferret out the truth.

I've decided to dial back my cuteness quotient regardless; there's no point putting so much effort into my hair and makeup if Jake is going to be looking elsewhere the whole time. Besides, we have work to do, and I'm not about to ruin my new designer jeans and cashmere sweaters just to impress Jake Spellman.

I'm sitting with Twila at the mahogany desk in the lobby, training her on our reservation system, when I hear tires crunching on the snowy driveway outside. I grab my puffer coat from the back of my chair and head out the front door, slipping on my jacket while Cassia's silver Honda CRV comes to a complete stop. As Jake climbs out of the passenger door, I bend down to say "Hey" to Cassia before she drives away.

I straighten at the same time as Jake, and this time, he looks directly at me. His large amber eyes are not sad so much as apologetic. "I'm sorry about yesterday. I really wasn't feeling well."

My heart does a backward flip inside my chest at the intensity of his gaze. It takes me a moment to find my voice. "It's alright; I was concerned something else was wrong. Or my dad said something to make you feel... awkward around me."

Jake swallows hard, and now he's staring at my mouth. I may have skipped my eye shadow today, but at least I'm wearing lash-lengthening mascara and my favorite cherry-flavored lip gloss. Jake licks his lips and tilts his head, almost like *he's thinking of kissing me*. I raise my face, realizing this is crazy but also wanting to feel his mouth on mine... and then the inn's heavy door creaks open behind us.

Waving my phone in her hand, Twila Peppertail chirps, "Oh Mona, there you are! You left your phone on the front desk. Looks like you missed a call from Emilio."

Immediately, Jake's broad shoulders droop, and he breaks eye contact. I want to scream, "Just kiss me already!" but instead I turn to my assistant—who clearly needs additional training when it comes to boundaries and privacy and a host of other things—and I force a smile. "Thank you, Twila."

She hands me the phone and heads back inside, completely oblivious she just ruined my magic moment with Jake Spellman. I feel like whimpering, but I'm nothing if not resilient. I look up at Jake, who's staring at my shoulder again, and say, "Where were we?"

He cocks his head, peers into my face, and gives me a crooked grin. "I was thinking... it would be nice to..." As he leans down, my heart beats out a drumroll beneath my puffer coat, and I tip up my chin—

"What are you two doing out there?" shouts my father, who's just thrown open the chapel door. "Did you forget your keys or something?"

Jake lets out the teensiest growl, which makes my stomach drop to my knees. I clear my throat and squeak, "We're coming."

As we walk toward the chapel's blue door, which my father is holding wide open, Jake whispers. "You're giving me a ride home today, right?"

"Absolutely," I murmur.

"Good."

Butterflies spin in my stomach at the smolder in his amber eyes... which probably mirrors the longing in my own eyes. Maybe being in a confined space with Jake isn't such a good idea?

Nah. He's completely trustworthy. Besides, I've waited fifteen years for Jake Grayclaw Spellman to look at me like this. I'm *not* missing my chance again, and my father will *not* be providing Jake with any more rides.

As we cross the threshold, I notice Dad giving Jake the weirdest smile, all teeth and gums like some loony Jack O' Lantern. If he grimaced like that at Jake yesterday, no wonder the hunky werewolf was a bit tense; he probably read it as some sort of a veiled threat.

I arch my eyebrows at Dad, who gives me a normal, fatherly smile. Sighing, I realize he's doing the best he can with Jake; my dad certainly remembers Jake rejecting me in high school, and the tears I tried but failed to hide. Everyone thinks trolls hold grudges the longest, but that's not true: it's faeries who never forget a slight.

I know from all the trucks parked around our property that the contractors—Gnome Sweet Gnome and Lamps, Amps, and Vamps—are working inside the chapel today, despite the fact it's Saturday. I suspect my dad's given them an extra incentive, since we have a hard deadline with Jake's reinspection in a few weeks, plus his sister's wedding, although I still don't see how the chapel will ever be ready in time for Cassia and Will's ceremony.

The gnomes and vampires call out greetings to me and Jake as we enter. Since there's zero risk of any non-supers entering the closed chapel today, the contractors don't bother to mask their pointy ears, tipped-up eyebrows, and razor-sharp fangs. Jake wanders over to shake their hands, ask about families, and listen to complaints with genuine concern. A cynical person would think Jake is just doing it for votes in the next mayoral election, but that's not the case; I've known him long enough to confirm he genuinely cares.

Despite the fact I'd like to stick close to Jake now that he's here and making eye contact, our repairs require us to split up. Jake remains with the vampires, who are rewiring the chapel office today. I accompany the gnome crew that will be cleaning up the mess in the basement and installing a new support beam. We're leaving the landing area with the half-opened exit for another day; the rewiring and the basement wall are the priorities for now.

Around one o'clock, Dad and Elmo bring over a boxed lunch for everyone. The spread looks so mouth-watering I suspect it's half the reason the gnomes and vampires agreed to work on Saturday. Jake starts to make his way over to me but stops when my dad plunks down in the pew next to me. Sighing, I try not to show my frustration.

And let's face it, Dad and I have limited time together too.

But I can't help feeling my father is being very intentional about coming between Jake and me. If I discover that's true, then we're going to have a heart-to-heart chat. I make my own decisions. Period.

After Dad and Elmo leave the chapel, and the gnomes and vampires are back at work, Jake stops me as I head down toward the basement. "Are you up for an errand?"

"Sure. What do you have in mind?"

"I have the measurements for the lumber we need to build the exterior staircase," replies Jake. "The lumber yard is running a sale through today, so I figure we can run over now, purchase the wood, and bring it back here. You'll be saving thirty percent on materials, and we'll be ready to start construction as soon as the exit is cleared."

"That makes sense, except the hearse can't accommodate that amount of wood."

"True... but if you give me a lift back to my place, we can switch vehicles. You can drive my Suburban over to the lumber yard."

I know Jake can't drive yet due to his surgery, but I'm not sure I should be the one to drive his pristine SUV. I'm a mermaid cruise director who hardly ever drives. I'm okay maneuvering the hearse, which has so many dings you can barely notice the new dents I made in the rear fender and driver's door.

At least Dad hasn't noticed, or if he has, he hasn't said anything.

Still... it would give Jake and me some additional time together in the car. "Sounds good. Let me grab my purse and keys. Meet you outside in ten minutes."

When I dash back to our apartment, I'm relieved to discover Dad is elsewhere. I tack a note on the refrigerator so he knows I'm taking the hearse, and then I freshen up my lip gloss, tame a few wayward curls, and manage to arrive at the parked hearse out back the same time as Jake.

The passenger side door always sticks, so it takes him a few tries to yank it open, but not before I notice him wince. Ugh. I hope Jake didn't overstrain himself because of our ridiculous "van," which I've been begging my father for years to replace.

Jake fumbles a few times with the frayed seatbelt because the buckle always manages to get stuck down behind the seat. When he's finally ready, he gives me a sweet half-smile, as if he's embarrassed by his weakened condition.

That little smile undoes me.

Jake Spellman, the triple-threat overachiever, is struggling to cope with his *helplessness*—which attracts me more than any demonstration of his *hunkiness*.

We chat about the chapel repairs on the short drive to his cottage; I park in front, and we clamber out of the hearse. Jake opens his garage door and hands me the key fob to his all-black Chevrolet Suburban, which is so shiny it looks like he just drove it off the showroom floor. "Here you go!"

The vehicle is massive, the size of a small bus, and consumes nearly all the space inside Jake's single-car garage. How am I supposed to drive that thing? And forget about parking it... I'll need a runway!

But there's no one else available to drive us, except my dad, who's not an option for obvious reasons. I clutch the key fob in my gloved hand, mumble "Thanks," and head around to the driver's side. That's when I notice the side mirror, which is as big as my head.

Sharks! Backing out of this garage is going to be harder than threading a needle. "Um... Jake?"

Jake tilts his head to the side, waiting for me to finish my thought.

"Do you think you could back this out of the garage —without bothering your stitches or anything?"

Jake chuckles. "Sure, no problem. It does take some practice to get comfortable backing out." I watch as he expertly maneuvers his dragon-sized transporter out of the garage, reverses down the driveway, and parks in the street.

Jake exits the driver's side and holds the door open for me. As I climb in, I hear him sniffle slightly, and I remember him doing the same thing on New Year's Eve. At the time I thought he had a cold, but now I realize Jake is using his wolf's powerful sense of smell to inhale my scent.

But why? I don't wear perfume.

Then it dawns me, maybe Jake likes my natural scent, and my silly heart skips a few beats. I lean back against the smooth leather seat with its new-car smell, willing my pulse to return to normal before I have to drive this behemoth.

When Jake climbs into the passenger side, I'm reminded again of his size (six foot two), bulk (solid manly muscle), and build (broad back, wide shoulders, powerful thighs). It's no wonder the man drives such a large vehicle; anything smaller would probably feel cramped to him. Jake leans left as he buckles in, and for a moment, we rub elbows... and arms...and shoulders.

Jake immediately leans right, opening up the gap between us. "Sorry for invading your personal space. I'm not used to sitting on this side."

"No problem. I know you well enough to know you're not getting handsy."

He glances at me, his brow lowered. "Who's getting handsy with you?"

Shrugging, I say, "No one in particular; it just goes with the territory."

"Of being a cruise director?"

"Of being a woman surrounded by a lot of men all day."

"Captain Emilio?" he growls. While I'm flattered by the note of jealousy I hear in Jake's tone, that's not fair to Em, who's a decent man undeserving of werewolf grumpiness.

Shaking my head, I set the record straight. "Nah. Em and the crew are courteous guys. It's our drunken male guests who cause issues, but it's nothing I can't handle."

Jake grunts, "It's not something you—or any other woman—should have to handle. Some guys are just animals."

Coming from a werewolf, that's pretty funny… and awfully sweet… but I keep my opinion to myself. Besides, it's time for me to get this monstrous vehicle on the road.

As I maneuver Jake's Suburban down the street, I notice a few of his dog-walking neighbors giving us a wide berth. One old faerie bends down to get a better look at the yokel behind the steering wheel. She's probably not used to seeing someone driving five miles an hour.

When we reach Highway 42, I accelerate to twenty miles an hour, which is still well below the speed limit. As I pull into the lumber yard, I notice a long line of cars behind me, and one driver making an offensive gesture as he speeds past. How rude! It's not my fault there's a double-yellow line down the middle of the highway.

By the time we've purchased the wood and two beefy guys have loaded it all into the back of Jake's SUV, the sun's already set. (After a decade cruising warmer climes, and despite the fact I grew up here, it still surprises me how early the sun sets during a Midwestern winter.) A nasty mix of ice and snow has started falling, making the parking lot and roads slicker than usual.

Sharks and shells! I still have to drop Jake off and then drive back to the inn with the lumber. I'm leaving the rusty hearse at Jake's house until tomorrow, when I'll drive him back home in the afternoon. Jake said Dad can borrow his Suburban for any errands in the meantime, and I'm sure Dad will think up a few just for a chance to get behind the wheel.

As for me, I never want to drive this freighter again.

I inch out of the parking lot and enter the highway, going even slower than before. I get the sense Jake has something to say, but if it's about my driving maybe he should keep it to himself.

He clears his throat. "Are you feeling okay?"

Now what kind of question is that?

I'm driving a tank down a twisty two-lane highway where the woods are thicker than in any faerie tale; the road is slicker than a Wisconsin pond in winter, and all the snow from the past month is piled up high on either side of us. I feel like I'm navigating a slippery, dirty white tunnel in the dark.

"Of course," I mumble. "Why do you ask?"

"You seem kind of nervous behind the wheel, that's all."

I'm about to confess my aversion to driving anything larger than a golf cart when Jake yells, "Look out!"

The headlights pick up a lovely brown doe, standing in the middle of the road, staring straight at us. I jam on the brakes, yank the wheel to the right, and the SUV starts fishtailing. Jake shouts something about easing up on the brake but that makes no sense to me, so I keep my foot pressed down and pray that the three of us—Jake, Bambi, and me—walk out of this alive.

We're careening so fast I feel nauseous; I think Jake's trying to tell me something, but I can't hear him over my own screams. I know we're leaning too far to the right, still going way too fast, but I can't seem to slow us down. The Suburban is skidding along the narrow shoulder, half on, half off the highway.

Suddenly the road drops out from under us. We're airborne as the SUV flips onto its side, but it seems to be taking a long time to land.

Then there's a thud... and a crunch... and the airbags deploy.

I'm screaming—screaming the name I keep buried in the deepest, loneliest recesses of my heart—the only name that matters to me in that moment.

"Jake!"

CHAPTER 20

MERMAID BEHIND THE WHEEL

JAKE

LATER, JANUARY 19

The Suburban is lying in a ditch on its right side, and I'm leaning against the cracked window, which is face down on the snowy ground. I passed out for a few minutes, maybe longer; I'm not sure. The airbags have deflated, so I push aside the excess fabric draped over my shoulders.

The emergency lights from my dashboard cast a faint glow, which is enough for me to see Mona suspended above me, held in place by her seatbelt. Her long, dark curls are dangling down, obscuring her face. When I realize she's not moving, my heart stutters in fear.

"Mona! Mona!" I shout. "Are you hurt?" I hear a whimper. Now I'm frantic with worry and strapped into my seat, the buckle buried underneath my hip. I reach my left hand toward Mona, my fingers briefly tangling in her coil of curls, until I feel the curve of her cheek. "Confound it, Mona! Say something to me!"

"Jake," Mona cries. "Oh Jake..." She's weeping, her wet tears trailing onto my hand. I'm terrified she's badly injured and growing more frustrated by the minute that I'm in no position to help her. My right arm is pinned against the window, and I'm afraid of moving too much until I know where we've landed; otherwise, we might find ourselves tumbling down a ravine. I briefly consider shifting to my werewolf form, but I decide against it for the same reason.

"Mona!" I need to get her attention. I caress her cheek, slowly repeating each word. "Are. You. Hurt?"

"It's broken!" she sobs. "I'm so, so sorry!"

"What's broken, sweetheart? Tell me."

"Your new Suburban!" she keens. "I broke your car!"

"I don't give a fuzzy wolf's tail about it!"

Mona takes a shaky breath and hiccups a few times. "But all guys adore their cars!"

Another tear falls onto my hand, and I desperately want to take her face in both my hands and kiss her until she believes me, but I'm unable to stretch out my right arm.

Do I feel a twinge of regret over my new Suburban? Of course, but it can always be repaired or replaced.

On the other hand, there's only one Mona—and she's irreplaceable.

"I'm not like other guys," I say gruffly. "I don't adore my car... I adore—"

Someone's pounding on the driver's side window

and shouting, "Stay put! We'll have you out soon; whatever you do, don't rock this vehicle!"

Mona starts at the interruption and then hiccups. "Finish what you were saying, Jake, please."

I feel awkward now the emergency crew's arrived, and I'm sore all over (we're both going to be pretty bruised tomorrow). Then I recall Mona's grumpy father, lecturing me about her mermaid heritage and her need to travel far beyond the shores of Door County for her happiness.

Was that only yesterday morning?

There's a lot of shouting outside and flashing red lights. I block out everything other than Mona's sniffles and force myself to stay focused on Mona's needs, not my confessions, and so I tell her a partial truth.

"I adore... mermaids who can't drive."

"Excuse me?"

The vehicle shakes again, and Mona screeches. I reach up to rub my thumb against her damp cheek. "I should have realized you haven't driven in a long time, and you've probably never gotten behind the wheel of a large SUV. I'm sorry I put you in this position."

I can feel Mona smile beneath my fingers; she reaches up and takes my hand. "I *can* drive, you know. I'm even certified to carry passengers in specially equipped golf carts."

She snorts, and we both chuckle.

Then Mona does something truly amazing. She kisses the palm of my hand, sending tingles up my arm and down my spine. "Thank you for being so gracious about the car wreck," she whispers. "I feel like such an idiot."

Sweet moonglow! I'm yearning to take this woman in my arms and kiss her until I muster enough courage to defy her father and admit my true feelings.

But there's a swooshing noise above us, followed by a blast of frigid air—the emergency responders are prying open the driver's side door. As they gently maneuver Mona out of her seat, I hear her murmur, "Barnacles! We almost went overboard!"

That confirms my suspicion the Suburban flipped over at the edge of a bluff.

"You're safe now, ma'am," replies one of the crew.

"But he's not!" cries Mona. Then she calls to me, "Don't you dare move a muscle, Jake Spellman!"

"He'll be out soon enough, ma'am," he reassures her.

That little exchange confirms it's going to take some time to extract me. My only consolation is that Mona is safe.

By the time the crew extricates me from my crumpled SUV, the first ambulance has already transported Mona to the hospital over her objections; she insisted she was "only a little banged up" and didn't want to leave until I was out of danger.

I wish I knew whether that's because she feels guilty over the accident, or because she has feelings for me. I honestly can't read Mona. If she's so enamored of her life at sea and Captain Emilio, then why would she plant that tender kiss on my palm?

As the paramedics lift me onto a stretcher, I make a

fist with my left hand, trying to recapture that moment... that feeling of Mona's soft lips pressed against my skin.

Although the accident occurred outside Riddle Hill, Marv must have heard about it on his police scanner, because he's leaning over me as the crew wheels me toward the ambulance. "Hey, Chief. You're really testing Lady Luck these days! Two fires and a car accident in a month; must be some kind of record." Marv pats my shoulder and murmurs, "Maybe you should ease up and take some time off, eh?"

I roll my eyes at him. "Very funny." As the medics lift me into the back of the second ambulance, I say, "Could you please call Cassia? And tell her not to worry."

"Sure thing, although I doubt she'll listen to the second part."

"Just try to reassure her, okay?"

"Of course," replies Marv. "You take care of yourself now. And I mean it."

I'VE BEEN ADMITTED to the hospital for observation, so once again I'm reclining in a hospital bed, although in a different room than before. This one is larger, with extra chairs, but with the same split-pea-soup color on the walls, and the same monitoring equipment humming and beeping nearby.

At least Aunt Phoebe and Cassia aren't crying this time; the emergency room docs want me to stay overnight, but nothing's broken (small miracle), my prior injuries are healing nicely, and my heart is behaving normally.

There's a soft knock at the door and in walks Mona.

Scratch that last part about my heart. Now it's beating out a parade march inside my chest.

Mona has a bandage on her neck but otherwise appears uninjured, another small miracle. She pushes back a fistful of her glorious, dark curls and says, "Oh, I'm sorry... I didn't realize you had company."

As she turns to leave, I call her back, but Phoebe and Cassia are way ahead of me. They hop out of their chairs and sprint over to Mona, hugging her and exclaiming over the cut on her neck. Mona puts her arms around each of them and sniffles a little, probably from all the feminine sympathy.

Which, by the way, I could use a dose of myself.

Hello, ladies, Jake Spellman over here. I'm stuck in bed... but is anyone hugging me? Or shedding a tear over my wellbeing?

Cassia takes Mona by the hand and leads her to one of the chairs by the window. Phoebe draws the blind closed and sits on the other side of Mona.

"Tell us what happened." Phoebe pats Mona's arm. "Start from the beginning."

"Well...there was a deer in the middle of the road—" says Mona.

"—You must have been so frightened," gasps my sister.

"I was so scared I didn't know—

"—Of course not, dear," Phoebe tsks in sympathy.

"That's one of the reasons I don't like driving at dawn and dusk, especially in the winter."

Cassia and Phoebe coax Mona to continue, interrupting her periodically, patting her arm, and at one point, giving her another round of hugs. Mona eventually finishes her story—leaving out the part about kissing my hand of course—and then she stands up to leave. "I better go; my dad should be here by now. Marv offered to give him a lift to your place, Jake, so he could pick up the hearse."

"Thanks for stopping by," I mumble, feeling sorry for myself.

Mona nods, stares at the bed a moment, and then glances up at me. Her large chocolate-brown eyes are filled with remorse. "I guess I'll see you... when you're feeling better. "

"Of course," I murmur. I want to tell Mona to stop feeling guilty about the accident, but I sense two pairs of faerie eyes watching me intently, so I don't say anything more.

Mona says goodbye to the room at large and hurries out the door.

"Wow," says my aunt with an eye roll. "Nothing like a heartfelt moment completely wasted. Must be your werewolf blood. A faerie man would never let his special lady walk out the door without calling her back and reassuring her all is well. Followed by a swoony, sizzling kiss that would melt every last bit of her resistance."

My sister glances over at me, tenting her eyebrows in silent comradery.

Phoebe believes in "telling it like it is," even if you

haven't asked for her opinion, and her daughter, Sophie, is the same. Poor Cassia has been on the receiving end of their free-flowing—and well-intended—advice for quite some time. I guess it's my turn now.

Cassia rises from her chair, comes over to the bed, and gives me a sisterly peck on the cheek. "Get some rest and text me when they discharge you in the morning. I'll give you a ride back home."

After my sister leaves, Phoebe stands, stretches, and transitions seamlessly into her faerie form. Her ears curve into dramatic points; her auburn eyebrows tip upward, and with a loud flutter, her black-and-gold wings extend six feet on either side of her sturdy frame.

One of Phoebe's gold wing feathers flutters to the floor. She picks it up, placing it in my hand, and we exchange a chuckle. When I was a boy I used to keep my aunt's wing feathers in a small box under my bed, convinced they were lucky charms.

"Three times, Jake," whispers Phoebe, her eyes moist. "You've had three close calls since Mona returned home to Riddle Hill. I don't think I can take much more of this."

My mouth drops open. "*You* can't take it? What about *me*?"

She flaps one wing. "You know what I mean. You're behaving so emotionally lately, not like yourself at all. Please resolve this situation with Mona before anything else goes wrong."

"You make it sound like I caused those fires and chased that deer into the road. None of those events were my fault, you know."

Phoebe shakes her head. "I'm not saying you created

those disasters... but I have a feeling you're an unwitting contributor."

"That makes no sense," I huff. "I certainly don't start fires."

"True... but you're nearly always the first one on the scene and the first to rush into danger."

"Now wait a minute." I cross my arms. "I'm a fire-fighter; it's my job to rush into burning buildings, with proper precautions of course."

"I spoke with Teddy after the apartment fire last month," says Phoebe gently. "He told me you remained on the roof longer than you should have, given the speed of the fire and the fact everyone had been rescued and accounted for."

"But one of my crew was still up there. You certainly don't expect me to leave anyone behind?"

"Of course not," replies Phoebe. "But Teddy told me the other firefighter was descending the ladder when the roof collapsed. You were the only one in immediate danger at that point... because you'd placed yourself in harm's way."

"That's a judgment call," I grumble. "And Teddy has far less experience fighting fires than I do."

"Alright," says my aunt. "I'll concede that point. But the next two disasters are different, and I think because of Mona somehow."

"Go on." I nod for her to continue, because she will tell me whether I want to hear it or not. "I'm listening."

"First—" Phoebe holds up one finger "—let's take today's accident. Why did you put Mona behind the wheel of that huge SUV? She's rarely on land long enough to drive anywhere; she must've been a nervous wreck in your Suburban."

I sigh. "Fine; I'll concede it was a dumb move on my part."

"I'm glad you agree, which brings me to my last point. If you hadn't been so determined to shut down the chapel and pressure Rick to get everything fixed at once, Mona and Cosmo wouldn't have been working overtime to get the repairs done. They probably wouldn't have been inside the building when the fire started, and you wouldn't have had to rush in to rescue them, almost getting yourself killed in the process."

"Your theory has a lot of holes." I scowl at my aunt, who I know loves me despite her bossy disposition. I'm not about to admit I've had some second thoughts myself about the way I handled the code violations. "Rick DeMaris has been skirting the fire code for years. It was high time someone held him accountable, and unfortunately that unpleasant task fell to me."

"Did the fact Rick doesn't want you dating his daughter impact your decision?"

I gape at my aunt. "How do you know about Rick's feelings on the matter?"

Phoebe waggles her faerie eyebrows at me. "It doesn't take a rocket scientist or a faerie godmother to know Rick still holds a grudge against you. Mona wore her heart on her sleeve when she invited you to that high-school dance. You had a good reason for turning her down, but then you really hurt her by inviting her best friend to senior prom."

I run a hand through my hair. "But that was fifteen

years ago! Besides, I've explained all that to Mona and apologized."

"Mona may have forgiven you, but Rick is a protective father who knows how badly you hurt his daughter once before. You're going to have to prove to Rick you're not the same teenage dolt you once were. You need to convince him you're an accomplished man who cares for his daughter."

"Mona is thirty-two years old! She's fully capable of managing her own life." Scowling, I add, "I don't need Rick's approval."

"Of course not, but you don't want his active opposition either."

Maybe Phoebe has a point; my aunt is an excellent judge of people's motives. I decide to tell her about my conversation with Mona's dad. "Rick gave me a ride and thanked me for rescuing Mona. We had a pretty good chat actually; I didn't know he was friends with my parents."

"Rick and Zeke used to hang out together all the time," says Phoebe softly, her eyes misting at the memory. She sniffs and refocuses her attention on me. "So after Rick thanked you and reminisced a bit, I'm guessing he brought Mona into the conversation."

I nod at my perceptive aunt. "Rick told me Mona has a shot at a big promotion on a new ship, and that she needs to be at sea to be truly happy. He mentioned Emilio is encouraging her to apply for the job, and then he suggested it's my fault Mona is dragging her feet. Rick seems to think there's some hero worship going on since I rescued her, and now she's... confused." I stop speaking and heave a sigh, feeling drained from the physical and emotional toil of the past few days.

"In other words, he implied you'd be disrupting Mona's plans and path to happiness if you ask her out?"

"Pretty much."

"Phooey," says Phoebe, kissing me on the cheek. She retracts her wings, which fold neatly inside the hidden slits of her sweater, and casts a glamour to hide her faerie features. "I have no doubt you'll figure this out on your own—without any advice from Rick DeMaris."

I watch her leave and then drop my head against the pillow, closing my eyes. I'm not sure what to think, except the emotional connection between Mona and me seems to run deeper than I imagined. If anything, I'm behaving as if she were my *mate*... but if that were the case, I'd know it.

No... this thing with Mona, this bond I think I'm feeling, is exactly what's preventing me from finding my true mate. I need to move past it. I need to break free from this near obsession with Mona Lisa DeMaris.

Tomorrow, I yawn as my weariness overtakes me. *I'll think about it tomorrow.*

CHAPTER 21
WATER THERAPY

MONA

Sunday to Tuesday, January 20-22

When Dad picked me up at the hospital on Saturday night, it was obvious he'd been crying. I guess I really scared him, which made me feel guilty all over again. I tried apologizing for frightening him, but my father held up his hand to stop me.

"You don't need to say another word about the accident. Let's be thankful you and Jake walked away without serious injuries... and apparently so did the deer that wandered into the road. I want you to take it easy—you're not to lift a finger around the inn until you've had some downtime. Twila, Elmo, and I can manage things, and even Cosmo can help out a little. I want you to relax, take long baths, and clear your head."

"Thanks, Dad," I reply shakily. "That sounds really good.

And that's exactly what I've been doing for the past

few days. It's Tuesday afternoon, and while I'm still stiff and bruised from the accident, I'm no longer on the verge of tears.

Quite the opposite. If anything, I'm feeling kind of... anticipatory... like something good is just around the corner.

Right now I'm lounging in the extra-large bathtub my father installed when he married Mama; I love it because I can stretch out my tail fin all the way without touching the other side. Of course, mermaids don't take traditional bubble baths, since soapy bubbles leave a residue on our scales. But we do enjoy an Epsom-salt soak for sore fins, which I'm relishing right now. I'll follow it up with a vinegar rinse to burnish my tail fin's pearlescent glow.

When Dad built the bathtub for my mother all those years ago, he also crafted a hickory shelf that fits across the top, perfect for holding a book, beverage, candle, even a phone. I'm leaning on the shelf, reading a romcom from Dad's collection, sipping a frothy mocha, enjoying the flicker of my favorite lavender-scented candle, and *not* scrolling through my phone. I've been ignoring social media, emails, and messages from everyone... well, almost everyone.

I *have* been replying to Jake's texts. When you share a near-death experience with someone, you're kind of obligated to respond, don't you think?

Jake's first text message came on Sunday; he sent me a sketch of a mermaid wearing sunglasses and reclining on an Adirondack chair in front of the inn. The caption reads, "Mooncrest's Marvelous Mermaid...

Mona Lisa DeMaris!" Then below it he added, "Pamper yourself!"

I wrote back, "Thanks for the artwork. Did you draw this yourself?"

Jake replied with a smiley face, so I think that's a "yes." I tacked the sketch up on the corkboard above the old desk in my bedroom.

On Monday, Jake sent me a second sketch. In this one, a mermaid is perched on a stool at the Sit for a Spell Café. A large slice of pie is on the counter in front of her. Beneath the image he wrote, "Mooncrest's Marvelous Mermaid is Sweeter than Pie!" and then he added, "Feel better soon!

I sent Jake another text. "Thanks! I do love your aunt's pies... How are you doing?"

He replied with two smiley faces. He didn't say anything more; I figured he must be feeling better and started sketching mermaid cartoons to stave off his boredom. I know how much werewolves hate being cooped up.

Then half an hour ago the doorbell rang. When I answered, Sophie from the Rhyme 'N Riddle Bakeshop was standing on our apartment's stoop, holding a white box tied with red string. "I hope you like chocolate cake with buttercream frosting!" She tucked a lock of brown hair behind her ear, started to leave, and then turned back around.

"Oops! Almost forgot this!" Sophie grinned, handing me an envelope.

"Hang on, don't I owe you something for this?" I asked.

Sophie called over her shoulder as she dashed down to her bakery van, "It's all covered. Enjoy!"

I carried the box into the kitchen, clipped the string, and opened the lid. One peek inside, and I knew who'd sent it. The cake's deep blue frosting was topped with pink seashells, yellow sand stars, and a mermaid with a green tail fin and curly black hair. In the enclosed card, Jake had written, "Mooncrest's Marvelous Mermaid is the Icing on Top... Remember, carbs are good for the soul! See you in the morning."

Two sketches and a custom cake with silly/sweet sayings? Jake must be trying to cheer me up for wrecking his car. Why else would he go to this much effort?

I had been heading to the bath when Sophie stopped by with the cake, so I should thank Jake now. "Carbs may be good for the soul but not my mermaid hips!" I text him. "Thanks for the beautiful cake. See you tomorrow."

Jake sends me three smiley faces.

But wait... he's not finished. He adds, "Mooncrest's Marvelous Mermaid has perfect hips. Enjoy the cake!"

Perfect hips? My heart flip-flops at the compliment, but I can't take it seriously.

Is this the same guy who struggled to make eye contact with me not that long ago? I just hope Jake hasn't had one too many knocks to the head because all this seems so out of character.

Since I'm not sure how to respond, I play it safe by sending Jake a thumbs up.

One thing's for sure... I'm glad he hasn't mentioned that little kiss in the car. I don't think I can explain it, except that I didn't know how else to express my feelings right then. Feelings of gratitude and grace and hope... and attraction. Very, very strong attraction.

My phone buzzes, and I snatch it back up, hoping it's Jake.

But it's another text from Em. I let out a long, low sigh of frustration because he's been reaching out more than usual. Apparently Em wants us to have "a heart-to-heart chat," but I've been putting him off, first because of the fire, and now because of the car accident.

Em asks me how I'm feeling, and when I reply that I'm much better, he sends me three sparkly hearts. Then he adds, "I miss you, Mona... terribly. I'm ready to take that next step in our relationship. How about you?"

My stomach feels queasy all of a sudden, like a small pit has opened up at the very bottom and all the contents are sliding downward. My hot mocha, which I adore, now tastes bitter on my tongue.

Don't get me wrong—I like Em, quite a lot actually. But I'm absolutely not ready for "that next step" for a number of reasons, including my confused feelings about Jake. Another reason is that Em and I didn't have an actual relationship. We never progressed beyond joint swims, hand holding, and quick, goodnight kisses, because neither of us was ready for anything more. And I'm still not ready.

But now it sounds like Em wants to commit.

Meanwhile I'm more ambivalent than ever about Em and the new job opportunity because we'd be working in close proximity again, which means we'd have to talk about the future, whether I want to or not. It's a good thing I'm home and Em's in Barcelona, because I'm not up for a serious conversation at the moment.

"Let's talk later, when we can see each other face-to-face," I write.

Em replies, "Great idea!" and signs off with a kissy face.

Hmm… I sure hope Em didn't misinterpret my last text.

I put down the phone, slip under the water, and debate which cute-but-practical outfit to wear tomorrow.

CHAPTER 22

AN INVITATION

JAKE

WEDNESDAY, JANUARY 23

Granny Catbeam parks her motorcycle in front of Mooncrest Inn, the engine purring as it idles. "Thanks, for the lift, Gran," I say, climbing out of the sidecar. "I'm glad you could pinch-hit for Cassia." My sister is home with Olivia, who's come down with a cold, so she lined up Granny to give me a ride.

I stow the black helmet beneath the seat and then lean down to kiss my grandmother's weathered cheek. Catbeam reaches out her hand, ruffling my hair like she used to when I was a small boy. "You take care now, Jakey—and don't overdo it. Yer still healing!" She nods, revs her engine, and pulls away so fast her wheels kick up ice and gravel.

I'm still chuckling as I watch her zoom up Main Street, going faster than she ought, when I hear the inn's front door open. As I turn toward the sound, I spot Mona checking me out. She's wearing a black-and-white Buffalo-checked flannel shirt and black jeans. Somehow, Mona manages to look both adorable and alluring in a Midwestern chic sort of a way.

I raise an eyebrow at her to let her know I've caught her red-handed staring at my backside. "Nothing's damaged or broken, in case you're wondering. All my parts are in good working order."

"Um... I'm... I'm so glad to hear it." Mona has the good graces to blush. She clears her throat and murmurs, "Thank you for the mermaid sketches and the cake... and for helping me feel a little less awful about wrecking your Suburban."

"The important thing is no one was injured. As for the car, I have insurance, so no more needs to be said about it." I walk over to where Mona is standing on the inn's wide front porch. She's two steps above me, so we're just about eye level. Mona licks her glossy red lips nervously, and now I can't look anywhere else. I lean in closer, and so does she, until our two breaths mingle to form a single frosty puff.

There's nothing I want more in this world at this moment than to kiss her.

I reach one hand behind Mona's neck, caressing the silky softness of her curls, and tilt my head just enough so that our mouths are perfectly aligned. I graze my lips against hers, and she trembles. Heat courses through my veins as she gives a barely perceptible sigh. Feeling more alive and energized than any time I can remember, I climb up one step, extend my free hand around Mona's waist and draw her into my arms.

This is it. I'm going to sweep Mona Lisa DeMaris off her feet with a kiss that captures all my pent-up need— and all my regret over fifteen wasted years of wanting this woman but doing nothing about it—until a squeal of tires on the driveway behind me stops me cold.

Mona pulls back with a gasp, and I let out an exasperated growl. "To be continued."

Mona looks me in the eye, her lovely lips so distracting I forget to release her. She gently pats my beard and then steps out of my arms to greet the new arrivals, a middle-aged vampire couple who apparently are checking in early. I suppose I should be grateful they're out-of-towners and not from Riddle Hill. Otherwise, the entire village would hear about our barely-a-kiss by lunchtime.

I'm so on edge it takes every ounce of willpower not to shift on the spot and run along the wind-swept beach, howling out my frustration. Instead, I murmur to Mona as I pass her on the steps, "I'm taking a short walk before heading over to the chapel."

Mona gives me a small nod as she escorts the couple into the inn's lobby. I cross the road and head down a narrow side street that takes me to the deserted harbor and frozen bay beyond; what a sharp contrast to the summer months, when the deep blue water is dotted with sailboats, catamarans, and yachts. I inhale the chilly air, thinking about merfolk and their adoration for the sea, which here in Riddle Hill is extremely cold and mostly frozen for months at a time each year. No wonder Mona loves the Mediterranean.

Still, there's no doubt in my mind she wanted that

kiss as much as I did. And whether that's because of some hero worship as Rick suggests, or because Mona actually likes me... I'll never know if I don't ask her out, which I'm fully prepared to do. I reach into my parka's inside pocket and pat an envelope addressed to *Miss Mona Lisa DeMaris*. Instead of a mermaid sketch inside, it contains an invitation to "an evening of light entertainment, delicious victuals, and stimulating conversation with your most ardent admirer."

I know it's ridiculously corny, but I've decided to pull out my Regency card one more time. I've got nothing to lose, except the last vestiges of my pride... and that's a small price to pay for an evening alone with Mona, without her father, her staff, or her Auntie Imogen around to interfere.

When I finally return to the chapel, Mona is conferring with the owner of Lamps, Amps, and Vamps, a vampire with a black unibrow named Benz. Mona looks up and gives me a mischievous grin that nearly buckles my knees.

"Miss DeMaris," I say, "Would you please show me the work that's been completed in the chapel office?" I plan to hand her the invitation and watch her reaction as she reads it, which will tell me a lot about how hard I need to work to convince Mona we belong together.

Mona nods, her curls bouncing on her head, but Benz says, "Hey, Chief, I'm happy to walk you through it."

I force a smile on my half-frozen lips. "That would be great. Thank you."

I spend the next hour or so going through the repairs with Benz, who's distantly related to Malaki. By then it's lunchtime, and Rick sits next to his daughter again in one of the pews. Elmo serves us turkey-and-Swiss on rye (or the vegetarian equivalent for Mona), as well as cottage fries, mixed berry salad, and chocolate bars for dessert.

It's close to four-thirty when Mona and I climb into the pockmarked hearse for the short drive back to my cottage. She drives slower than usual, gripping the steering wheel as if it's a life preserver. I don't know whether she's nervous because of the car accident or our truncated kiss, but I decide to wait until we're in my driveway before I say anything.

"Would you please read this?" I ask, handing her the invitation. "I'll wait, if you don't mind."

A thin line forms on Mona's smooth brow. "Of course."

I watch as she opens the envelope, withdraws the note, and reads it. When Mona glances back at me, her large brown eyes are shining as she deadpans. "It would be my pleasure, kind sir, to join you for an evening of light entertainment, delicious victuals, and stimulating conversation."

Grinning, I say, "Excellent. How about this Saturday night?"

Mona smiles. "That's perfect."

I unbuckle the ancient seatbelt and climb out of the hearse. "I'll be able to drive by then and will pick you up at seven."

"But I destroyed your Suburban."

"I'll figure something out." I start to close the door, think better of it, and then lean down to eye level. "Um, you might want to hold off mentioning anything to your father until the weekend."

Mona chuckles and gives me a small wave. I step back and watch as she reverses down the driveway, barely missing my neighbor's garbage cans across the street, and pulls away.

When Mona and the hearse turn the corner, I let out a happy howl and pump my fist in the air. "Finally!"

I'm ecstatic until it dawns on me I need to pull off the perfect date.

No pressure.

CHAPTER 23
FAERIE ADVICE

MONA

Later, January 23

It's all I can do to remain calm and collected as I drive away from Jake's cottage, but inside, my stomach is fluttering with a thousand faerie wings, and my pulse is chugging faster than a ship's engine pulling out of port.

I bring my fingers to my lips, recalling Jake's sizzling but short-lived kiss on the porch this morning. If that was an indicator of how he feels about me, then I'm ready to dive into the deep end... and see what happens. I can no longer deny I'm strongly attracted to him, especially after he sent me those adorable sketches and notes, followed by the swooniest, Regency-like invitation I've ever received for a date.

I'd have to be made of stone like one of Phoebe Spellman's gargoyles to resist.

I park the hearse in the reserved spot behind the inn, still daydreaming about Jake's kiss, when I hear rattling and clanking beneath the hood, followed by a loud bang and a long hiss.

Uh-oh. That sounds like the death throes of an ancient engine. When I turn the key in the ignition and try restarting it, nothing happens. My father's going to be very sad about the hearse, but I'm totally ready for something a bit more... oh, I don't know... Modern? Stylish? Non-creepy?

I enter our apartment, toss my purse onto the hall table by the door, and wander into our blue-and-white kitchen where Dad is whistling as he tosses a salad.

I kiss his cheek. "That salad looks great... much better than the poor hearse."

Dad puts down his tongs. "What happened to the hearse?"

"I have no idea—" I shrug "—but the engine appears to have called it quits."

"Do I need to call a tow truck?"

"Nah, it gave up the ghost out back; it was polite enough to wait until I parked."

"At least you made it home safely," he says. "I'll take a look at it in the morning."

After dinner, a glass of Sauvignon Blanc, and a warm soak in the tub, I pull on a soft flannel nightgown. I lie down in my old twin bed and stare up at the glow-in-the-dark constellations Mama tacked onto my ceiling a few months before she left home for good. When I was young, I used to imagine my mother staring up at the same set of constellations and pretend she was only a room away... instead of an ocean.

Dad did the best he could after she left, but he was

grieving too, and sometimes a girl simply needs to talk to another woman. I was luckier than most; I had a handful of amazing supernatural women around to offer me encouragement, including Catbeam and Phoebe Spellman, Trixie Wolferman, and even Auntie Imogen, who wasn't quite as ghostly back then.

Sighing, I wish I could speak with someone right now about Jake, who makes me feel unsettled and fluttery inside. He's so very different from Emilio; I'm never nervous or trembly around Em, who's as low-key and comfy as a pair of broken-in jeans. I roll over onto my side, waiting for sleep to take me but after an hour, I rise, slip into my fluffy robe, and tiptoe out the back door connecting our apartment with the rest of the inn.

I wander down to the library for a book, but I'm a mood reader and nothing appeals to me. I head to the deserted lobby and sit on the couch facing the fireplace, which has been swept clean by Elmo. Grabbing a wooly throw from the curved back of the sofa, I burrow beneath it, listening to Auntie Imogen's soft snores above me.

Awakening a few hours later, I stretch, push myself up, and brush my mop of curly black hair out of my face.

"Having trouble sleeping?" whispers Auntie from the wall.

I glance up at my ancestor, who's dressed in a flowing pink and white satin dressing gown with a matching stocking cap on her head. Her wings are partially extended, making her appear almost angelic, but then I remind myself angels don't have bad tempers, break furniture, and flirt ruthlessly with every male super between the ages of seventeen and seventy.

"A little bit," I admit. "I have a lot on my mind."

"Is he a good kisser?" she asks breathlessly.

My head snaps up. "How did you..."

Imogen tee-hees into her hand. "I overheard the vampire couple whispering about 'the young lovey-dovey pair out front.' I put two and four together and came up with... um, let's see... six, that's right. Six." She peers down at me. "Well? Is Jake Spellman a good kisser?"

"Yeah." I admit with a small chuckle. "Yeah, he definitely is."

"Ah... how I miss my dear Martel and his kisses; we used to sneak behind the—" Fortunately, Auntie clears her throat before she overshares about necking with her second husband. "So now what?"

"What do you mean?"

Imogen gives me a dramatic eye roll. "You're being courted by two eligible bachelors, dearie. Jake Spellman and Emilio Costa. You've got a classic love triangle brewing—" she clasps her hands to her breast and exclaims "—lucky you!"

It's my turn to roll my eyes. "I don't feel very lucky. If anything, I'm more confused than ever."

My auntie snorts and shakes her head. "Silly billy. It's really a very easy choice."

"It is?"

"Of course," says Imogen with a flutter of her hand. "You just..."

I wait for the punchline, assuming Auntie Imogen has paused for dramatic effect, but then I hear the soft murmur of her snores.

I chortle under my breath, wondering why I was contemplating listening to her in the first place. What can my mostly ghostly faerie auntie tell me that I can't figure out on my own?

Still... it was kind of fun talking about love and men with her.

CHAPTER 24
VAMPIRE ADVICE

JAKE

Thursday, January 24

I haven't seen Mona since arriving at the chapel this morning; apparently Twila Peppertail is taking a few days off, so Mona needs to cover the front desk today and tomorrow. It's a good thing I worked up the nerve to ask Mona out on a proper date yesterday... which I still need to plan.

It seems Rick is also preoccupied today; a few of the gnomes helped him push the defunct hearse into the shed before I arrived. Now he's busy trying to figure out whether it can be resuscitated.

I decide it's time for me to descend the stairs to the chapel's basement and have another look around. I'm determined to face the scene of Mona's and my near demise without a panic attack, but I start panting halfway down. By the time I reach the bottom, my heart is hammering away like an over-the-hill jogger's. This is just plain embarrassing, but I'll have to work through it.

The foreman, a burly gnome with oversized, pointy ears and a long beard he tucks inside his flannel shirt, greets me. "Hey, Chief, good to see you."

"Hey," I huff, swiping my perspiring brow. "Figured I'd see how you're coming along."

He doesn't appear to notice my overly anxious state, or if he does, he's politely ignoring it. The foreman takes me over to the new electrical panel installed by Benz and tells me most of the chapel's been rewired; the contractors will have no trouble completing the electrical work before my final inspection. Then he points out the new support beam and drywall his team installed. "We're taping and mudding today, and then painting the whole shebang tomorrow."

I take a few deep breaths and swipe my brow again. "The basement's already looking better than it has in years, and that's without a fresh coat of paint."

The gnome grins. "Yeah, well, Ricky's had his hands full, and this basement was at the *very bottom* of his list." He chuckles at his own joke.

I chuckle along with him, despite the fact I'm sweating heavily and can't wait to head back up the stairs. "Anything I can do to help you down here?" I'm praying he says no.

He shakes his head. "The only thing left is the landing area. My boys have cleared out the rubble; now we need to frame out the new exit. Maybe you can give us your opinion on the best location for the door?"

"Sure. I'll go take a look."

I mount the steps with intentionality, reliving each moment of my dash up that same staircase with Mona, reminding myself she's fine, I'm fine, and there's no reason to stress out every time I'm down here.

But I know I'm still going to feel anxious whenever I return to that basement... and when I inspect the charred remains of the old apartment building that caught fire last month... and when I drive past the section of road where Mona and I had the accident.

With time and distance, my anxiety will lessen; at least that's been true with other traumas, including my parents' accident. The first few New Year's were really rough, and then gradually they got easier—until this last one. I think the apartment fire and Mona's return to Mooncrest Inn somehow triggered me. But I'm still not sure why.

Is it because I'm crazy in love with her?

Frowning, I pause on the steps. This is the first time I've admitted to myself *I'm in love with Mona Lisa DeMaris.*

I inhale deeply and exhale a few times. My heart rate is slowing down and returning to normal.

I swipe my brow. It's a little clammy but no longer dripping.

Holy conflagration!

I must've been mentally blocking, or at least strongly denying, the depth of my feelings for Mona. And now the truth's finally dawning on me.

Not only do I *love* that woman... I *need* that woman... She's my *mate!*

Why have I missed this truth for so long?

I have a sudden flashback to the first time I laid eyes on Mona on our first day of kindergarten. A rush of memories flood my head, and now I remember the way my heart stuttered in my chest and my breath caught in my throat when she walked past me. My feet seemed to have had a mind of their own because they carried me across the playground, stopping directly in front of the prettiest girl I'd ever seen.

Her mother—at least I assume it was her mom back then—had pulled Mona's unruly hair into a ponytail. I watched as little Mona reached behind her head to yank off her hair tie, and a cascade of dark curls tumbled down her back. I gulped and sniffed the air, detecting her enticing scent of sea breeze and citrus. Then I said something that made Mona frown at me before stalking away.

Confound it all... what did I say to her? Scratching my beard and concentrating so much my head hurts, the final memory from that long-ago day floods into place.

I stood before five-year-old Mona and asked, "What's your name?"

"Mona Lisa DeMaris," she said so softly I had to lean in to hear her.

Straightening, I blurted out, "Mona Lisa DeMaris, when we're grown up, I'm going to marry you."

Mona's mouth dropped open; she stared at me as if I'd said something truly awful. Scowling, she stomped to the other side of the playground, as far away from me as possible.

How could I have forgotten all this until just now?

For years I assumed I'd eventually "outgrow" my schoolboy's crush on Mona; even though my crush lasted a whole lot longer than anyone else's, I kept telling myself that's all it was. Instead, I've been in denial about the depth of my attachment to her.

My date with Mona on Saturday night is more important than ever.

I pull out my phone and call the most debonair man in Riddle Hill, Malaki Acheron.

Malaki's sleek, all-black Tesla cruises to the curb in front of Mooncrest Chapel. As I climb in, I say, "Thanks for the ride... and for the advice, which I'm going to need even more than this lift."

Malaki grins, his fangs on full display. It's just the two of us, so he's not bothering with a glamour. "Of course, Jake. Anyt'ing fer you and Mona Lisa."

"What?" I say, recalling the Bid for a Bachelor fundraiser and Malaki's sneaky orchestrations. He definitely set up our disastrous "date" that night, and now I'm wondering why.

"You wanna some advice about Mona Lisa, right?"

"Why do you think this is about Mona?" I ask. "It is, but I'm wondering how you know that."

Malaki doesn't answer me right away. Instead he parks in front of his shop and waits for me to climb out of his car. Pulling open the door, he ushers me inside Malaki's Menswear. The lighting is always dim to accommodate sensitive vampiric eyes, and the walls are papered in a black-and-ivory geometric print and topped with gilded crown molding.

I greet one of Malaki's nephews, who's assisting a customer. Malaki leads me to the back and parts the black velvet curtain separating the shop from the storage, office, and tailoring areas.

Malaki removes his camel hair overcoat and drapes it on a padded hanger dangling from a hook next to the rear service door. He pats his silver-streaked black hair, picks an invisible piece of lint off his dark slacks, and offers me a tart cherry juice cocktail. I shake my head, because Malaki's cocktails are disgusting. Who adds hot pepper sauce, salt, and savory spices to *cherry juice*?

It dawns on me he's stalling, and now I'm really curious. I sit down in one of the black director's chairs in his neat-as-a-pin office. "What gives, Malaki? What aren't you telling me?"

My vampire friend places his spicy juice cocktail on the desk, pulls up another chair, and takes a seat. "I've been waitin' a long time now."

"Waiting for..."

"To remind you about yer first day of school. I needed to be sure you ver ready fer da truth."

I draw my brows together, wondering what Malaki is up to. Then I shrug; there's no use trying to press him for details before he's ready to spill them. Malaki's as stubborn as he is good-hearted. "It was the first time I met Mona. I know I liked her immediately... but I'm not getting the connection here."

"I drove you home from school dat day. Zeke vas out of town; Phoebe vas busy at da café, and yer mama, she had ta take little Cassia somewhere, doctor's I think."

"I have no memory of you picking me up after my

first day of kindergarten... So what happened? Why all the mystery?" I prompted.

Malaki gives me a wistful smile devoid of fangs. "Ven you got into da car dat day... you like a little glow-vorm. Happiest I've ever seen you, Jake. So I ask vhy you so happy, an' you told me all about Mona Lisa... an' I knew."

"What did you know?"

"You'd met yer mate... but you ver only five years old! Of course I told yer parents... who could see fer themselves I vas right. They told one other man... da pack alpha. They needed his advice, because meetin' yer mate at such young age eez... unheard of."

The pack alpha at the time was Rob's grandfather, Max; after he passed away Rob's mom, Trixie, became pack alpha. She ran our pack until four years ago, when she decided to retire and join the elder council. Trixie demanded I challenge her... which I did... and that's how I became alpha at twenty-eight.

"What did Max tell them to do?" I ask warily.

Malaki sighs. "He told Zeke to cast a spell so you'd forget Mona Lisa vas yer mate...'til you ver much older. And den we took a blood oath to tell no one. Not even Nash and Pheobe know."

"You're kidding me!"

Hot anger courses through me as I jump up from the flimsy director's chair, knocking it to the ground. I can feel my wolf rising to the surface as my canines sharpen inside my mouth. Malaki breaks eye contact and glances away, which is the right move. He's been around werewolves long enough to know how to help us get a grip on our powerful emotions.

Malaki waits until I'm no longer ready to howl. I take a few stabilizing breaths, right the chair, and sit back down. He shakes his head sadly. "'Fraid not, an' with no one else left... eet's up to me to tell you da truth."

I run both my hands through my hair, shocked my parents would have messed with my memories... until I examine my feelings for Mona, which have been deepening with each interaction. Even without the hormones of a grown man, I still would've struggled if I reacted strongly to Mona every day in school. I probably would've followed her around the playground, peppering her with questions or making her daisy chains; without a doubt Mona would've hated my guts by the time we turned six.

Even so, I'm pretty upset right now. Righteous anger and all that, but the last person to take it out on is Malaki, the only one left who knows the truth. "I'm not sure how I feel about all this," I sputter. "It's a lot to process."

"I'm sorry, Jake; I didn't know ven to tell you about eet." Malaki clamps a well-manicured hand onto my shoulder. "I hope you can forgeev me."

"Of course," I sigh. "Besides, it was my step-dad who cast the spell, not you." My head snaps up. "How long was the spell supposed to last?"

Malaki shrugs. "Who can say fer sure? At least a dozen years."

"Well it wore off sooner than that," I snort. "My massive crush on Mona started when I was twelve and lasted all the way through high school. At least my overwhelming attraction and urge to protect her makes more sense now."

I'm not sure how Mona feels about the overprotective aspect of my alpha wolf nature, but it's innate—even more so with the woman who's my intended mate—and impossible for me to switch it off. "Although I've been ignoring my feelings for Mona for a long time, I'm hopelessly in love at this point."

"Bein' hopelessly in love... eet's a good thing!" exclaims Malaki.

"Except that I'm petrified Mona is going back to cruising; she has a great job opportunity, and there's another guy in the picture. Plus Rick has dropped strong hints that Mona belongs at sea and not here in Riddle Hill."

Malaki raises his beringed hands in the air, as if he's chasing away all my doubts. "Nonsense. She's yer mate! Now tell me how I can help... you said somethin' about needing advice?"

Nodding, I tell Malaki about my Saturday night date. He gives me a sly vampiric grin. "I'll plan da whole evening fer you. It'll be da perfect date."

Now if anyone else told me that, I'd have my doubts. But trusting Malaki Acheron to plan the perfect date is the easy part.

The hard part? Waiting until Saturday night to see Mona again.

CHAPTER 25
THE PERFECT DATE

JAKE

Saturday, January 26

I'm standing in front of the mirror in my gray-and-white bathroom, examining my appearance one final time. I trimmed an inch from my beard this morning, losing the bushy wolfman look, and applied an extra bit of gel so my hair doesn't flop onto my forehead. I check out my new navy blazer, courtesy of Malaki, which I've paired with a light gray turtleneck and darker gray slacks.

Sternly addressing my image, I point a finger at my heart, which is one hundred percent at risk of breaking if things don't go well. "Don't blow it tonight, Jake."

Malaki has definitely come through, pulling out all the stops for my first official date with Mona. He's letting me use his own private lighthouse for the evening, which is so well hidden non-supers don't even know it exists, and he's lending me his red BMW X5 so I can drive Mona in something other than Granny's motorcycle.

I think Malaki feels guilty for the part he played in my memory loss, but I certainly don't blame him... or my parents, for that matter. I've had a couple of days to think it over. I'm sure they believed they were doing what was best, and if they hadn't died far too early, they would've told me at the appropriate time.

I turn out the lights in the bathroom and bedroom, slip on my parka, and reach for the key fob to Malaki's Beemer. It's six-forty-five... time to head over to Mooncrest Inn.

I pull around to the back and park in the spot normally reserved for the hearse, which is still being diagnosed in Rick's shed. After I ring the doorbell, I pace around the tiny stoop; I'm not sure whether I'm more nervous about seeing Mona tonight or her father. I have no idea when she told Rick about our date, but I'm sure he knows by now, and he can't be very pleased with me.

Rick opens the door, juts out his bottom lip, and trains his steely blue eyes on me. He's not using a glamour in his own home, but I might feel better if he were; Rick's faerie eyebrows are drawn together in a menacing scowl, and even the pointy tips of his ears appear sharper than usual.

"Mona's almost ready," he grumbles. "Come inside and have a seat."

I follow Rick into the family room, which is simply furnished with a beige sectional sofa, a few tables with lamps, and a flat-screen television. Knotty pine paneling covers the walls, and a tweedy oval rug protects the oak floors.

"Have a beer," says Rick. When I murmur no thanks, Rick barks, "Have a beer. That wasn't a question." Rick grabs a hanger from the hall closet and extends his hand toward me. I remove my parka and reluctantly hand it over. If he's hanging up my coat, then this is going to take a while.

Looks like Rick is back to being the grumpy father figure again. Although I easily stand five inches taller than the man glowering at me, and I'm mayor, fire chief, and pack alpha, Rick DeMaris still manages to fill the room with his presence.

I tug the collar of my turtleneck and adjust the sleeves of my navy sport coat, feeling warmer than I ought. "Okay, sure." I perch at one end of the sofa.

When Rick leaves the room and returns a few minutes later with two chilled bottles of local ale and a couple of pilsner-style glasses, I wonder how to translate "Mona's almost ready." Does that mean fifteen minutes? Thirty minutes? Not that it matters—I'd wait forever for that woman—but I have to make small talk with Rick in the meantime. I pour my beer into the glass and take a few sips, wondering what to say to the man sitting across from me.

Rick saves me the trouble. "So you think you know what's best for my daughter. Like maybe I don't know what I'm talking about. Huh?"

I try unpacking Rick's sentence. Is the man asking me a question? Making a statement? I can't tell. I aim for a diplomatic response. "I'm sure you have Mona's best interests at heart, Rick."

Rick quirks his faerie brows at me. "Don't patronize me. You may be the mayor and fire chief and alpha-man for your pack, but you're still the arrogant football captain who broke my daughter's heart her senior year."

I gulp down some beer to buy myself some time and figure out how to respond in a way that won't alienate Rick further. "I'm sorry," I say quietly. "I don't mean to sound patronizing. As far as high school is concerned, I was young and stupid back then."

"Yeah, well, weren't we all," mutters Rick. He takes a long swallow from his glass, glaring at me as if sizing me up. "You still look pretty young to me. But the question is, are you still stupid?"

I shake my head. "No, sir, I don't believe that I am."

Rick huffs and puts down his glass. Scowling, he says, "I sure hope that's the case, because so help me, if you hurt her again, I'll... I'll..."

I raise one palm. "Can I say something without you biting my head off?"

"Fine," grunts Rick. "Go ahead."

I put down my glass, frowning at the contents as if the amber liquid can provide me with just the right words to set Rick's mind at ease. I ask, "Can anyone overhear us?"

Rick gets up and closes the door separating the family room from the kitchen and bedrooms beyond. "Solid walnut; she won't hear a thing."

Nodding, I say, "What I'm about to tell you I just learned from Malaki this week, and you have my permission to confirm the truth of it all. I also ask that you hold this in strictest confidence."

"Humph," mutters Rick, but he leans forward. I have his attention now.

"Mona is my mate," I blurt, with all the awkwardness of a teenager.

"What!" shouts Rick, jumping up from the sofa, his fists curled at his sides. Gah! I think he thinks something else entirely... and now he's about to sock me in the face to defend his thirty-two-year-old daughter's honor.

I throw both my hands up defensively. "That came out wrong... please, let me explain!"

Mona's dad sits back down, but it's obvious he's still ready to strike me if he doesn't like what he hears. I quickly relay to him everything Malaki told me; to his credit, Rick listens without interrupting. When I'm through, Rick is rubbing his white beard, but he no longer appears ready to launch a frontal assault.

"That's a pretty weird story," he grumbles, "which I fully intend to verify with Malaki, just so you know."

"I'd expect no less," I reply, adding, "At the very least, I hope this allays your fears about me hurting Mona... if anything..."

"Mona may wind up hurting you," finishes Rick softly. Sighing, he rises from the sofa, wanders over to the bookcase, and gazes at an old photograph—a wedding photo, perhaps?—of Rick with his arms around a pretty, raven-haired woman. He's in a naval uniform, and she's wearing a short white dress; both of them are grinning at the camera. "Love is the deepest, truest, fiercest of all emotions," he says, still gazing at the photo.

"It can fill you with joy and happiness all your days. But the opposite is also true. Love is despair... and pain."

Rick returns to the sofa and drops back down onto the cushions. He looks older all of a sudden, and I find myself feeling sorry for the grouch. "But is it worth it?" I ask.

"Of course it's worth it!" Rick's head snaps up, his blue eyes blazing to life. "I'd never trade an eternity of smooth sailing for the wild, rocky, twisty path of true love."

He looks like he's about to say more, but there's a tap on the other side of the walnut door. Rick and I glance at each other; he gives me a small nod and goes over to open the door.

When Mona steps into the room, she's so stunning I momentarily forget to breathe. I hop up from the sofa, gulping for air like a fish out of water. She's wearing a form-fitting ivory knit dress with black trim, lacy black leggings, and a pair of dark red leather boots.

"Sorry I'm late. I couldn't decide what to wear. I wasn't sure how to interpret 'Dress comfortably.'" Mona adds, "Roses are my favorite. Thank you."

I ordered two dozen red, pink, and white roses from Bibbidy Bouquets and Baubles, which Cousin Bibbidy delivered this morning along with my handwritten note: *Dress comfortably. See you at seven. Jake.* I remembered that Mona loves roses, and regarding how to dress... I figured I'd leave that up to her.

The weird combination of Rick's grumpiness and Mona's gorgeousness has rattled me. "You look comfortably fashionable," I tell Mona. "And um... just perfect."

Mona smiles and then pulls a black wool coat out of the hall closet, which I help her into before donning my parka. She slips on a pair of leather gloves, pops a red beret onto her dark curls, and gives Rick a quick wave on the way out the door.

"So how did that go?" she asks once we're inside the car.

I start the engine. "You mean with your dad?"

Mona nods. "He asked me to take my time getting ready, since he wanted to talk to you."

"So you're not normally thirty minutes late for a date?"

"I average ten minutes, tops. Tonight was an exception."

"Good to know." I chuckle. "Your dad and I had a friendly conversation, after he made sure we understood each other."

"Oh no." Mona glances over at me. "Please don't tell me he brought up senior year and my broken heart."

"Hm-mm."

Mona winces. "How embarrassing! I don't know why Dad thinks he still needs to protect me."

"I think it's kind of sweet. But I'm glad we had the conversation fifteen years after high school; I wouldn't have wanted to face him back then. Your dad can be a pretty scary guy. I might've run away." We both laugh.

After we leave Riddle Hill, I point the red Beemer north until we reach the tip of the peninsula, where Green Bay and Lake Michigan commingle, forming ice-bound waves under the starlit sky. I continue following the road as it curves around the windswept shoreline, heading east toward the lake side of the county.

Mona is peering outside the window, probably trying to figure out where I'm taking her. Thick trees, their branches laden with snow, hug both sides of the road. There isn't a restaurant in sight, no rustic cottage by the side of the road, not even a road sign. As I turn onto a trail barely wide enough for the car, I catch glimpses of the frosty lake between the trees, the almost-full moon reflecting off its rippled surface.

"Where on earth are we going?" asks Mona.

"You'll see." I follow the twists and turns of the trail, the BMW's headlights picking up the base of a tall white tower in the distance. As we round the last bend, Mona exclaims, "We're having dinner *here...* in an abandoned *lighthouse*?"

"It's actually not abandoned; Malaki owns it." Then I add with mock seriousness, "Fear not, milady. Your evening of light entertainment, delicious victuals, and stimulating conversation awaits!"

We exit the vehicle and follow a shoveled path up to the wooden door. I extract an ornate brass key from my coat pocket, jiggling it in the lock until it clicks. After pulling open the heavy door, I step back so Mona can enter first. A light has been left on in the entrance, and a low fire burns in the front room of the lighthouse, which would've served as living room, family room, parlor, and even sick room for the lighthouse keeper and family.

Classical music is playing softly, piped in from a pair of speakers above the door. We remove our coats and hang them up on the coatrack in the foyer before entering the front room, where a linen-draped table for two sits on a hand-loomed Turkish rug.

I pull out Mona's chair for her, light the candles on the table, and toss a couple logs onto the fire. Several chafing dishes, a carafe of water, a small tray of petit fours, and several bottles of wine sit on a vintage sideboard beneath the window.

I pour out two glasses of chilled Pinot Grigio, handing one to Mona. She nods her thanks and clinks her glass against mine. "You really know how to impress a girl."

"It's good to know some things back home still impress you." Although I'm grinning, I'm also serious. What if Rick is right and Mona could never be happy in Riddle Hill?

"What's that supposed to mean?" Mona tilts her head to the side, and I'm distracted by the way her hair cascades over her shoulder in dark, glossy waves. I desperately want to take her into my arms right now and pick up where we left off on the inn's front porch... but I force myself to slow down. There'll be plenty of time after we've eaten and chatted and hopefully laughed a few times before I kiss her again.

"You've been cruising the high seas for the past decade," I reply. "Your home base is the Mediterranean, which sounds a lot more glamorous than the Midwest. I'm a hometown guy who's content hanging out with my family and friends right here in Riddle Hill."

Mona pushes a coil of hair out of her eyes as she explains, "First of all, while the Mediterranean is breathtakingly beautiful, it's not home, which I've started missing. I was more than ready to take a leave of absence to come back to Riddle Hill to help my dad. And cruising is really fun the first year or two, when everything is new, but after a decade, it's the same ports, the same types of problems, the same guest complaints, with every tour."

"What about hometown guys versus those swanky Europeans? You must've met some pretty interesting characters through the years... such as Captain Emilio."

"Jealous?" teases Mona.

"Curious, I guess," I answer her honestly. "Maybe a little bit insecure."

"You? Insecure? Give me a break."

"Yes, even I can be occasionally insecure, particularly around bright, beautiful women." I serve Mona first and then myself. Malaki's foodie cousin, Vlad, made us butternut squash ravioli in a white wine sauce, with roasted vegetables drizzled in balsamic vinaigrette and crusty sourdough bread on the side. "Especially around you. I believe I already told you my sad story about crushing on you while asking Gracie to prom? Which seems to have caused a family vendetta, at least with your dad?"

"Okay, okay," Mona laughs. "The truth is most European men think American women are easy pickings, which I'm not. So I've been pretty much on my own during the past ten years. And as for Em... he's a good friend."

I decide to press her on Captain Emilio, for my own peace of mind if for no other reason. "You mentioned you and he were dating 'on and off.' Where do you stand now? Are you and Emilio on, off, or idling in neutral?"

Mona wrinkles her brow as she considers my question. Finally she says, "I guess we're sort of idling right now."

I inhale and exhale slowly, deliberately, willing my pulse rate to remain steady. There's no need to worry, I tell myself; after all, I'm here and the charming captain is somewhere in Europe. Then I recall the heat behind Mona's kiss on the porch, and the way she gently patted my beard afterward, and I start breathing normally again... until Mona adds, "But I think Em is hoping for more."

I raise one eyebrow. "And what about you? What are you hoping for?"

Mona hesitates, pausing to take a sip of wine before answering. I realize Rick isn't entirely wrong about his daughter; she probably is confused, conflicted even, about her feelings and her future plans. She murmurs, "That's what this date is supposed to help me determine."

"No pressure, huh?" I mumble under my breath, not wanting to let on what this night means to me. Even though it feels like she just jabbed a hot poker into my unprotected chest, I can't argue with Mona's logic. I can, however, do everything in my power to demonstrate how important she is to me.

Mona takes a bite of the ravioli. "Hmm, this is delicious. My compliments to the chef."

"I'll tell Vlad," I smile, determined to put Captain Emilio firmly out of my mind for the rest of the evening.

We have a leisurely meal, reminiscing about school days and old friends we share in common, the conversation eventually coming around to our families. We chuckle over her Auntie Imogen's flirty ways, Granny Catbeam's crazy motorcycle, and even the gargoyles in my aunt's café. "Did Phoebe ever tell you what they did to earn one hundred years of servitude?" asks Mona with a laugh.

I shake my head, chuckling. "Nope. My aunt's still mad about it, whatever it was." Pausing, I consider the possibilities. "If it was an insult to her cooking skills or her hospitality, I think she'd let that slide; frankly, she'd let most things slide. But the one thing Phoebe places above everything else is family. If those gargoyles tried to interfere in any way with Sophie, Cassia, or me, I think that would make Phoebe very angry. Her mothering instincts would definitely be roused."

Mona nods. "Phoebe's a pretty amazing woman to have as a mother, or aunt, or faerie godmother for that matter."

"Yeah," I say softly, realizing I'm treading on sensitive ground with Mona, whose own mother scarpered when she was barely ten. "Losing my folks was the worst thing that's ever happened to me, but at least I had Phoebe and Nash as surrogate parents. I don't know what Cassia and I would've done otherwise."

Mona fiddles with her napkin, suddenly wistful. "Sometimes I'm jealous of Cassia and Sophie because they have Phoebe... and all I have is my ghostly Auntie Imogen."

Nodding, I feel that I have to ask this next question. "Have you or Rick heard from Karyn?"

"Apparently my father and mother have been in

touch more frequently than I realized. Dad might even find a way to visit her... when um... sometime in the future."

"Well I'm glad for Rick, but what about you? How would you feel if your parents started seeing each other again?"

Mona looks out the darkened window above the sideboard and whispers, "I've seen my mother three times since she left Riddle Hill twenty-two years ago."

"You don't have to talk about this... unless you want to."

"It's fine; I'm fine." Mona tosses her head. "Mama showed up unannounced each time, entering my life quietly and then slipping away again, just as quietly: when I received the MVP trophy senior year for softball, during the induction ceremony for the history honors society in college, and last year when I had shore leave in Naples. I was walking down this crooked little street and heard someone calling my name. My mother found out where my ship would be docking and traveled there hoping for a glimpse of me." Mona stops suddenly, her lower lip quivering as she fights for control. She quickly stands up and turns away from me.

I leap from my chair and rush around to the other side of the table. Mona gazes up at me, her large brown eyes glistening. A tear rolls down her cheek, which she swipes away. I gently cup her face in both my hands and lean down, brushing my mouth across her pillowy lips. Just one small, simple kiss that sends tingles across my shoulders, down my chest, and into my heart with the force of a flaming arrow.

Mona reaches around my back and draws me closer, which is all the invitation I need. Dropping one hand to her waist, I reach behind Mona's head with the other, entangling my fingers in her rich, silky black curls. Stifling a moan, I pour all my hopes and needs into one single, perfect, scorching kiss. My heart is on fire with so much love and joy that I never want to stop, never want to let her go.

My wolf needs this woman in my life like I need the air I breathe, solid ground beneath my paws, and a full moon overhead.

But I feel Mona trembling in my arms and taste the saltiness of her tears. I realize her face is damp and reluctantly pull away, loosening my grip around her waist and disentangling my hold on her dark waves. My chest is heaving; as I wait a few beats to catch my breath, I wipe away her tears with my thumbs. "What's wrong, Mona? Have I done anything—"

Mona steps out of my embrace, shaking her head. "It's not you, it's—"

"Please... hear me out," I whisper, putting a finger to her lips before she says *it's not you, it's me*, which is the worst break-up line ever. "If you're confused, I'm a very patient man; I'll wait for you. If you want to continue working as a cruise director, I'll do everything I can to support you. If you're worried about your dad, I'll bend over backward to get along with him."

Squaring my jaw I add, "Just don't tell me you don't feel anything for me, because I refuse to believe it."

Mona sniffles and takes a shaky breath. "I'm in a muddle over a lot of things right now—including my feelings for you—which have definitely reawakened since I've been home. I'm also conflicted about my job and Emilio and even my dad and mother possibly reuniting. I'm going to need some extra water therapy to figure all this out."

I'm riding a roller coaster of such highs and lows I'm almost lightheaded. On the one hand, Mona has just admitted to having feelings for me, which is something for me to hold on to in the midst of everything else, including the fact she's also conflicted about Captain Emilio. An unpleasant surge of jealousy courses through my veins at the mention of his name, but I tamp it down, reminding myself I'm here, while the good captain is an ocean away. Proximity has its advantages.

I'm still processing when I ask, "What sort of water therapy? It's too cold to take a dip in the bay."

When Mona tells me about the extra-large, specialized tub Rick installed for his mermaid wife, I feel another stab of sympathy for the grouchy, lovelorn innkeeper. Mona excuses herself to freshen up in the restroom, while I proceed to douse the fire, put out the candles, clear up the dishes as best I can, and wait for Mona by the entryway. As she walks down the narrow, dimly lit hall toward me, I'm struck again by her beauty, which is otherworldly.

Although we're both supers, Mona's merfolk heritage makes her somewhat unique here in Wisconsin; mermaids rarely make a permanent home on land because the sea has just too strong of a pull for them. With a sharp pang, I wonder how a werewolf and a mermaid could ever make a go of it... until I remind myself *she is my mate.* My wolf's instincts can't be that misguided, can they?

I pull Mona's coat down from the hook and hold it open for her. She turns around, sliding her arms inside the sleeves. Still standing behind her, I gently place my hands on her slender shoulders. "Take all the time you need, Mona Lisa DeMaris. I'm not going anywhere."

Mona nods, her glossy curls brushing against my hands, which I slowly drop to my sides. I slip on my parka as we head outside to Malaki's car. As we pull away, Mona whispers "thank you" so softly I almost miss it.

CHAPTER 26
EXPECT THE UNEXPECTED

MONA

Saturday, January 26

Jake and I are silent on the way back to the inn. He's been pretty closed off since we left the lighthouse, like he's hurting but doesn't want me to see it, which makes me feel twice as bad. I'm sure Jake must be disappointed with how this evening turned out. A private lighthouse, a candlelit dinner, and a kiss that melted my insides and nearly brought me to my knees—who could top that?

No one... but I managed to ruin the magic moment anyway.

I never should've talked about Mama tonight because once I opened up, the tears started flowing. I'm terrified of becoming like her... a wife who leaves the arms of her adoring husband for the pull of the open sea... a mother who abandons her only child and never comes home again. Jake could see talking about her pushed me over the edge, but he was so sweet about my meltdown, so kind and caring, that I almost used the *L* word when he asked about my feelings.

But the word caught in my throat, lodging there along with all my doubts and fears. I won't—I can't—mention *love* to Jake Spellman in my present state of mental overload. I'm not entirely positive whether what I'm feeling for him is leftover swoon from high school or something deeper. Besides I still need to figure out my job, what's up with Em, and how I feel about my dad selling the inn, which I almost told Jake about tonight, stopping myself at the last minute because it's still a secret.

And then there's the whole topic of my dad wanting to see Mama again; I'm afraid he's read one too many romance novels, but it's too late now. Dad has started humming to himself, staring off into space at the oddest times, and sneaking off to call her when he thinks I'm not around. (I've eavesdropped a few times but stopped when I overheard too much sweet talk. *Yuck.* They're still my parents.)

I definitely need multiple rounds of water therapy to sort everything out.

The BMW's headlights sweep across the nearly empty lot behind the inn. Nearly empty? What's that black Toyota RAV4 doing sitting in the hearse's normal spot?

"Looks like your father has company," says Jake.

"I have no idea who it could be; Dad didn't mention anything to me."

Someone, probably my dad, flips on the outdoor spotlights, and our car is flooded with bright light. The door to our apartment opens, spilling two men out onto the stoop. One is my father, and the other is almost as tall as Jake, with broad shoulders and ramrod-straight posture. He's wearing a dark woolen jacket with two rows of silver buttons that reflect the light. I can't see his face, but I'd know that coat anywhere. "*Em?*"

Barnacles! What's Em doing here?

Jake clenches the steering wheel, squinting through the windshield. "Captain Emilio is here in Riddle Hill?"

My mouth opens and closes a few times before I manage to sputter, "Um... yeah. That's definitely Emilio."

I sense Jake tensing next to me, almost like his werewolf form is rising to the surface. He practically growls, "I hope you won't mind if I don't walk you to the door."

"Of course not," I murmur, gathering my purse and opening the car door. "Thank you so much for tonight... and for everything."

Jake nods wordlessly as I close the door, but it doesn't take twenty-twenty vision to see the rigidness in his shoulders or the angry set to his jaw. As I'm stepping back from the car, I notice his hands are shaking... and *his fingernails are elongating into claws.*

Sharks! Jake's wolf is showing!

He accelerates out of the lot without a backward glance, obviously trying to put as much distance as he can between his wolf and the rest of us. I just hope he can maintain his human form long enough to get safely home.

I didn't think I could feel any worse but seeing Jake

struggling to control his emotions, and his wolf, brings on another wave of guilt. But Jake's reaction to Emilio tells me I'm only partly to blame for how he's feeling at the moment; I had no idea Em was planning to cross the Atlantic Ocean for an unscheduled stopover in Wisconsin.

"Mona!" cries Em, who hurries down the steps, crosses the lot, and sweeps me into his wool-clad arms. Before I have time to say anything other than a surprised "hey," Em tilts my head back, brushes the hair from my forehead, and moves in for a kiss, but I quickly turn my head so he grazes my cheek instead.

There's no way I'm letting Em kiss me on the lips. Not after Jake's kiss left scorch marks all over my heart.

Besides, Em has never been so eager before. Pleasant little pecks are all we ever shared, which was fine by me, because I wasn't ready for anything more, the same as Em.

But this is a whole new Em, and I'm reeling from the change. What's gotten into this merman? Could my absence have made his sea-faring heart grow fonder?

I have no clue... all I do know is my head is spinning right now. I pull back at the same time Dad harrumphs his annoyance.

Em flashes me a crooked grin, his olive-brown eyes twinkling as he gazes down at me. He's a handsome man; with his wavy brown-black hair, trim beard, and high cheekbones, Em's nickname on board the ship is Captain Jack Sparrow. Em dislikes the title, since he hates rum, abhors drunkenness, and doesn't see his obvious resemblance to a young Johnny Depp.

"You look stunning tonight," he says huskily. "I hope I didn't scare off your friend. Your father mentioned you were having dinner with an old school chum."

Ignoring his comment about my old school chum, I finally find my voice. "What a surprise, Em! I never expected to see you here in Riddle Hill!"

My mind races with all the questions I'm not asking him right now: *What are you doing here? Why didn't you tell me you were coming? How long are you staying? Where are you staying?*

Then it dawns on me, Em must've booked a room at the inn... which means my father knew about it and didn't say anything. I peer over at my dad, who's standing behind Emilio. When our eyes meet, Dad gives me a half-shrug.

There are far too many men in my life who seem to think they know what's best for me. As Em and I follow my father up the steps and into our apartment, I realize there *is* one man who hasn't tried to tell me how to feel or where to live or advise me on job prospects. But Jake has just driven off to lick the wounds I inflicted on him tonight; I'm feeling lower than an eel's belly, which is about as low as a mermaid can sink.

Em's black Tumi suitcase is sitting in our foyer. Nodding down at it, I murmur, "Looks like we need to get you checked in, Em."

He gives me the sweetest smile, dissolving most of my annoyance at his surprise visit. "Would you do the honors, Mona? I told your father I would wait for you."

Em's words strangely echo Jake's from earlier this evening. Clearing my throat, I slip into my innkeeper's persona. "Of course! Let's get you settled. You must be exhausted."

"A little bit," acknowledges Em, "but seeing you after such a long absence gives me renewed energy. Perhaps we could go for a short drive to the harbor? Hmm?"

I stifle a sigh; this seemingly endless night has worn me to a frazzle. But I hear such hopefulness in Em's voice that I don't have the heart to turn him down. Besides we need to talk without my dad, Auntie Imogen, and the Peppertail elves' eavesdropping. "Sure. Meanwhile, do you need something to eat?"

Em shakes his head, explaining he grabbed something before he left the airport. We enter the inn through the back door of our apartment. I guide him across the carpeted hall, past the library and Dad's office, and finally into the front lobby. Em glances up at Auntie Imogen, snoring in her frame.

"Is that your—" he starts to ask in a normal tone of voice, but he stops when I pinch his arm.

"That's Imogen Althea Belvedere DeMaris, my faerie ancestor, godmother, and great-great-auntie," I hiss. "It's best not to wake her now; I'll introduce you tomorrow. And, um... don't be surprised if she flirts with you."

Em raises one dark eyebrow and lowers the other. "I shall look forward to meeting your flirty faerie auntie," he teases.

Rolling my eyes, I sit behind the antique desk, open up the laptop, and start scanning reservations. I'm unable to find Emilio's until I realize my sneaky dad booked him under *Mister M*. When I hand Em the key to a second-floor guest suite, his fingers brush mine, lingering longer than necessary.

"I'll wait down here for you," I murmur, gently withdrawing my hand.

As Em carries his suitcase up the stairs, I rub my fingers together. I may not experience the same tingles and shivers at Em's touch that I do at Jake's, but Em is my closest friend. He's steady and stable, someone I can depend on in stormy weather.

Jake is gorgeous and swoony, and my heartrate sputters and spins at his touch, but sometimes I think *Jake is the storm itself.* Jake feels like the rain and wind and waves of a raging tempest... while Em feels like the calm at the center, the eye of the hurricane.

Auntie Imogen might have enjoyed a love triangle in her day, but I want a simple, uncomplicated life; I don't want to be forced to choose between two good, decent men because I will inevitably hurt one of them.

I don't need to give Em directions to the marina; all merfolk have an innate sense of direction when it comes to finding the nearest body of water. He pulls the Toyota into the harbor's deserted lot, pointing the front of the car toward the frozen bay, and turns off the engine.

"It's far colder here than I expected," says Em, and I wonder whether he's referring to more than the outside temperature. It's true I've been distant since Em's arrival, but his unexpected visit, on top of Jake's lighthouse date and smoldering kisses, have thrown me off-kilter. If I wouldn't keel over from hypothermia in a matter of minutes, I'd dive into that frigid bay right now and go for a long, head-clearing swim.

Em reaches over, picks up my hand, and starts to peel away my glove, but I stop him. "Em, what's going on? Why the surprise visit?"

Em sucks in a lungful of air and slowly releases it. "I've missed you, Mona. More than I could have believed possible, and I've been hoping you feel the same. Based on our last text messages, I thought you did, but now I'm not so sure... have I misjudged the situation... and your feelings for me?"

"Oh, Em," I sigh. "Of course I've missed you and our moonlight swims and our late-night chats. You're my best friend and the most amazing mentor anyone could ever have."

"A friend and mentor, eh?" Em cocks his head at me. "I was hoping for a more permanent arrangement Mona... and more intimate."

Barnacles! The *I* word scares me almost as much as the *L* word.

I can not... I will not... be *intimate* with a man unless I'm absolutely certain I *love* him. And since I've never been that sure about anyone... well. Ahem. Let's just say I still blush at the spicy scenes in movies and leave it at that.

Wait... What sort of permanent arrangement?

Sharks and shells! Is Em talking about marriage? We may have known each other for years... but our friendship... our relationship suddenly feels like it's moving way too fast.

When I don't answer because I'm temporarily tongue tied, Em reaches over and grips my hand. "I've obviously surprised you in more ways than one tonight. I can see you need more time, and I'm fine with that. Take all the time you need."

"Thank you," I mumble, grateful Em is giving me an easy out, at least for now. "I'm sorry you traveled all this way only to be disappointed."

Em shakes his head. "I have no regrets about traveling to Wisconsin in January. I'm sitting here beside you, which cheers my heart to no end, and you haven't rejected me outright, which gives me hope. Besides, I now have a much better appreciation for our guests who flee the Midwest during the winter."

I snort, which makes Em chuckle, and then I laugh along with him, thankful for his friendship and his grace. When I tell him as much, Em waves his hand. "You should know me well enough to realize I only want what's best for you... and that I only hold very small grudges."

Still smiling, I lower my brow. "What sort of small grudges are we talking about?"

Em raises his hands, palms up. "Only against old school chums who appear to be standing in the way of my happiness. I shouldn't be surprised someone from your past would pop up and try stealing you away now you're back home."

"Oh, I don't know about that..."

Em shakes his head at me. "Don't deny something that's so obviously true, Mona. Your mind... and your heart... are wandering elsewhere." Em reaches over and takes my hand again. "But I'm a very stubborn merman, and I will not give you up without a fight."

"A fight?" I sputter, horrified at the notion of Em and

Jake locked in some weird supernatural combat; images of pitchfork-hurling merfolk and growling, snarling werewolves flit through my weary brain.

Em pats my hand before releasing it, turns on the car's engine, and eases out of the spot. "Yes, my lovely mermaid. A fight."

CHAPTER 27
HEARTACHE HOWL

JAKE

Sunday, January 27

A low growl escapes my throat as I stare down my long snout at my paws. A red mitten encases each one—four paws, four red mittens. Raising my head slightly, I survey my surroundings; I'm lying on an ivory leather sofa in someone's dark-paneled office.

Confound it all! What happened last night? And where am I now?

I need the answer to the second question before I shift from my werewolf form, since the only covering I have at the moment is a silky-smooth blanket that probably cost more than the monthly payment on my wrecked Suburban.

Who in their right mind would drape a gold Pashmina throw over an unconscious werewolf? And place mittens on his paws?

Never mind; there's only one man fastidious enough to be concerned about protecting his leather sofa from claw marks, and kind enough to ensure I don't wake up with a chill. After shifting seamlessly, tossing aside the mittens, and securing the gold blanket around my waist, I amble over to the six-panel door.

Opening it cautiously in case one of Malaki's sisters is visiting from Transylvania, I tiptoe over to the second-floor railing and hiss, "Malaki! Where are you? I'm awake… and in need of some pants!"

Among supers, werewolves have the best sense of smell, but vampires have superior hearing; they can hear a pin drop onto a wooden floor from fifty yards away. Malaki glides into the cavernous marble-tiled foyer below, wearing a black chef's apron, and waving a spatula at me. "Ah, purrfect timing! Da waffles are just 'bout ready. Look in da office closet for a change of clothes."

"Thanks," I call down as he disappears into the kitchen.

Ten minutes later I've showered and changed into brown slacks and a beige sweater that fit so well I suspect Malaki maintains some of his menswear over-flow in that closet. We're sitting in his breakfast nook, a hexagonal room with tinted-glass windows on five sides that provide an excellent view of the snow-covered ravine and frosty bay behind his mansion, which sits on ten acres of prime waterfront real estate. Malaki is the wealthiest super in Wisconsin, possibly in the entire Midwest.

"Vell?" says my host after topping up my coffee. I've just polished off two helpings of fluffy waffles with fruit compote and a generous side helping of hickory-smoked bacon. "Vhy did yer wolf show up last night, howling at da moon?"

I vaguely recall leaving Mooncrest Inn and zipping along the highway, barely maintaining control over my wolf, and heading straight for Malaki's place because it was closer than my cottage. Rubbing my brow, I mutter, "Last night did not go the way I'd hoped. Mona is... confused about a lot of things... including her feelings for me."

"Eet's not so surprising... but eet doesn't explain vhy you shifted and vas whiney and refused to shift back." Malaki crosses his arms, pinning me with an inquisitive stare.

"Captain Emilio," I grumble.

"Who ees dis captain?" he asks, his fangs catching on his lower lip.

If there's anyone who deserves the full scoop, it's Malaki, given how hard he worked to help me pull off the less-than-perfect lighthouse date. I unload all of it, telling him about my chat with Rick, my dinner with Mona, her meltdown over her mother, and the captain turning up on her doorstep.

By the time I'm finished speaking, Malaki is shaking his head. "Eet's messed up."

"Yeah, it sure is."

"So vat you gonna do now?" Malaki seems to think I've figured out my next move.

But I lift my shoulders and then let them droop in defeat. "I'm going to give Mona some space so she can sort out her feelings."

"Vat you talkin' about? She doesn't need space... she needs you!"

"How do you figure that? She may be *my* mate, but that doesn't necessarily mean I'm *hers*."

Malaki's furrowed brow accentuates his dramatic widow's peak, making him look even more like Bela Lugosi than usual. "I'm no wolf... but even I know da mating bond runs both ways. Mona must feel eet too."

I close my eyes and think about kissing Mona; truthfully, there isn't much else I want to think about. "While that's true for two werewolves who are mates, I've never heard of a werewolf-mermaid pairing, so we can't be sure. I'm not sure of anything when it comes to Mona, except that I don't want to live the rest of my life without her!"

"Then do somethin' about eet!"

"But she has company," I point out. "And the captain is sort of her boss too, so I have to tread carefully."

"He's only here because of you."

"How do you figure that?"

"Eet's easy—she's probably not acting da same around him—so he came here to tell her how he feels."

I realize Malaki is probably right. "Okay," I shrug. "But I have no idea what to do about it."

"You must fight back. Fight fer Mona."

"Fight?" An image of my wolf biting Captain Emilio's tail fin pops into my sleep-deprived brain, which I immediately dismiss as undignified. Besides, as mayor of Riddle Hill I'm supposed to welcome all visitors to our supernatural village... even dashing mermen here to sweep my mate off her feet and out of my arms.

"Yes... you fight. You win her heart," says Malaki firmly.

Grimacing, I drop my head into my hands. "How? He's not a werewolf, so it wouldn't be a fair fight."

Malaki throws his hands in the air, the three-carat ruby ring on his right hand glinting. "Not as a wolf—it isn't da nineteenth cent'ry—but as a *man*. A man who ees about to loose his soulmate."

Raising my head, I lean back in the chair, mulling over Malaki's words. Even he thinks I'm on the brink of losing the only woman who will ever satisfy my deepest longings.

But how can I demonstrate my love for Mona without coming out and saying so, which I fear will only make her bolt; she's like a skittish kitten right now, unsure of everything, even her own feelings.

Somehow, I need to prove to Mona no matter how far she wanders from home, I'll always be here for her.

AFTER WRACKING my brain and bouncing ideas off Malaki —who thinks I should immediately declare my love for Mona and propose to her, which is just plain ridiculous. When I tell him that's very nineteenth century, he goes off to the kitchen in a huff.

I finally land on the same idea I had before the car accident. Mona and Rick could still use my help bringing the chapel up to code as soon as possible—preferably in time for my sister's wedding—and definitely before Mooncrest Inn loses its spring and summer wedding business.

Thanks to the efforts of Gnome Sweet Gnome and Lamps, Amps, and Vamps, most of the infrastructure work has been completed in near-record time. The contractors have started on the third exit, which still needs to be finished before the chapel can officially reopen. They'll finish the interior work within the next week or so, but there's still the issue of the exterior staircase, which I was planning to build with Mona's help before she flipped my Suburban into a ditch.

A couple days ago, Rob and Teddy retrieved the lumber Mona and I had been hauling before the accident; they delivered the wood to Mooncrest Inn, where it's sitting in the shed beside Rick's hearse.

Since I'm cleared to swing a hammer and lift up to twenty pounds, framing out a staircase is definitely within my wheelhouse, but I could still use some help. While I'd love for that help to come from Mona, now is not the time. Rob's often occupied with his real estate business on Sundays, so I text Teddy to see if he's available; he sends me an immediate thumbs up.

I explain my plan to Malaki and ask for a ride to Mooncrest Chapel. We stop at my cottage on the way so I can pick up my toolbox and change into work clothes (comfy jeans and a fleece-lined flannel jacket). Malaki pulls around to the back of the inn and parks his Beemer.

Teddy's already here, sitting in his pickup truck. He gives us both a friendly smile.

With my hand resting on the BMW's door handle, I turn to look at my vampire friend. "Thanks Malaki... for everything you've done for me. I appreciate—"

But Malaki waves off my thanks. Lowering his black eyebrows, he hisses one final reminder. "Mona ees yer mate; don't give up on her!"

I mumble my thanks, climb out of the vehicle, and grab my toolbox from the trunk. Teddy joins me, holding up a key in his right hand.

"Rick gave me the key to the shed, after first grilling me about why I wanted it." Teddy lowers his voice. "I think he's worried someone is going to cart off that ridiculous hearse, but who in their right mind would want that thing?"

We're both still chuckling about Rick and his hearse when Teddy gives one final tug on the shed's double doors. As the doors swing open a variety of scents, mostly saw dust, engine oil, and mouse droppings, assault my nostrils. The hearse sits off to the left, its hood propped open. The battery's been removed and a variety of parts are scattered on the concrete in front of the vehicle. An old snow blower, an even older riding lawn mower, various gardening tools, and several rickety ladders are stored in the back. To the right sits the lumber for the staircase, plus a circular saw belonging to one of the contractors. I set down my toolbox next to a stack of two by sixes.

"Have you seen Mona?" I ask.

Teddy bends down to examine my tools, avoiding eye

contact. "I spotted Mona leaving with some fellow as I was pulling up."

My heart gives a single, painful shudder. "Yeah, that's Captain Emilio," I reply, trying to sound casual. "They work together."

"Huh," says Teddy, straightening up.

"What's that supposed to mean?"

Teddy grimaces. "I know you like Mona... and I think she likes you... but the way that dude was hanging all over her made my skin crawl."

My chest squeezes uncomfortably, and I take several deep, calming breaths. I can only hope my actions will speak louder than any words uttered by the captain, and that Mona will have no doubts about my feelings for her.

Kneeling on the hard cement, I start pulling out tools. "Let's get to work."

"Sure thing, Chief," replies Teddy softly.

"Why don't you double-check all my measurements." I hand Teddy my tape measure and folding yardstick before grabbing a ladder and heading over to the chapel. Heavy-duty plastic covers the opening where the gnomes are installing the new door. Pointing at four wooden stakes driven into the ground, I say, "This is the landing area, which I'll be prepping tomorrow."

Teddy nods and carefully measures the distance from the bottom of the doorway opening down to the middle of the landing area. He runs through the calculations needed to construct the five-step staircase and confirms my original measurements.

We return to the shed and start working on the stringers, chatting occasionally, mostly about Riddle Hill, the fire station, and Cassia and Will's upcoming wedding. Teddy and I make a good team, and I'm thankful my cousin wound up marrying him despite their rough start. Reflecting on Teddy and Sophie's happy ending gives me hope for Mona and me.

Around one-thirty we break for lunch; Malaki packed enough to feed three werewolves, so Teddy and I are well fortified when we pick up our hammers again. By the time dusk falls, we've cut and measured the stringers, the risers, and the treads, and we've applied a coat of stain. I'll be back tomorrow to clear the snow, level the ground, and lay down fresh gravel for the landing area beneath the third exit.

Teddy offers to give me a lift back to my cottage, and I hesitate. I've been hoping for a glimpse of Mona and the captain, but they've been gone all day. I can't hang around the shed like a loveless puppy with nothing to do, so I figure I may as well go home.

Before I answer Teddy, Rick pops his head into the shed. Jutting his jaw at the staircase-in-progress, Rick says, "Looks good, fellas. Thanks... I really appreciate the extra help."

"Sure, no problem," I reply, packing up my tools and preparing to leave with Teddy.

Rick's tipped-up faerie eyebrows arch even higher on his forehead. "You as handy with cars, by any chance?"

Teddy stares at the hearse's propped-up hood and clears his throat. I clap a hand on his shoulder; the poor guy's a newlywed and wants to spend time with his wife. "Why don't you go on home to Sophie. I can give Rick a hand and hitch a ride later."

Teddy gives me a wide grin as he waves goodbye. Nodding at the hearse, I say, "I'm more than happy to help if I can... but is it worth it?"

Rick's face twists briefly, as if he's in pain. Then he snorts. "If you're asking whether it's economically worth it, the answer is a resounding no." He stops, swallows, and adds with a soft chuckle. "As you've probably realized by now, my mermaids are terrible drivers."

I smile, not sure where he's going with his story. Rick walks over to the vintage vehicle and pats its roof. "Karyn wrecked my old Ford pickup on her way home from Green Bay... let's see, I guess Mona Lisa had just turned five. I didn't care one whit about the truck; I was grateful Karyn walked away with nothing more than a black eye. A few weeks after the accident, I'm in the lobby doing some paperwork, and Karyn is chatting with Auntie Imogen.

"The door opens and in walks a tall, gaunt vampire dressed entirely in black; it was Mobley the undertaker. He gives Karyn a friendly nod as he walks past her, and she's smiling ear to ear. Mobley stops at the mahogany desk, hands me his keys, and asks me to give him a ride back to the funeral home in my 'new van.' When I tell him I don't own a van, he laughs and tells me of course I do... although I might want to paint it a cheerier color.

"By now Karyn and Imogen are both tittering, and I rush outside to see... this hearse... which Karyn bought me. I asked her how we could afford it, because our tourism trade wasn't nearly as strong back then, and we hadn't gotten into weddings yet, but she simply shrugged. Turns out Karyn had bartered her pearl necklace, a gift from her mother, to purchase this crazy old thing." Rick rubs at the chipped paint on the driver's door with his knuckles. "I figure she has a little life left in her."

I don't know whether Rick is referring to the hearse or his relationship with his absent wife, but I realize it doesn't matter. "I figure you're right." I walk over to the scattered car parts and kneel down on the cold cement.

Rick kneels next to me, points at the battery on the ground, and says, "That's less than a year old, but it's dead." Nodding at the open hood, he adds, "I'm getting a new radiator hose tomorrow, and a replacement battery, but I'm not sure what else is wrong. Any ideas?"

Bending over the hearse, I examine the engine, mechanical components, and exhaust system. "How often are you replacing the battery?"

Rick sighs. "Too often. Maybe every year and a half."

"You need a new alternator." Running my hands over the gunky spark plugs, I add, "And new spark plugs too."

"Shoot." Rick dashes a hand through his hair, and I get the sense he's running on empty, with the cost of the chapel repairs and now the hearse.

Straightening, I glance at him. "If you can cover the parts, I can do the installation."

The tips of Rick's pointy ears turn pink. "I can't accept that kind of help from you."

"Why not?"

"Because of Mona. I'll not be beholden to you."

I roll my eyes. "This isn't about Mona. It's about me... realizing I mishandled things with you and the fire inspection."

"Yeah, how so?" Rick's voice is gruff.

"I should've done a better job explaining the issues and given you one more chance to make things right before shutting down the chapel. This is my way of apologizing."

Rick sniffs and squaring his jaw, peers down at his beloved hearse. He lifts his shoulders ever so slightly. "Fine. Apology accepted. I'll get the parts; I figure it'll take a few days, maybe longer, given the age of the hearse."

"Sounds about right." I nod.

Rick's phone buzzes. He withdraws it from his jeans pocket, scans it, and texts a reply. I get the sense it's a message from Mona, who's still out with the captain. He stuffs the phone back in his pocket, but I notice he's chewing his bottom lip.

My heart cracks a little bit more, and I need some fresh air to steady myself. "I'm heading out, Rick. I'll leave my tools here. See you tomorrow."

"Wait... don't you need a ride? I can ask Elmo to run you back home in his Jeep."

I shake my head. "No thanks. I'll walk."

Rick purses his lips together. "You sure you're up to it?"

I sense he's asking me about more than walking a few miles in the dark. "Yeah." I tell him goodnight, step out of the shed, and withdraw my wool beanie from my coat pocket.

As the snow crunches beneath my work boots, I take a couple of deep breaths. It's clear and crisp, the stars twinkling like tiny diamonds in the black canopy of the sky, a perfect evening for a run with my pack. But I'm not allowed to run for another week, and my wolves are where they belong on a cold winter's night—home with their mates.

Picking up my pace, I tug my hat more firmly over my ears.

Sometimes a man just needs to walk alone.

CHAPTER 28
SPLASH

MONA

Sunday, January 27

My phone is buzzing on the nightstand next to my bed. I open my eyes and groan at the sunshine streaming through my half-closed window blinds. Blinking a few times, I stare up at the glow-in-the-dark constellations pasted to my bedroom ceiling, barely visible now that it's daytime. I've obviously overslept, but my brain is so foggy I don't recall why.

Then it hits me—Jake, our romantic lighthouse date, his searing kisses—and Emilio, who traveled all the way to Riddle Hill just to see me. Unfortunately, Em's timing couldn't have been worse. The image of Jake's shoulders hunched over the steering wheel and his fingernails elongating into claws pops into my foggy brain, and with nauseating clarity I realize just how much I've hurt him. What a date-night disaster!

Why did Em have to choose that precise moment to

turn up on my doorstep? I'd already ruined the perfect date Jake had planned with my tears, but Em's surprise appearance was the final insult. Jake probably thinks I'm a two-timing mermaid who enjoys pitting two decent men against each other.

Shaking my head, I dash a hand through my messy curls and realize Auntie Imogen is right about one thing: I *am* in the midst of a classic love triangle. But unlike her, I hate it. I like clear lines and absolute certainty, or as certain as things can be when it comes to love. Blowing out a puff of air, I swing my legs over the side of the bed and reach for my phone.

The first message arrived an hour ago from my dad: "Sorry I didn't tell you about the captain's visit. He wanted it to be a surprise, but I should have known better."

I send him a text. "Yeah, pretty awkward. Let's talk after Em leaves." Dad and I need to have a frank chat about father-daughter boundaries.

Then I move on to the second message, which is from Em. "Good morning, Mona! I hope you slept well. Please pack your mer-gear and an overnight bag. Meet you at eleven."

Mer-gear is what mermaids call the little extras we need when we transform for a swim. Popular misconceptions aside, seashell coverings do not magically camouflage our chests when we extend our tail fins. We need to plan ahead, otherwise we'll be swimming in our bras or doing the mermaid equivalent of skinny dipping. My mer-gear consists of bikini tops in various shades of blue and green that compliment my sea-green tail fin, plus hair ties to keep my ridiculous floaty curls out of my face in the water.

Wait a minute. *Why an overnight bag?* "You know I don't do casual dating, Em," I text him.

Em sends me a bunch of hearts, followed by, "Separate bedrooms, I promise."

"What's up?" I ask.

"Water therapy... in a private pool... just for two."

I have no idea where he's taking me, but Em has obviously done his research. My fingers hesitate over the phone. Em is probably stressed after the long flight and my cool reaction to his surprise visit; he needs this swim as much as I do. I send him a thumbs up, followed by, "See you at eleven."

I shower quickly and change into black jeans, a teal sweater and matching wool jacket, and short black boots. I toss a couple of bikini tops, a toothbrush, makeup, hair products, and my frumpiest jammies into a canvas duffle. Not that I don't trust Em, but I'm going to make sure there's absolutely nothing to tempt either of us to cross a line that we shouldn't be crossing later tonight. There's something about swimming with a handsome merman, our tail fins brushing against each other beneath the surf, that can turn a mermaid's head; I'm taking no chances.

Em greets me in the back parking lot with a dazzling grin. "You look radiant."

I shake my head, flushing under his heated gaze, which is so different from the way *old Em* would look at me. I'm not prepared for the way *new Em's* olive-brown eyes are focusing on my lips. I'm having major second thoughts about our joint swim, but I can't think of a graceful way to get out of it now.

"Thanks, Em… but I think you need more coffee."

"Don't, Mona… please." Em takes my duffle bag, and draping an arm around my waist, guides me over to his Toyota.

"Don't what?"

He plunks my luggage into the trunk and then turns to face me, drawing me closer. "Don't be so self-deprecating. You are a beautiful woman. Will you please allow me to acknowledge it?"

I ignore the tires crunching on the gravel behind us, and stiffening slightly, I give him a wordless nod. Em places a hand on my back, escorts me to the passenger side, and opens the door for me. As I dip my head to enter the RAV4, I glance up and lock eyes with Teddy Barker, who's staring at me through the window of his pickup. He quickly looks away.

Teddy, who's a member of Jake's pack and married to Jake's cousin.

I heave a sigh; there's no way Teddy missed Em's body language. Unfortunately, there's also no way Teddy could've noticed how stiffly I was holding myself. Jake will no doubt hear about the former… but not the latter… and there's nothing I can do about it now.

I need to put Jake firmly out of my mind for today; I need to be fair to Em, who traveled four thousand miles to see me. Even if my feelings are a jumbled mess at the moment, I owe Em the courtesy of my undivided attention.

Less than an hour later we pull onto a long private drive that winds past snowy farm fields and cherry orchards, their trees bare and swaying slightly in the winter wind. Wherever Em is taking us is so far off any main road I'm feeling a bit like Dorothy in Oz. I know we headed in a southeasterly direction when we left the inn, but otherwise I'm lost. "Are we still in Door County?"

Em chuckles. "Yes, but barely. How is it I have a better sense of your home than you do?"

I give him a fish-eyed glare, which makes him laugh harder. "You know I'm hopeless on land. But give me the open sea—"

"And you could navigate to Shangri-la and back," quips Em. He rounds a bend in the road, and we both let out an "ooh."

A large, rambling farmhouse with white gingerbread trim sits in a snow-covered clearing. But what makes me lean forward and lower the window despite the chilly air is the color of the painted wooden siding—it's the deepest, richest turquoise blue, a shade so lovely it catches in my throat, leaving me breathless and reminding me of the sea on a cloudless summer day.

White-tipped firs, spruces, and holly bushes edge the driveway and surround the home in a dark green embrace. A wide wraparound porch, painted a lighter blue, encircles the house on three sides; I can almost visualize a row of Adirondack chairs out front in warmer weather. To the left of the drive is a large frozen pond, perfect for ice skating in winter and swimming in summer.

"What *is* this place?"

"Mariner Meadows."

"Really?" I turn to look at Em. "What an odd mashup of two names."

"Precisely. It's owned by a faerie man and his selkie wife. They serve those of us who are marked by two different worlds, who must learn to balance our lives on land with the call of the sea."

"How did you hear about this place?"

Em grins as he pulls around the circular drive. "SuperSuite, of course."

SuperSuite is the social media app used by all supernaturals everywhere. "It's funny I've never heard of this place, especially if they advertise on SuperSuite."

Em shakes his head. "Oh no, they don't advertise at all. Strictly word-of-mouth. I asked my network for a recommendation, and one of my aunts had heard about this bed and breakfast in Wisconsin that offers private saltwater pools for merfolk and selkie guests. It was pure luck Mariner Meadows is less than an hour from Mooncrest Inn."

Touched by the effort Em has put into his visit, I decide to set aside my reservations about his budding romantic intentions and simply enjoy myself. I'm positively itching for a swim in non-chlorinated water.

We're greeted by a tall, blond faerie who tells us his name is Quinn. He's dressed casually, in jeans and a fleece jacket, his pale blue wings partially unfurled against his back. The faerie takes our luggage, and we follow him up the steps, across the porch, and into the lobby, which is painted in variegated shades of teal, green, and blue. A large aquarium filled with gorgeous, multi-colored fish lines one wall.

A stunning woman with long, straight black hair and expressive brown eyes smiles as we enter. "Mister Emilio Costa and Miss Mona Lisa DeMaris?" she asks softly.

When we nod, her smile deepens. "Welcome to Mariner Meadows! Please consider this your home away from home while you are staying with us. My name is Lura. I can see you've already met my husband."

The selkie woman quickly checks us in while Quinn heads off with our overnight bags. After we sign the guest register, Lura guides us down a blue-tiled hallway to the right. She opens a door painted a paler shade of blue and moves aside so we can enter first. "This is our Aquamarine suite."

We step into a great room with an open kitchen and dining area that merges seamlessly with the living space. As with the lobby and hallway, the suite is awash in soothing blue-green tones, and a nubby, wavy, teal fabric covers the sofa and chairs.

"It's beautiful! And... and is that salt air I'm smelling?" I inhale deeply as Lura nods. "But how?"

"A regular sprinkling of Quinn's faerie dust does the trick."

"It's amazing," says Em. "If I close my eyes, I'd think I was standing on my ship's deck."

"I'm glad Quinn's magic is so accurate." Lura chuckles. "Let me leave so you can explore on your own. I've stocked the fridge with soup, quiche, cheese, fruit, veggies, and beverages. Breakfast is served between eight and eleven in the dining room, which is on the other side of the lobby. Please enjoy your stay and let me know if you need anything."

After Lura leaves, Em looks over at me and says, "Race you to the pool!" Then he grabs his bag and heads off to the far end of the living room.

"No fair!" I holler, lugging my duffle toward a pair of lapis-blue doors labeled "Gents" and "Ladies" in bright pink lettering. Em dashes through the door on the left as I yank open the other one and jog inside.

"Whoa!" I shout, nearly plunging headfirst into a deep channel of dark blue water that runs down the center of the changing room. Several lockers and a bench line one side of the channel, with a shower stall, powder room, and floor-length mirror on the opposite side.

There's a loud splash from the other locker room, followed by a string of rapid Spanish. I start tittering; I sure hope Em packed a change of clothes, because I'm pretty sure he just belly flopped into the other channel. I shrug out of my layers of clothing and toss everything into a locker. Reaching into my bag, I select a green bikini top and slip it on. Then I pull my messy curls into a sloppy ponytail and sit down at the edge of the channel, dangling my bare legs over the side.

Oh my... oh my... I heave a sigh as the saltwater washes over my feet and calves. Closing my eyes, I feel the pull of the sea stirring deep within me, calling to my mermaid spirit. Filling my lungs with air, I slowly exhale as I extend my tail fin. In a few blinks, my girlie tummy, hips, legs, and feet are replaced by a curvy green tail fin with a pretty pearlescent glow.

With a shout of pure joy, I drop into the channel and follow the water as it flows beneath the locker room wall. I emerge in a grotto-like area, complete with a small, sandy beach, large rocks for lounging, and a deep blue pool perfectly sized for swimming and diving. A clear, domed ceiling arches above me, rays of sun peeking around the edges of a puffy cumulus cloud.

This is the best inland water therapy imaginable. Aside from swimming in open water, there's nothing that can compare. Em must've spent a small fortune on our suite.

I hear a powerful splash behind me and spin around. Em's bronze tail fin sparkles as he propels himself toward me, his well-defined back and shoulder muscles clearly visible beneath the water. He stops a few feet away and lifts his head, his black hair sleek, his beard dripping beads of moisture. Em's powerful fishtail is swishing back and forth below us, maintaining his upright posture.

"I won!" I tease him and dive down, circling around him in a victory lap before popping up again. Small ripples swirl around us and crash against the tiny beach.

"So it would seem." Em grins. "In my haste I managed to fall headfirst into the channel, drenching my clothes."

"Oh, Em," I wince. "I'm sorry."

Em lifts his shoulders. "At least I packed a fresh shirt and jeans. But I don't think my coat can be salvaged; I'll have to ask Lura if she can rustle up a jacket for me." His brown eyes soften when they land on mine. "Would you care to dance?" Em swims over to me, closing the distance between us.

It's one of the games we used to play when we had shore leave and would meet up for a swim. Using the beat of the waves or the lap of the current against the shore as our music, we would pretend to be ballroom dancing in the water.

"Of course, kind sir." I bow my head with a soft chuckle.

Em curves his tail fin around mine and draws me into his powerful chest. I place my left hand on his shoulder and hold my right hand out, which he grips in his palm. He wraps his free arm around my waist and with a mighty swish of his tail, Em whisks us both away, swirling and undulating to a rhythm all his own, sea foam spraying the air around us. As Em propels us through the water, the scales along his fin brush continuously against mine, giving me tingles from the tip of my tail to the top of my spine.

Hmm... perhaps this water dancing game was a bad idea, because I'm beginning to tremble all over.

And while I'm very fond of Em, these shivers are not caused by his proximity; this is my body's natural reaction to swimming for the first time in almost three months. The simple truth is I've gone too long without a good swim, and I silently berate myself for not doing a better job of self-care. Just as the pull of the moon draws out the wolf in Jake, the water draws out my mermaid spirit. Merfolk need to swim every month or so—even taking a dip in a chlorinated pool counts—and I'm no exception.

Some of the stress I've been carrying around for months begins to leach out of me. As another tremor passes through my body, I let out a small sigh of relief. Water therapy is exactly what I need most right now.

Suddenly, Em is all over me. He entwines his tail fin around mine so firmly I can't wriggle free and buries his fingers in my curly hair, which has come loose from its tie. I'm about to ask Em what's going on—he's holding me way too tightly, and we're no longer swimming, we're sort of just bobbing—when he crushes his lips against mine, his beard damp against my face and throat. I can feel his heart pounding in his chest; my heart is speeding up too, but not with passion.

Nope. I'm flipping mad at this merman, who should know better.

Wrenching my head away, I give Em a hard punch in the shoulder.

"Ouch!" he yelps. "What was that for?"

"Back off, Em! Now!"

Em raises his hands, palms up like he's surrendering to the local sheriff, and then rapidly unwinds his tail fin from mine, releasing me from his vise-like grip. I pivot away from him and dive immediately, skimming along the bottom of the pool as tears stream down my face.

I can't believe Em just used my water craving, which is an overwhelming physical need all merfolk have, as an excuse for squashing his body—and his lips— against mine. That's so not cool.

I stay underwater a long time, swimming laps until

I'm no longer crying, until I can think more clearly again. Em's brain must've reengaged, because he's swimming on the opposite side of the pool, almost like there's an invisible dividing line right down the middle.

Eventually I stop swimming and flip over, enjoying the blurry view of the domed ceiling and blue sky arching above my watery cocoon. I use my arms and gentle flaps of my fin to remain like this, swaying slightly with the water, letting my mind wander freely.

For the first time, I'm beginning to understand my mother's intense need for regular access to the sea. Mama is one hundred percent merfolk, which would've made her water cravings even sharper than mine. I also know that's not why she left; although not ideal, a swim at the local YMCA could've satisfied her immediate need.

I finally learned the real reason this morning, when Dad poked his head in my room as I was packing. He nodded at my mer-gear lying on the bed. "Brings back memories."

I glanced up at him. "I hope some of them are good memories."

Dad drew his faerie brows together. "They're *all* good memories, Mona."

"But Mama left us because of this." I waved my bikini tops in the air. "She loved the sea more than she loved us!"

Dad's mouth dropped open, and he clutched his head with both his hands. "Sharks! Is that what you really think?"

"Well yeah... everyone in town thinks so." I narrowed

my eyes. "What have you neglected to tell me about Mama?"

Dad dropped down into my desk chair. "I guess you don't remember Karyn... before her meds stopped working."

"Her meds?" I swallowed hard, thinking about the woman who left me behind, the woman I've missed so much through the years. "What meds? What was wrong?"

"Karyn's mental illness has had different labels through the years, and for all I know, the terminology has changed again. She relied on medication and therapy to help her maintain an even keel, and she was really careful about never missing a dose. But her body chemistry changed when you were around eight, and from that point on her doctors couldn't find the right combination to alleviate her wild mood swings and other symptoms."

Dad rubbed his eyes before continuing. "Karyn struggled at times to properly care for you, and she was terrified her illness might negatively affect you. She knew I was capable of raising you alone, so she made the heartrending decision to leave. Your mother didn't desert anyone, and she certainly didn't leave because of her mermaid's yearning for the sea. She tried to do what was best for all of us—especially for you."

I cried when Dad told me, and when he hugged me, I noticed his cheeks were damp too.

I flip back over on my stomach and swim more laps. As I move through the water, I let the hurt and pain from my mother's abandonment wash over me... and drain away.

Mama didn't leave because she didn't care about me. *She left because she loved me.*

The truth hurts, but in a different way than believing a lie. Instead of feeling sorry for myself for being abandoned, now I feel sorry for my mother because of her illness and my coldness toward her.

And then I feel it... I feel the sweet release that comes from forgiving another person. I've finally forgiven my mother for leaving me.

When I break through the surface of the water, I'm more refreshed than I've been in a long time. I still have a lot to figure out, including my job situation, and I want to help my dad sell the inn so he can retire and visit Mama. And at the very top of my list is Jake: I can't wait to see him again.

But first, Em and I need to talk about what just happened.

I hoist myself onto one of the rocks, stretch out my tail fin, and wring out my wet curls. Em's head and torso emerge from the water; he's obviously been watching me swim. He eyes me warily as he treads in place. "Is it safe for me to join you?"

"I could ask you the same question."

Em drops his head to his brawny chest. "I am really sorry, Mona. Please forgive me. I wanted to believe your trembles were because of me and not your water cravings, and I got carried away. I promise to keep my distance from now on."

I point to a rock ten feet away. "You can sit over there." I'm not ready to forgive Em just yet. He raises himself out of the water, twists his body, and lands on the rock with fluid grace, his back and arm muscles bunching as he moves. Em is a fine-looking merman; I suspect Auntie Imogen might have a hard time choosing between dashing Em and handsome Jake. But it's no contest for me.

"We can't work together again, Em." He starts to interrupt me, but I hold up my hand. "One day you're going to find the right mermaid for you. But that day is not today, and that mermaid isn't me. In the meantime, it's going to be too awkward for us to be on the same ship."

Em runs both his hands through his wet hair. "I really blew it, didn't I?"

"Yes, you did. But even without your unwanted advances, my feelings would still be the same. I like you as a friend. Period."

"But I don't want to be the reason you turn down a good job offer. That would make me feel even worse than I do right now."

I arch my eyebrows. "Who said anything about refusing a good offer?"

Em furrows his brow. "I'm not following."

"The chief of cruise operations sent me an email yesterday, offering me a promotion if I stayed with our old ship. I told her I needed to think about it."

Em goes into mentor mode, which is a relief after everything that's happened, and he peppers me with questions about the job and financial package. I tell him the details, and he nods. "With all your experience, you can ask for a higher base salary, at least five thousand more. You're worth it, Mona."

"That's good advice. I'll think on it some more and will negotiate if I decide to take the job." I lean over the side of the rock and drop my hand into the pool, tracing lazy circles in the water with my fingers. "I'd like to take one more swim before we head back."

Em sits up straighter. "Head back? But why? We have this suite until noon tomorrow."

I shake my head. "Because of what we just discussed. Nothing is going to happen between us."

"Exactly. Nothing is going to happen between us. You have your bedroom, and I have mine." Em waves his hand around the pool. "Besides, wouldn't you like to swim again in the morning?"

I glance around. Em's right; another swim in the morning would be heavenly.

Em adds, "There's fresh popcorn."

Drat. I am hungry, and popcorn is a definite weakness, which Em knows all too well. "Salty caramel?" I roll my lips together; I can almost taste it.

"Yep," says Em. "And I planned a movie night... all your favorites."

I rattle off the cheesy movies we used to watch with the staff. He nods at each title. Finally I snap my fingers, trying to stump him. "*Jaws.*"

"Even *Jaws.*"

"Alright." I cross my arms and squint at Em until I'm sure he's paying attention. "I'll stay for movie night and a morning swim, on one condition: there will be no touching and no kissing. Deal?"

Em sighs. "Your negotiating skills are definitely improving, Mona." He gives me a wistful little smile. "Deal."

CHAPTER 29
NO GOOD DEED

JAKE

MONDAY, JANUARY 28

It's a chilly gray morning, a quarter past seven, when I arrive at Mooncrest Chapel in Granny Catbeam's borrowed motorcycle. Before she handed over her keys, Granny made me promise she'd be the first passenger to ride in my new Suburban, which I ordered to replace my wrecked one. Poor Granny has a bit of a wait, and so do I; according to the dealer it'll be a month before I can get my new SUV. Meanwhile, at least I have a set of wheels.

I park around back and notice the black Toyota is missing. Does that mean Captain Emilio has finally left Riddle Hill... or that he and Mona never returned last night? That last thought makes my mouth go dry; I just can't go there, not if I want to get any work done.

The shed doors are already open, and the contractors are banging away inside the chapel. Time for me to prepare the landing area for the exterior staircase. I grab a shovel, head over to the square section of ground beneath the partially completed third exit, and start clearing away the slightly slushy snow. It's warm for the end of January, the temperature hovering in the upper thirties, making my job this morning a little easier. Once I've reached dirt, I begin digging around in the soil, carting off large stones and clumps so I can create a flat surface for the stairs.

One of the gnomes helps me finish the digging, and then we use heavy-duty tampers to level the ground. By now it's mid-morning, and I've worked up a good sweat. I glance over at the parking lot; still no RAV4 and no sign of Mona.

My heart gives a painful lurch, which I dutifully ignore.

I have one final task to complete today, and that's to lay down fresh gravel over the newly leveled soil. After the gnome returns to his other assignment inside the chapel, I uncover the pile of gravel sitting next to the shed, toss the tarp aside, and begin carrying shovelfuls over to the landing area.

I'm transferring the last of the gravel into place when I hear a car pulling into the lot behind me. I force myself to smooth out the gravel and take one final look at the new exit taking shape above me. I've prepped the lumber, materials, and landing area for the exterior staircase. Once the contractors finish constructing the doorway, they'll be able to assemble the steps without delay.

Soon, Mooncrest Chapel will be ready for its final inspection. Cassia and Will may get their dream wedding after all, but I'll wait to tell my sister until after the inspection. It's entirely possible one of the vampires crossed a wire somewhere in the building, causing another setback until it's sorted out.

In any case, the chapel will be able to open in time for the spring and summer wedding season, and Rick DeMaris won't lose his business because I closed him down. Whatever is going to happen—or not happen—between Mona and me, at least I can take a small measure of comfort in that.

My work here finished, I grip the shovel in my right hand and slowly pivot around toward the rear parking lot and the car that just arrived. Something deep in my gut tells me I'm not going to like what I'm about to see.

CHAPTER 30
TERRIBLE TIMING

MONA

Monday, January 28

Em has behaved admirably since I chewed him out last night; I wouldn't have stayed otherwise, despite the appeal of Lura's remarkable saltwater pool. As our car crests a snow-covered ridge, the farms and meadows of south-central Door County fall behind us. The bay comes into view, icy and steely gray this cloudy winter morning, but by summer Green Bay's turquoise waters will be sparkling as vividly as the Mediterranean, and Riddle Hill will beckon supers and non-supers alike with its quirky small-town charm.

I wrap my arms around myself, a lump forming in my throat when I think of a certain Riddle Hill werewolf. Em's surprise appearance on Saturday night, coming on the heels of my teary breakdown at the lighthouse, must've hurt Jake deeply. This may sound strange, but I could almost *feel* Jake's sadness washing over me.

After Em leaves for the airport in a couple hours, I'm going to find Jake. I'll do whatever I can to repair the damage and hopefully, rekindle our relationship. Whether I take that job on my old ship or find something else, I still want Jake in my life. I don't know how... and I don't know where or when... but I do know *why* we need to be together.

Jake Grayclaw Spellman has captured my heart all over again, and this time, I want no misunderstandings keeping us apart. This time we're going to figure out this thing between us, and this time, we're going to get it right.

At least that's what I want. I can't be sure what Jake wants until I see him again.

As Em pulls around to the back of the inn, I spot a tall, bearded man in a fleece-lined flannel jacket and faded jeans shoveling gravel by the chapel. I examine him more closely; he's too big and muscular to be one of the gnomes. My hand flies to my mouth.

Sharks and shells! It's Jake!

This is horrible! Much, much worse than Em's unscripted appearance on Saturday night. Jake is going to see me arriving with Em, and he's going to assume the obvious. Why wouldn't he? It's noon, and I'm coming home from a date with Em.

How can I possibly explain this away? I had a hard enough time explaining to my dad (in several texts) that absolutely nothing was going on between Em and me.

Not that it's any of Dad's business, but he's still over-protective... and I got the distinct impression he doesn't like Em very much. Oddly, I think Dad and Jake appear to have struck some sort of accord.

Em switches off the car and then opens his door. I compress my lips and do the same, dreading the moment when my eyes meet Jake's. I slowly climb out of the Toyota, close the door, and turn to face the gorgeous man standing opposite me, one hand gripping a shovel so hard I think he's using it for support.

CHAPTER 31
A WOLF FOR ALL SEASONS

JAKE

Noon, January 28

It's the black Toyota, and both doors are opening. The smarmy captain climbs out of the driver's side, although he looks kind of bedraggled. Instead of his sleek wool coat with all the shiny buttons, he's wearing a shabby flannel poncho.

And then I see Mona's slim, jean-clad legs emerging from the passenger side. *She's been out all night with the captain!* How could she? And so soon after I poured my heart out to her?

My stomach plummets, and my vision goes blurry. I slam the tip of the shovel into the ground to keep myself from swaying, because I'm feeling lightheaded all of a sudden, probably due to hunger. My appetite's been off since Captain Emilio showed up in Riddle Hill; all I had for breakfast was a boiled egg.

Mona closes the car door, glances up, and sees me

256

staring back at her. A pained expression passes over her face, like maybe she was hoping I wouldn't be standing here watching as she returns home after spending the night with Captain Lover Boy.

It's a good thing I didn't eat anything else, because I'd be puking it all up right now. The captain must notice something is amiss, because Mona is frozen in place and so am I. Glancing from her to me uncertainly, he scurries over to Mona's side, draping an arm around her waist, and I break a little bit more.

Grief and pain course through my body, and I'm afraid, so afraid of lashing out, of doing something I'll regret later. I glance down at my trembling hands, my claws already tearing through my work gloves.

My wolf is struggling to break free to claim my mate, and I do the only thing I can: I turn my back on Mona and her captain, avoiding a fight that would only hurt her in the end.

I stride purposefully toward the front of the inn, climb onto Granny's motorcycle, start it up, and leave without looking back. I don't bother with a helmet because I want the cold air to sting my face; at least it helps to keep my wolf at bay a little longer.

I park in the fire station's lot, rip off my ruined work gloves, and scramble into the maintenance bay where Teddy is showing our newest firefighter how to clean his gear. Teddy glances at my hands, which are covered in gray fur, and then up at my face. I can feel my canines pushing through the gums inside my mouth.

"How can I help?" is all he says, and I'd hug the guy if

I could, but there's not enough time. I'm shifting now, and it's not going to be pretty.

"Lock me in."

"But Chief..." objects our new crew member, his eyes widening when he sees my nose stretching into a snout. The kid's a werewolf, so he's not surprised by my furry features, but he probably expects his pack alpha to display more self-control. After all, the moon won't be full for another thirty-six hours.

Sorry, kiddo. If you've ever loved and lost your mate... and then loved and lost her again... maybe you'd get it.

Teddy dismisses the young man, grabs my arm, and half drags me toward the dorm rooms next door. We dash down the steps to the holding pen, with its cinder block walls, concrete floor, and steel door that even the strongest wolf can't break through. I dump my keys, wallet, watch, and phone into a basket next to the door before scurrying into my prison.

As Teddy hurries to close the door—now I'm stripping off layers as fast as I can—I manage to bark two words, "Pack pledge."

"Pack pledge," repeats Teddy as the door clicks shut, confirming no one in the pack will breathe a word of this. He throws the bolt, and I sag to the floor with relief.

There's only one reason to lock a werewolf inside the holding pen, and that's because the wolf's control and discipline might slip during a full moon. In order to preserve the pack and keep both supers and non-supers safe, an alpha sometimes orders a werewolf to remain inside the holding pen until the morning after the full moon.

However, alphas never place themselves in lockdown —they don't need to order such Draconian measures against themselves—and no one can remain a pack alpha with so little self-control.

I can't worry about that now; I have to do the right thing, which means protecting Mona's captain from my teeth and my claws. She obviously loves him, and as much as it tears my insides apart, I won't lay a finger on the captain. I refuse to do anything that could hurt Mona or the man who's captured her heart.

Growling as my undershirt rips apart, I lift my shaggy gray head and cry, pouring all my brokenness and heartache into every howl.

CHAPTER 32
FULL MOON

MONA

Monday to Tuesday, January 28-29

My eyes welled with tears at the stricken look on Jake's face. When Em rushed to my side and placed an arm around my waist, I shrugged out of his grasp. Dashing after Jake, I reached the front of the inn just as he roared away on his grandmother's motorcycle. I called after him, "Jake! Wait—please!" but I don't think he heard me.

"Is *that* your old school chum?" asks Em as he joins me on the driveway.

"Yes."

Em shakes his head, disbelief evident in his voice. "You're in love with a *werewolf?*"

Sucking in a breath, I hesitate before answering. Am I ready to use the *L* word with Jake? "Yes." I give a firm head nod before repeating, "Yes, I love him."

Em lets out a long, low whistle. "Then I suppose you need to explain things to him."

I glance over at Em, my friend and captain for so many voyages. "I will, but let me help you get checked out first."

Em's mouth twists, as if he's trying to smile but can't quite manage it. "I'd like that, Mona. Thanks."

An hour later, after Em has left for the airport, I send Jake a short text. "Jake, we need to talk. Please."

No response. He's upset; I get it. I'll try again later.

The hours fly by as I help Twila with several summer bookings, all large groups of supers coming to Riddle Hill for various events. It's a relief to see the reservations booking up; at least the inn will remain in the black while Dad searches for a buyer. Now all we need is for the chapel to reopen soon, and we'll be as busy as ever.

It's nearly five o'clock before I try texting Jake again. "Jake, what you saw...it's not what you think. Please, I'd like to explain."

When another hour goes by with still no response, I find myself becoming agitated. Jake is clearly hurting and upset, and possibly also angry. Fine. But I know Jake; he believes in talking through issues. Jake doesn't normally clam up and disappear like this.

I'm sitting at our old maple table in the kitchen, staring out the window, when Dad hands me a bowl of his homemade veggie stew and a chunk of fresh sourdough bread. I barely manage a few mouthfuls before pushing it away. He glances at me, worry etching his face. "You've been quiet all afternoon. What's wrong? Did that merman do anything to—"

I hold up my hand. "This isn't about Em, or at least not directly."

Dad draws his faerie brows together in a mighty scowl, and I see the resemblance to Auntie Imogen, just as she's winding up for a rant. "What did that sneaky water serpent do?"

"There's no cause for name calling!" I fold my arms across my chest. "Mama would never have permitted that language in our home!"

At the mention of my mother, Dad exhales and scratches his head, his hair sticking up in little white tufts. "You're right. I'm sorry... it's just that captain of yours was so... gropey. I wanted to slap him on the side of the head a few times."

"Em's gone now, and he's definitely not my captain, not any longer that is." At Dad's quizzical expression, I tell him about the job offer to return to my old ship.

My father gives me his *proud Papa* smile. "That's fantastic, Mona... what an opportunity! You're going to take it, aren't you?"

"Probably." But even as I say it, I feel such a longing for Jake that I can hardly breathe. What's going on with me? "We'll see."

Dad cocks his head to the side. "So let me see if I've got this straight. You're not upset about Captain Emilio; you've got a great job offer on the table, and you're moping around like you lost your best friend. What's wrong?"

I tear my bread into tiny little pieces so I have something to do with my hands. "I had the loveliest date with

Jake on Saturday night," I whisper. "Until Em showed up…"

"That was really awkward," agrees my father. "And I apologize again for my part in it."

A small sigh escapes my lips. "It gets worse."

"Oh?" Dad leans forward.

I explain about Jake spotting Em and me arriving at the inn together this morning… and the obvious conclusions Jake would've drawn.

"O-oh…" says Dad, drawing out the syllable. "That poor guy."

My mouth hangs open. When has my dad ever had a kind word to say about Jake… let alone a sympathetic one? "What are you talking about?"

Dad clamps his mouth shut and draws his tipped-up eyebrows even closer together. "You need to speak with Jake right away."

"I realize that… but he's not responding to my text messages."

"Then call him. If that doesn't work, ask Elmo for a ride over to Jake's place. Talk to the man, Mona. Don't let him stew in his own juices."

I'm confused by Dad's reaction and the sense of urgency I hear in his voice, but I don't argue because *I have to do something.* I head to my room and dial Jake's number. Twice. Both times my call goes directly to voicemail.

Thirty minutes later, I'm ringing Jake's doorbell while Elmo waits for me in his Jeep. Jake's cottage is dark, and there's no answer. Climbing back into the Jeep, I say, "Let's try Howling Shores Pub."

Howling Shores is a werewolf hangout and the unofficial "home" of Jake's pack, the Bay Howlers. I pull open the heavy wooden door with the porthole window and step inside the nautical-themed tavern. Scanning the room, my eyes finally land on Rob Wolferman. I figure Jake's beta and best friend should know where I can find him. Rob is sitting alone at the oak bar nursing a beer.

I climb onto the stool next to him. "Hey, Rob."

Rob glances over at me and then stares back down at his beer. "Hey."

Wow. Normally gregarious Rob is practically morose. He's not on his phone; he's not telling me about his latest real estate deal, and he's not his typical salesy self. "I'm looking for Jake. Have you seen him?"

Rob splutters, clears his throat, and refuses to meet my eyes. "Haven't seen him."

"Any idea where he's at?"

"Nope," he replies, drawing out the *P* so it pops.

I narrow my eyes at Rob. Something is very, very wrong. "Is Jake... hurt?" I grimace at my choice of words; Jake is almost certainly hurting right now.

"Just leave it be, Mona," mutters Rob. "You've done enough." He drops a bill on the bar and stands to leave.

"What are you talking about?" Rising, I step in front of him.

"You broke the man's heart," hisses Rob. "Of course he's *hurt*." Rob pushes

past me.

"Wait, please," I call out. When Rob turns to face me, I almost lose my nerve. But I have to know. "How do you know I broke Jake's heart?" I whisper.

Rob narrows his eyes at me. "As Jake's beta, it's my job to know his emotional state—and the reason for it. Besides, the entire pack feels the strain when the alpha is suffering." Rob spins on his heels and hurries out the door.

Tears sting my eyes, but I blink them away. Thanks to Rob's brutal honesty, I feel even worse. I really need to see Jake so I can set the record straight, but how? He's gone... somewhere to be alone, it sounds like. And Rob Wolferman, the most talkative extrovert in Riddle Hill, won't tell me how to find Jake. What am I supposed to do now?

My entire body droops with exhaustion, and I realize I can't do anything else until I get some rest. I push open the heavy porthole door and head out into the cold.

Elmo takes one look at me as I climb into the Jeep beside him and asks, "Home?"

"Yes, please." I lean my head against the seat, close my eyes, and think back over the most emotionally draining weekend of my adult life.

Two men declared themselves in ways I wasn't expecting—Em got carried away and infuriated me— while Jake took me in his arms and told me he would wait for me, for as long as I needed. I swipe at a tear trickling down my face and sniffle. There's no way Jake feels that way about me now.

This is all far too much drama for a mermaid who craves normalcy and likes to stay on an even keel. Something rattles around inside my head, and I recall Dad using that same phrase when he explained about

Mama's illness and why she left, toppling all my old assumptions about her.

I rub my temples wearily, unable to process anymore emotion without rest. The lights are dim in our apartment when I return, which is just as well. I'm so tired I can barely see straight.

Tomorrow. I'll find Jake tomorrow and will explain everything to him then.

It's my turn to take the early shift in the lobby, so at seven I'm sitting at the mahogany desk, replying to emails and booking a few more reservations. Every so often I check my phone, but Jake hasn't responded. I look up the lunar cycle and realize tonight's the full moon. Since he's still healing, Jake won't be able to run with his pack. Does that mean he'll be all alone? I don't like that idea at all. I get the sense his werewolf form is more emotional.

I have to speak with Jake as soon as I can, before he shifts. It's late morning when I dial Jake's number again, but there's still no response. I slap my phone on the desk, startling Auntie Imogen out of her nap. "Sweet moon-glow, whatever is the matter, child?"

"I'm sorry to wake you, Auntie. It's nothing."

Auntie Imogen leans out of her frame and squints at me. She's wearing a day gown in a lovely shade of violet, and the fake fruit on her hat is purplish today, plums, grapes, passion fruit, and blackberries. "I can see as plainly as the nose on my face you're sad this morning.

Although I don't understand why. You sent the merman packing, which was the right thing to do under the circumstances. I would never recommend prolonging a love triangle when the answer is so obvious, eh?"

Rising from the desk, I walk into the center of the lobby and stand in front of the fireplace, facing Imogen's portrait. I try to unpack her words but soon give up. "What's so obvious?"

My faerie auntie's silver eyebrows tilt dramatically upward. "Why he's your mate, child!"

I put my hands on my hips, wondering why I'm even bothering to listen to my ridiculous faerie godmother. "My mate? Who are you talking about?"

Imogen gasps. "You don't know? But how can this be?"

"Auntie!" I stomp my heel on the thick rug, which muffles the sound. "Please explain!"

"Well," Imogen replies, bringing one hand fluttering to her throat. "I'm not sure I ought; I mean, *he* should have told you. I only know because I overheard your father and that dreamy vampire talking about it... oh, let's see. I suppose it would've been Sunday. You'd just left for your date with the merman."

I grab two fistfuls of my hair and plead, "Who were they talking about Auntie?"

Auntie Imogen shakes her head stubbornly. "You need to speak with that vampire, dearie. I only caught snippets of conversation, a bit here and there. I might be mistaken." She covers her mouth to hide a yawn. "It's best you talk to Malaki Acheron directly. He can explain about—"

Imogen emits a garbled snore. I swallow down a scream of frustration and rap on the gilded frame of her portrait. Auntie wakes with a start, spreading her silvery-white faerie wings as if prepared to take flight. Then she glances down at me and shakes her head. "What are you still doing here? Go see Malaki without delay." She falls back asleep.

I dash to the desk, grab my phone, and dial Malaki's Menswear. The call is transferred a few times until I hear a familiar accented voice greet me. "Mona Lisa, eet's so good to hear from you."

"Malaki!" I blurt out. "Something's wrong with Jake—and I think you're the only man who can help me."

"Vhere are you?" Malaki sounds worried.

"Mooncrest Inn."

"I peek you up at noon."

My hand is shaking when I hang up the call.

CHAPTER 33

HEART TO HEART

JAKE

WEDNESDAY, JANUARY 30

"Chief?" I hear someone's muffled voice. "Can we open the door now?" I growl out a garbled "N-no" through my canine lips and lay my head back down on my paws.

I felt the moon's pull slowly waning hours ago, so I know it's safe for me to be around other people, even Mona's captain. I'm not going to snap; frankly, I don't have the energy.

And I'm definitely getting hungry. I've been tearing into the dried jerky and kibble my packmates periodically shove through the opening at the base of the door, and lapping from the water bowls they've been supplying, but it's not enough. Somewhere in the back of my scrambled brain I know I need to get cleaned up and sorted out. I know I need to eat a real meal; I know I need to emerge from my self-imposed exile.

I know I need to face the rest of my life without Mona.

There's shuffling on the other side of the door, and I hear a male voice with a thick Transylvanian accent shout, "We need ta talk, Jake."

I roll my eyes. What's Malaki doing here? He may be my friend, but he's not my packmate.

"Eet's very important. Cannot wait."

Sighing, I realize my timeout is over. "Fi' min'its," I manage to yip.

"Dat's fine. I'm geeving you five minutes. Den I'm opening dis door."

Who does Malaki think he is? Pack alpha?

The idea is laughable—a fashionable, cashmere-clad vampire leading a pack of large, grungy werewolves—and I snort at the thought. But then I glance down at my matted fur and take a whiff.

Confound it all! I stink!

It's time for me to emerge from this slab of concrete, where I've wept and wailed and whined for almost two days, if for no other reason than to take a hot shower and eat something more appetizing than desiccated beef strips.

It's time for me to face reality.

My mate... my Mona... loves someone else, and there's nothing I can do about it.

I take hold of the blanket someone shoved through the hole a few hours ago. Shifting into my man form, I toss the blanket around my torso and wrinkle my nose. I think I smelled better as a werewolf.

"Ready!" My voice is raspy after all that howling.

The bolt is thrown back, and Marv and Malaki enter the holding pen. Malaki coughs and quickly covers his nose with a silk handkerchief; Marv just stares down at me impassively.

I glower up at the huge cop. "What ever happened to the concept of pack secrecy, Marv?" Then I nod at Malaki and murmur, "No offense."

Malaki waves one beringed hand in my direction. "None taken."

Marv crosses his beefy arms. "Three women registered a missing persons report on you, Jake. Three! I've been doing paperwork for hours!"

Three women? I run a hand through my snarled hair.

One would have been my sister; I just remembered I was supposed to have dinner at her place... um... Monday night. Almost two days ago. Okay, I can understand why Cassia freaked out. Then she would've called Teddy, and he wouldn't have spilled the beans, so Sophie would've probably gone with Cassia to the police station. That's two women.

But who was the third? If my aunt and uncle weren't on their annual Caribbean cruise this week, I'd add Phoebe to the list.

Rubbing my forehead, I grumble, "Cassia and Sophie were two of them, right?"

Marv nods. "Yup."

"Alright, I give up. Who was number three?"

Marv glances at Malaki and says, "Why don't you do the honors, since you drove her to the station."

Now I'm really stumped. Who would've asked Malaki for a ride to the police station?

"Eet vas Mona Lisa," murmurs Malaki.

I sit up straighter on the hard floor, not sure I've heard him correctly. "*Mona?* But why?"

"I'll tell you after yer bath. I'll vait fer you up in da kitchen—I'll fix you somethin' to eat," mumbles Malaki through his handkerchief. I think he's hamming it up a bit to make a point, but I can't deny the scent of unwashed dog mixed with manly body odor lingers in the air.

Rising, I follow the two men out the door, a tiny shaft of hope piercing my gloom.

Maybe, just maybe, I haven't lost Mona after all.

"So Mona really knows? You told her about my step-father's spell and the whole werewolf-mate thing?" After showering and changing into one of my spare uniforms, I found Malaki in the fire station's sleek, stainless-steel kitchen, which he's commandeered for our private use. He treated the two guys and one gal on duty to carry out from Vlad's Victuals; they're having lunch downstairs in the training room.

Meanwhile I just finished my second helping of cherrywood bacon, scrambled eggs with chives, and buttered toast, because Malaki refused to tell me anything until after I'd eaten breakfast twice over. I'm starting to feel human again—barely.

"Dat's vat I've been tryin' to explain. Mona Lisa, she knows."

"And she didn't run away screaming?"

"Nah. She went to find you, and ven she couldn't, she went to da police. An' I went with her. We both were very worried by den."

"I'm sorry about that Malaki... I really am. It was the safest solution under the circumstances."

"Tell dat to Mona 'n Cassia 'n Sophie. Eet's a good thing Phoebe 'n Nash are out of da country this week." Malaki is right about that; my aunt and uncle would read me the riot act for disappearing without letting anyone outside the pack know what was happening and that I was safe.

I wipe my mouth with a napkin. "I don't understand Mona at all. Why would she be so worried about me if she's in love with the merman?" The image of the slimy captain with his arms around Mona pops into my brain, and my skin starts to crawl all over again.

"She send da sea captain packin'."

"What? When?" I shake my head, more confused than ever. "That doesn't line up with what I saw."

Malaki puts his hand up. "Mona tell me vat happen. Eet's not vat you think."

"I know what I saw, Malaki." I cross my arms, scowling.

Malaki checks his phone. "Den let Mona explain. She prettier than me, an' she's in da lobby." He rises from his chair. "I'll send her up."

I start to object that I don't want to see her—this isn't the right time; I'm not sure what to say to her—but by the time I manage to voice my concerns, Malaki is long gone. With vampiric efficiency he's cleared away my plate and mug, leaving just my phone sitting on the table in front of me.

I start swiping through two-days' worth of texts and phone calls from family and friends, all of them worried about me. I owe my sister a huge apology, and my cousin too. I come across a rather ominous-sounding text from Trixie Wolferman. She requests my presence at a special pack meeting tomorrow night and suggests I come prepared to demonstrate my fitness. In other words, I need to be ready to fight to retain my alpha status. Trixie's only doing what's best for the pack; I'd do the same in her fur. But it still rankles.

I continue to scroll, pausing when I see Mona's name. She sent me three texts... and tried calling a few times too... but why? What can Mona possibly say to me after spending the night with the captain? I start reading her messages:

"Jake, we need to talk. Please."

"Jake, what you saw...it's not what you think. Please, I'd like to explain."

"Jake, where are you? We're all so worried. Please come home."

Those last words stick in my craw. Mona has some nerve telling me to *come home* when I'm the one who's never left. I'm the one who's always valued home and family and community above everything else. I haven't spent the past decade wandering the big blue sea.

I'm so busy feeling sorry for myself I'm stunned when Mona pulls out a chair at the table, her intoxicating scent of sea breeze and citrus overwhelming my senses. I plunk down my phone, take a stabilizing breath, and peer up at her, fully prepared to hold on to all my hurt and anger.

One look at Mona and my resolve crumbles; she's beautiful as always, wearing a rose-colored jacket, white blouse, and blue jeans. But she's paler than usual, with purplish circles beneath her eyes that makeup can't hide, and she's lost her sparkle. Mona is like a star that's suddenly dimmed, all the twinkle and brightness gone.

Confound it all! Her lower lip is trembling!

I want to kiss this woman—this mate of mine that another man has claimed—with every fiber of my being! Instead I close my eyes, my heart stuttering so painfully in my chest it hurts to inhale. *Just breathe, you fool of a wolf,* I berate myself. *Mona clearly has something to say, and the least you can do is try to listen.*

"Jake, look at me. Please."

"Can't," I mutter.

She hesitates. "Why not?"

With my eyes still firmly closed, I clench my fists on the tabletop. "Because... despite everything that's happened, everything you've done with the captain and *not* done with me... I want to kiss you."

I feel a sharp jab in my right pec and yowl in pain. "Ow! Did you just punch me?"

"Yes!" Mona's brown eyes are fiery; she hasn't entirely lost her sparkle. "And I'll do it again if you don't listen up and keep those amber eyes of yours opened wide. I'm not going to repeat myself, werewolf, so pay attention!"

Glowering, I rub the spot where Mona hit me. "Go on. You've got my attention."

Mona nods and says more softly, "I know how it looked on Monday."

"You mean when you showed up at noon with Captain Kissy Face after spending the night with him?" I can't keep the sarcasm out of my voice.

"Yes... I mean no, not exactly."

"Which is it Mona? You can't have it both ways."

Mona runs a hand through her curls, which are as lustrous and bouncy as ever. "Em and I had separate bedrooms; we spent most of the time swimming and watching old movies."

"Are you trying to tell me nothing happened between you and the captain? That merman was all over you, Mona. I find it hard to believe he was well behaved."

Mona looks at me, her eyes moist, and takes a deep breath. "The truth is Em did slip in a kiss when I wasn't expecting it—"

"I knew it!" I explode, pounding my fist on the table. "I knew he was a sneak!" My wolf is itching to track down that merman and make him pay for kissing Mona without her consent.

Mona places her hand over my fist; the calming effect of her touch soothes me like balm on a burn. My anger at Captain Emilio abates somewhat. "I punched Em a whole lot harder than I hit you just now, and I told him to back off because nothing was ever going to happen between us."

I tear my gaze away from her pale, smooth hand covering my much larger, calloused one and peer into her eyes, two liquid brown pools I'm prepared to drown myself in. "And he listened?"

"Yes. Em behaved like a gentleman for the remainder of the evening." Mona's voice drops to a whisper, and I lean forward to ensure I catch every word. "He had no choice when he realized there was someone else in the picture... someone I care deeply about... someone I love."

Did Mona just say she *loves* me? I'm still pondering that miraculous possibility when she does something truly remarkable. Mona leans across the table, puts her arms around my neck, and kisses me full on the lips.

"Oh, Mona," I groan. Tugging her out of her chair, I rise and draw her into my arms, threading my fingers through her long, dark waves. I nip at her perfect bow-shaped lips and then gently press my mouth against hers. Her arms tighten around me, and I deepen the kiss, sending shockwaves through my body that sear me, heart and soul. I realize I'll love this woman for the rest of my life, but it won't be enough. I'll never have my fill of Mona Lisa DeMaris. "You're killing me."

Mona pulls back, her brow furrowed. "I'm *killing* you?"

I plant tiny kisses all along her jawline until I feel a sharp pinch in my side. "Ouch! What was that for?"

"Explain yourself, or I'll pinch you again."

I chuckle, my heart lighter than it's been in years. "According to a very wise man, love is pain. I'm so in love with you it hurts."

Mona pats my beard gently. "Poor Jake. I hope I'm not wounding you too deeply."

I pull her against my chest and nuzzle her hair, inhaling deeply. "I'm in agony, Mona dearest, but I wouldn't have it any other way."

Laughing, she stands on her tiptoes to fit her mouth against mine, and I feel myself going weak in the knees. This woman is positively deadly. "Um, there is something I do have to tell you," she says.

An iron fist slams into my gut at the serious tone in Mona's voice. I know what's about to go down: she just told me she loves me, and now she's going to tell me she's leaving. Because let's face it, that's just my luck. "What is it?" I murmur, bracing myself.

"My boss offered me a substantial promotion to return to my old ship, but she needed my answer by today. I signed an eight-month contract." Mona tilts her head to the side, waiting for my reaction.

"Eight months?" I huff. "That's practically a year!"

"Don't be ridiculous." Mona tosses her head, her hair tumbling around her face like a dark halo. Gah! She's so distracting. "It's little more than half a year. And I'll have a week off at the halfway point."

"Are you working with Captain Emilio again? Because I don't trust that guy around you."

Mona takes both my hands in hers and squeezes. "First of all, you need to trust me when I say that Em is the past. But to set your mind at ease, he'll be cruising on the Adriatic Sea while I'll be sailing the Mediterranean. Two entirely different bodies of water."

My rancor toward the merman cools somewhat when I realize he won't be anywhere near Mona while she's away. "I told you I'd support your decision to continue cruising." I lean forward, touching my forehead to hers. "If this is what you want, we'll figure out a way to make it work."

Mona wraps her arms around my waist and tucks her head into the hollow of my chest. "I don't intend to cruise forever, Jake. But there's been so much upheaval with Dad's injury and his plans for Mooncrest that I need this; I need one more tour at sea."

I hold her close and kiss the top of her head, already mourning her departure. Eight months—with only one week in the middle when I get to see her! But then little alarm bells start going off in my head that have nothing to do with Mona's cruise director job. "What's your father planning to do with Mooncrest?"

Mona pulls away with a small scowl, pursing her rosy lips, which are so delectable I nearly forget my question. "Dad's plans are just that, his plans. I'm not at liberty to say."

Now it's my turn to scowl. "I don't like secrets between us, Mona."

Mona takes a step back, crossing her arms. "Neither do I, but like I said, this isn't my secret. My father can do whatever he likes with the inn."

"Now wait just a minute. As Mayor of Riddle Hill and the people's representative, I do have a vested interest in your father's plans for Mooncrest Inn."

"I don't believe this!" Mona throws her hands in the air. "Not everything in Riddle Hill revolves around you, Jake Spellman! And if my dad decides to do something with Mooncrest Inn, that's none of your concern!"

I narrow my eyes at her, not liking where my thoughts are heading. But I'm a wolf, and wolves are nothing if not direct. "So that's why your father has finally decided to spring for a contractor. The chapel

279

repairs have moved along so quickly I've been asking myself why he dragged his feet for so long. The expense is one reason, obviously, but I've been thinking there has to be another, and now the answer is obvious. Your dad is going to sell Mooncrest, isn't he?"

Mona brings a finger to her lips. "Shh! Dad will strangle us both if word leaks out."

"I've been there practically every day for the past few weeks, helping with the chapel repairs, and you never breathed a word. You didn't trust me enough to tell me the truth!" I stammer, rubbing the spot on my chest directly above my heart, which feels suddenly fragile, like it's going to shatter any minute.

"Don't be so dramatic," sputters Mona. "My father swore me to secrecy."

"But Mooncrest Inn is crucial to Riddle Hill's economy. What happens to the inn could affect all of us. Surely you can see that?"

Mona grabs her purse from the table and slings the strap over her shoulder. "All I see is a werewolf who's such a workaholic he can't find the forest for the trees!"

"Oh that's rich, coming from a mermaid who'll go out with anyone, just so long as she can get in a good swim!" Mona's mouth drops open, and I immediately regret those words, but it's too late to recall them.

She stomps her bootheel on the tile floor, which I'd find endearing if I weren't so upset. "Don't bother showing up at the chapel unless it's to perform the final inspection." Mona spins around and stalks over to the stairs.

"Don't worry—I have more important things to do than babysit your repairmen!" I call after her.

"You are impossible!" Mona shouts at me over her shoulder and then clomps down the stairs.

A few minutes later Malaki pokes his head into the kitchen and smirks. "I see dat went well, eh?"

I drop my head in my hands. "I blew it again. Sometimes I think I'm going to be spending the rest of my days messing things up with Mona."

"Prob'ly." Malaki chortles. "But dat's not so bad. You get to make up vis her too—which ees da best part!" The cagey vampire grins, showing me a bit of fang.

I give Malaki a weary smile but keep my thoughts to myself. There's no doubt in my mind Mona is going to be piping mad for a while, because I intend to find out everything I can about Rick's plans to sell Mooncrest Inn.

I have no choice. It's my civic duty.

CHAPTER 34
MARRIED TO THE PACK

MONA

Wednesday, January 30

As I stalked through the station's lobby, I passed
Malaki heading toward the stairs. He must have heard
the yelling because he arched one black eyebrow at me,
waiting for an explanation. I told him the same thing I
told Jake. "That man's impossible!" Malaki chuckled
softly as I continued walking right through the front
door.

"Oh... um, sorry about that." I nearly collide with
Sophie and Teddy Barker making out on the sidewalk.

They both laugh, and then Teddy leans over to plant
one final kiss on Sophie's lips before heading into the fire
station. Sophie has a slightly dazed look on her face; this
girl is seriously in love. She adjusts her green beret at a
jaunty angle on her long brown hair. Then she pats down
the lapels of her wool jacket, which Teddy was just grip-

ping, and gives me an assessing gaze. "I have a feeling you just saw Jake."

I shake my head. "I don't know how you stand it." I'm referencing the whole being in love with a werewolf thing, but Sophie zeroes in on Jake.

"Well, as far as cousins go, he's actually pretty sweet."

"As boyfriend material, he makes my head spin." I snort in aggravation. "One minute Jake's got me on a pedestal so high I'm practically floating, and the next he's lecturing me with all the sternness of a papa wolf. Sharks and shells! Are all werewolves so exhausting?"

"Werewolves are certainly a breed apart." Sophie loops her arm through mine, guiding me down the sidewalk in the direction of her bakery. "Sounds like his alpha wolf is asserting itself, which is probably a good thing. Jake is going to be challenged tomorrow night."

I stop walking and stare at Sophie, horrified. "Do you mean *physically* challenged? Like he has to *fight*? Jake just spent the past two days in the werewolf equivalent of solitary confinement! He needs to rebuild his strength."

Sophie lowers her voice. "It's as much a mental challenge as it is physical." She gives my arm a gentle tug. "Let's talk inside the bakery rather than out here in the cold." I allow myself to be pulled along a few blocks until we arrive at the Rhyme 'N Riddle Bakeshop, which Sophie inherited from one of her ancient faerie aunties.

Sophie nods at the little wrought iron table and matching chairs parked beneath the plate glass window at the front of her shop. "How about coffee and something sweet?" Sophie bustles away without waiting for my reply, just like Phoebe, who has a sixth sense about what I need at any given moment. Sophie appears to have inherited her faerie mother's foodie gift.

While I wait for Sophie to return, I prop my elbows on the table, rest my chin on top of my folded hands, and relive the moment when Jake returned my kiss. If I hadn't had my arms around his neck to hold myself up, my legs would have given way. Jake is without doubt the most infuriating man I've ever known, but his kisses bring me to my knees.

Everything inside me softens when our lips touch, and I can't imagine anywhere else I want to be, except in his arms. Until he goes all alpha, channeling his inner mayor or chief inspector vibes; then Jake's as bossy as when he was student council president. But even then I used to secretly swoon over him.

We finally confessed our true feelings—my heart lit on fire when he told me *I was killing him*—and then he has to ruin it all by focusing on Mooncrest Inn. He behaved as if I betrayed a sacred trust because I didn't tell him my father's secret.

Barnacles! Why couldn't I have returned Em's affections... or the half dozen other mermen who flirted with me through the years?

Why did I have to go and fall in love with a werewolf?

And why does it have to be Jake Spellman—who makes me dizzy with yearning one minute—and rigid with fury the next?

Sophie returns to the table carrying a tray with two coffees and a platter of flaky mini croissants filled with chocolate and marzipan. One of her assistants brings us plates, napkins, utensils, and cream and sugar for our coffee. "Thanks," I say, doctoring my coffee with extra cream.

Sophie gives my hand a sympathetic pat. "I'm probably the only woman in Riddle Hill who can truly understand what you're going through right now."

I glance up at her. "Because you're a faerie in love with a werewolf?"

"Yes, I'm in love with Teddy... but it's so much more too."

I tilt my head. "I'm not following."

"Teddy and I are mates. His wolf needs me, and my faerie heart returns his love with a fervor that leaves me breathless." Sophie shakes her head and stares down at her half-eaten croissant. "For the longest time I rebuffed Teddy, refused to believe we could ever be happy together."

She glances up, her gaze locking on mine. "I wasted so much time in denial. Teddy was miserable and heartbroken... and so was I. Don't make the same mistakes I made. Tell Jake how you feel."

"I just did."

Sophie's eyes widen. "And what did he say?"

"Everything that would melt a gal's heart."

"Sweet moonglow! Then what's wrong?"

I sigh. "He's angry because I didn't tell him something that is none of his business. He wanted me to spill someone else's secret, which I refused to do."

"Of course you need to keep someone else's secret. Jake should know better."

"Stubborn werewolf," I grumble.

"Stubborn werewolf," agrees Sophie.

"Tell me about this challenge tomorrow night."

Sophie wrinkles her nose. "I guess it makes more sense if you are a wolf and accustomed to living in a pack. Teddy says when an alpha appears unable or unwilling to perform his duties—such as when Jake put himself in lockdown—

the pack calls a meeting and invites any and all challengers to fight him for the top spot."

I'm suddenly horrified. The only reason Jake is in this predicament is because of the misunderstanding about me and Em. Now he has to fight to retain his status? "That's just plain... neanderthal."

"Not really," says Sophie softly. "It's typical wolf behavior."

"But could Jake get hurt tomorrow night?"

Sophie hesitates. "I guess you don't know much about wolf packs, do you?"

I shake my head.

"Most of the time, an alpha knows when to admit defeat and allow a stronger wolf to take over the pack. Like when Trixie Wolferman ordered Jake to challenge her. They had a good fight for maybe ten minutes, and then Trixie allowed herself to be pinned down. That was it; Jake assumed the alpha role. But sometimes an alpha will keep fighting until—until he can't."

I wish I hadn't eaten that last croissant because now I'm nauseous. Jake is so stubborn that's exactly what he'd do.

Sophie adds, "But it's also quite possible none of the werewolves will challenge Jake."

"Really?"

Sophie nods. "Teddy has no intention of fighting Jake. He doesn't think anyone else in the pack wants to oppose Jake either. Teddy thinks this is just a formality, nothing more."

"Let's hope Teddy's right." I stand up. "I better get going... thanks for the comfort food and the chat."

"Look, I need to make a couple deliveries. Why don't I give you a lift back to the inn in my van?"

Fifteen minutes later Sophie pulls in front of the inn. "Thanks again," I say, opening the door.

"No problem... and um," Sophie hesitates before plowing ahead with what's on her mind. "Just in case another werewolf decides to challenge Jake tomorrow night... you might want to patch things up."

I narrow my eyes at her. "But he started it."

"Even if he started it, he's probably regretting it now. All I'm saying is you want Jake to focus on the pack meet tomorrow and not be distracted because..."

"Because he's stubborn and foolhardy and thinks he knows what's best for everyone else."

Sophie chuckles softly. "Yeah, exactly."

CHAPTER 35
PACK MEET

JAKE

Thursday, January 31

I'm in the men's locker room in the attic of Howling Shores Pub. I hang up my leather jacket, jeans, and chambray shirt, remove my boots and socks, and change into a pair of loose gray sweats in case I need to shift quickly to meet a challenger. My packmates are doing the same right now, the guys in here with me, and the gals in their locker room across the hall.

I haven't checked my phone once since Mona stormed off yesterday—per doctor's orders. Doc Demetrius told Malaki to retain my phone until after the pack meet; I wound up yelling at Malaki, but he merely extended his fangs at me and shrugged. Argh. Vampires are so toothy.

I suppose Doc's concerns are legitimate; he thinks I'll be too distracted if I hold on to my phone in my current state. The truth is I'm having trouble thinking about anything other than the feel of Mona in my arms, her lips on mine, and then the emptiness that settled in my gut after she left.

Confound it all! Mona is the most aggravating woman on land or sea. Why can't she understand that I only want what's best for everyone, including the supernaturals who call Riddle Hill home? I'm not opposed to Rick selling Mooncrest, but I'd like to be consulted before he signs on the dotted line, since his decision could have huge ripple effects across this community.

I slam my locker door shut and see Rob staring back at me. "What?" I grumble.

"Make sure your head's in the game, bro."

I snort. "I wish this were high school, and we're suiting up for the homecoming game senior year. Now that was a game."

Rob grins. "Yeah, it was quite a rout. What was the score again?"

"Thirty-five to seven," I reply, smiling at the memory. "And you never forget a score. I know what you're doing."

Rob claps me on the shoulder. "I've got your back."

"I know... and thanks."

We file into the gym, its wooden floors retaining the scent of pack meets through the years, a mixture of damp fur, sweat, and blood. Trixie is standing in the center of the room, her perfectly coiffed blonde bob gleaming beneath the overhead lights. Like the rest of us, she's wearing sweats, although hers are pale blue and fashionably form-fitting, which means she has no intention of challenging me. I stand directly opposite her, and all my packmates, twelve men and nine women, stand off to my left.

"Jake Grayclaw Spellman," intones Trixie without preamble. "You placed yourself in lockdown for over forty hours, potentially jeopardizing your pack with your absence and calling into question your competence as pack leader. We're here tonight to invite any werewolf—packmate or loner—to challenge you for the alpha role. Before we begin roll call, I will give you one minute to respond."

I bow my head in submission. "Thank you, alpha emeritus, for the opportunity to address my pack." I turn toward my friends and packmates. "What Trixie said is true; I did place myself in lockdown, an unprecedented move for an alpha. I fully understand—and will not begrudge—anyone who wants to challenge me tonight. However, I must disagree with my alpha emeritus on one point."

I turn back to Trixie and meet her piercing green eyes. "Placing myself in lockdown did not jeopardize my pack, for several reasons. First, I'd already asked my beta, Rob Wolferman, to lead the pack during the full moon. This was Doc Demetrius's recommendation after my injury earlier this month."

Trixie nods. "Duly noted."

"Second, I was in a highly emotional state. I chose to lock myself away rather than act out and bring shame on the pack."

"An alpha must retain control at all times, regardless of his or her emotions."

"Yes, alpha emeritus, under normal circumstances

that is the case." I bow, exposing the back of my neck as a sign of respect. "However, for the record, I was suffering from mate blight."

"Mate blight?" Trixie arches her pale eyebrows. "Is this true Jake?"

"Yes, ma'am." I nod, mentally crossing my fingers that Trixie will acknowledge this as a legitimate reason for an alpha to lock himself away. A werewolf suffering from mate blight—which is the sudden loss of one's mate due to any number of reasons—has the potential of going mad with grief during their next full moon. Without a doubt, I was suffering from mate blight when I thought Mona had left me for Emilio.

Trixie blows out a puff of air, obviously choosing her words carefully. "Your mate blight is duly noted, and under the circumstances, your lockdown was warranted." A few of the younger pack members clap and whistle, but their applause quickly dies at Trixie's withering stare. "However, a call for challengers was issued, and so we will proceed."

Trixie points at the men and women lined up against the wall. "Step forward, look into your alpha's eyes, and either issue a challenge or pass him by."

One by one, each werewolf locks eyes briefly with me, then drops their gaze and crosses to the other side of the room. Teddy quirks a smile when he breezes past, and Marv gives me a quick head nod. As my beta, Rob goes last; he gives me a wink when he passes me.

I exhale in relief—not because I'm unwilling to fight, but because I honestly don't believe any of my wolves are ready to assume the alpha role. "Very well," says Trixie. "The pack stands behind their alpha."

I smile and start walking toward my packmates, but Trixie's next words stop me cold. "Not yet, alpha. There is one more challenger. A lone wolf."

My head snaps back to Trixie, who gives me a grim look. She doesn't like this anymore than I do. Lone wolves are unpredictable. Some, like Teddy, turn up for legitimate reasons, and they're able to integrate into another pack with minimal trouble. Others... well, they're loners for a reason.

"Very well, alpha emeritus. I'm ready."

Trixie flings open the door to the fire escape, sending an artic blast across the room, and the last werewolf I expect to see in Riddle Hill enters the pub's attic. Rafaellus MacTire is huge even for a wolf, with jet-black hair, skin so pale he must loathe sunlight, and body-builder muscles that strain beneath his sweater. I square my jaw and raise my hand, pointing at him. "I issued multiple restraining orders against you. You shouldn't be anywhere in the vicinity of Sophie or Teddy Barker, or any non-super in Riddle Hill."

Rafe smirks. "Relax, alpha trash. I'm not here for any dumb human, nor Teddy and his pretty little mate. I'm here for you."

Teddy darts forward, his fists curled at his sides, and I spin on him. "Leave now, Teddy! Go home to Sophie. That's an order." Teddy's face turns beet red, but he drops his eyes in submission and heads for the locker room.

"Rafaellus MacTire," barks Trixie. "Step forward, face

Alpha Jake Grayclaw Spellman, and issue your challenge."

Shrugging out of his sweater, Rafe kicks off his boots and saunters, bare-chested, to the center of the room. I remove my sweatshirt and toss it aside; there's no way I'm walking out of this room without a fight. Rafe nods respectfully at Trixie before turning toward me with a defiant glower. The loner's irises quicken from brown to yellow, and suddenly his dark werewolf form leaps across the wooden floor and tackles me to the ground.

But my wolf is ready for Rafe, who's merciless in a fight. I should know; this is the second time he's challenged me for control of my pack.

We tussle on the floor, our back legs entangled in our sweats. Rafe manages to kick his legs free first and attempts to pin me down, his canines bared. One of my paws slips on the polished wooden flooring as I try to rise. Rafe lunges for my neck, but I twist away in the nick of time, his jaws snapping empty air instead. I manage to break away and leap to my feet, waiting for another attack that's sure to come.

Out of the corner of my eye I see my packmates; they haven't shifted, but I can sense their highly strung emotions from across the room. None of the werewolves who recall my last fight with Rafe have any love for the loner. Rob's sweatshirt is off; as my beta, he's prepared to take on Rafe if I fail, protecting our pack from the wrong sort of alpha. Marv's shirt is off too; as second beta, he's ready to charge into the fray as well.

Rafe paces back and forth in front of me, saliva dripping from the corners of his mouth. I hold my bushy, gray tail high, waiting for Rafe to realize I'm taunting him with my show of dominance. He finally catches on and growls ferociously, charging me head on. I pivot toward him, but Rafe is a cunning opponent. He switches direction at the last moment, hurtling into my flank.

"Oof!" I yip, as Rafe's broadside maneuver sends me skidding across the floor.

We're both big werewolves, but Rafe is heavier. My paws scramble for purchase, but I'm not fast enough this time. Rafe scrapes his claws down my side, and I howl at the sting of his razor-sharp nails on my hide. Then he clamps his jaws around the back of my neck, his canines digging into my skin. Blood trickles to the floor, and for the first time it occurs to me I might lose this fight.

I'll admit I'm scared—a little for myself, because I know Rafe will claim his pound of wolf flesh—but mostly for Rob, Marv, and the rest of my pack. And Teddy and Sophie, who rues the day she ever dated Rafe.

As he flattens himself on top of me, his mighty jaws dig even harder into my fur, tearing at my skin. I growl and writhe in pain, struggling to shift out from beneath his rangy torso. Rafe is breathing down my neck, literally, and in a moment of blinding clarity, I realize this crazy wolf isn't here to pin me to the ground and spill a little blood with a victory bite.

Rafe intends to slice my jugular!

I think of my sweet, sassy Mona. We just confessed our love for each other, right before we had another argument, and now this vicious werewolf is trying to kill me! I haven't even had a chance to tell Mona I'm sorry, and beg for forgiveness, and kiss her until my insides turn molten.

Confound it all!

I'm not dying today. No. Blasted. Way.

With an angry roar, I draw upon every ounce of my dwindling strength and rear up on my hind legs, flinging Rafe onto the hard floor. He lands on his back, and I pounce on top of him, pinning his legs beneath me. Clamping my jaws around his throat, I hold him down without drawing blood, and I wait.

Finally, he whines in submission, and I slowly, carefully release his neck from my jaws. I stare at him, waiting until he lowers his eyes and looks away. Trixie is watching closely, and when Rafe finally breaks eye contact she shouts, "Jake Grayclaw Spellman remains alpha of the Bay Howlers Pack!"

I hear cheers and a few whoops behind me as I cautiously rise from the floor. My back, shoulders, and neck are bloody and aching from Rafe's bites and scratches. But the fight is over, and although I'm the victor, I'm too weary and hurting to celebrate. I turn toward the locker room, ready to shift back into my man form and stand beneath a hot shower, when I hear shouts behind me—and something else too—paws clacking against the gym's floor.

I turn just in time to see Rafe's muscular werewolf form sail through the air. He knocks me over, pinning me to the ground, and wraps his jaws around my neck. A garbled yelp escapes from my lips, as I realize too late that I should never have turned my back on a beast like Rafe. A hundred random thoughts race through my head

—ranging from Rafe's despicable nature to my regret at missing Cassia's wedding day—but most are wordless lamentations about loving and losing Mona.

Rafe is squeezing my neck harder, cutting off my air supply, and my vision is blurring. I see stars twinkling above me. And each shiny, starry sparkle reminds me of my mate, my heart, my love.

Forgive me, Mona, I whimper as the bright lights fade to darkness. Forgive me.

CHAPTER 36
HEALING TOUCH

MONA

Thursday to Friday, January 31–February 1

It's nearly eleven p.m., and I'm sitting in our front lobby listening to Auntie Imogen's quiet snores. I keep checking my phone, wondering whether anyone challenged Jake tonight, hoping he'll call me himself when he sees my text, praying he's not injured. My phone vibrates, and I swipe to answer.

"Mona... It's Rob."

My heart jolts in my chest. Why is Jake's beta calling me? I'm afraid to ask, "How's Jake?"

"It all happened so fast."

A strangled cry escapes from me. "What? What happened? Tell me!"

"A lone wolf by the name of Rafaellus MacTire showed up and challenged Jake. They fought hard, and Jake won fair and square. But when Jake's back was turned... Rafe attacked him," Rob pauses and sniffles.

"Marv and I brought down Rafe, but not before he hurt Jake real bad."

"No!" I whimper, gripping my phone harder. "Where's Jake now?"

"Doc Demetrius sedated Jake while he was still in his werewolf form, because some of his injuries are easier to patch up that way. Doc's working on him right now in the pub's attic."

Sobbing, I manage to croak, "I'm coming."

I leave a note for my dad and rouse Elmo to ask for a lift in his Jeep. "Thanks," I tell the loyal elf a short while later as he pulls up in front of Howling Shores Pub. "I'll hitch a ride home."

Elmo nods, his little red cap bouncing. "I just hope Mister Jake is alright."

"Me too," I whisper.

I've heard a few stories about Rafaellus MacTire, but I've never met him. Nearly all the drama between Rafe, Teddy, and Sophie happened while I was at sea. I guess Rafe managed to disrupt this year's Firemen's Ball when he punched Will Rossi's lights out. He was arrested for that because it's illegal for a werewolf to hit a non-super. If Rafe hasn't been hauled off to the police station yet, it's going to take a couple of werewolves to hold me back. I'm itching to give him a piece of my mind—and my fist.

I pull open the porthole door, rush through the pub, and dash up the stairs to the attic gym, where Jake and his packmates work out and hold their meetings. I notice all the fitness equipment and mats have been pushed back against the rear wall, I guess to make room for the pack meet. Jake's entire pack is hanging out here, sitting on the benches lining one of the walls, or standing around, talking quietly. I spot Sophie and Teddy speaking with Cassia and Malaki, who gives me a grim nod.

I start heading their way when Rob intercepts me. He has a bandage over one eye, which is bruised and swollen, and his hands and forearms are covered with bite marks. I swallow hard as I realize Jake's injuries are far worse. Rob takes my elbow and guides me toward the men's locker room. "Doc wanted to see you as soon as you arrived."

Fear turns my voice raspy. "Is Jake—"

"He's still fighting."

I'm shaky with apprehension as Rob knocks on the locker room door. One of Doc's veterinary assistants, a middle-aged vampire with a silver-and-black beehive, thrusts her head out. "Are you Mona?"

When I nod, she tells me her name is Elvira. Tugging me into the locker room, she closes the door behind us. "Doc wants to try something while Jake is still in his werewolf form."

She guides me to a makeshift operating room, where an IV drip dangles on a stand behind a massage table, and a portable heart monitor is squeezed into the space between the table and the wall. A rolling cart, littered with surgical equipment, soiled gauze, and stacks of bandages, is shoved into the corner. In the center of the table, a large gray werewolf in torn sweatpants lies on his side facing me, his fur marred with bite marks, his exposed throat shaved and stitched.

I bring a hand up to my mouth but don't say

anything. I can't. Shock has stripped me of my voice. Doc finishes tying off another set of stitches on Jake's back, and then he glances at me. "Mona," he says softly, "I understand you're Jake's mate."

When I nod, Doc says, "That's good. Your presence is going to hasten Jake's healing process."

"How?" I whisper.

"Hug him, careful to avoid his stitches. Let him know you're here... and you care."

"That's all?"

Doc smiles, his fangs glinting in the well-lit room. "A loved one's touch packs a lot of healing potential. And while that's true for all species, it's especially true for werewolves and their mates."

Gently, and oh so delicately, I lay my hands on Jake and murmur, over and over, "It's me, Mona. Please, please, get better Jake." My voice hitches. "Hurry up and heal." I lean over and whisper, "I love you, you ridiculous, obstinate wolf."

Doc is watching the heart monitor. "Good, keep it up. He's stabilizing."

Elvira brings me a chair, and I sit next to Jake, running my hands over his fur and whispering endearments. Ten, maybe fifteen minutes pass, before Doc says, "Okay, he's stable enough for me to wake him, at which point he's going to shift. Elvira, tell the paramedics we'll have a patient ready for transport in a few minutes, and then let his family and packmates know we're moving him to the hospital. They can meet us over there. Mona, why don't you step around the corner, but don't go far. I want you to hold Jake's hand in the ambulance."

"Anything he needs," I say, my voice cracking.

I pace around the locker room, sending up prayers for Jake's recovery, and periodically wiping my teary face. I hear the paramedics barreling through the door and wait until they've moved Jake to a stretcher before peeking at him. I wince, stifling a sob.

All I can see is Jake's bruised face and bandaged neck peeking above the blankets swathing the rest of him, but it's enough. My brave, gorgeous, stubborn Jake fought so hard.

Doc Demetrius waves me over, and I follow the medics and Doc down the service elevator and out to the ambulance. Once we're seated, I take one of Jake's battered hands in both of mine. I don't bother wiping my face; the tears keep trickling down my cheeks. A few fall on Jake's hand, and I feel movement beneath my fingers. I squeeze his hand, and he squeezes back.

I glance up, and Doc nods his head, looking pleased. "I'll let the staff know you need to stay in the room with Jake for the next twenty-four hours. Can you do that?"

"Of course." I lean over and brush my lips over Jake's forehead.

Something starts beeping, and the paramedic—one of Malaki's nieces—whispers, "Maybe hold off on any more kisses for now."

I arch my eyebrows, and Doc chuckles softly. "Our boy is going to be just fine, Mona, just fine."

~

THE NEXT FEW hours pass by in a blur. Other than when Jake is transferred onto a hospital bed and examined by the ER doctors, I'm with Jake the whole time, along with Cassia and Malaki, who claims he's Jake's "uncle." Around three in the morning, the staff moves Jake to a private room. By then everyone, including Malaki and Cassia, has wished me goodnight and left for home.

I'm so, so weary, but I'm afraid to fall asleep in case I drop Jake's hand. I want him to know I'm right here beside him, no matter what. The hard plastic chair provided for visitors is definitely not designed for overnight stays. I shift around, still gripping Jake's hand, but it's impossible for me to get comfortable. Eyeing the hospital bed, I realize there's room for me to squeeze up next to Jake if I lie on my side.

I kick off my ankle boots and carefully slide in next to him. Leaning my head against Jake's shoulder, I'm comforted by the steady rise and fall of his chest next to me. I lay my arm across his torso, careful to avoid all the tubes and wires, and close my eyes. When I wake up a few hours later, my head is resting on Jake's pillow and his bruised, swollen hand is cradling my hip.

I reach my free hand up to Jake's face, which looks so different without his full beard. Elvira had to shave it off so Doc could examine his injuries and stitch up a cut along his jaw. Poor Jake; he's not going to be happy about his missing facial hair.

Jake's eyes are still closed, but his hand is moving. His fingers trace the curve of my hip, follow the dip of my waist, edge along the rise of my shoulder, and finally sink into my hair, which is so wild and curly I'd contemplate one of Elvira's beehives if I thought that would tame my mane.

"Mona," his voice is low and raspy, which is due to his throat injury. Doc told me Jake's vocal chords were damaged in the attack. "Tell me I'm not dreaming."

"You're not dreaming," I whisper, leaning over to plant a kiss on his cheek. Then I recall the paramedic's warning about not kissing, but I figure that only mattered when Jake was unconscious. His roving hand tells me he's very much awake.

"And it's really you."

"It's really me," I assure him. "And if you'd open your eyes, you wouldn't have to ask."

The corners of Jake's mouth turn upward, and I'm sorely tempted to plant a kiss on each side of his mouth, but I don't want to set off any alarms. "My wolf heard you, Mona, and smelled you, and felt you beside me," he whispers. "Your touch—it brought me back. You brought me back, sweetheart."

I don't care whether I start another round of beeping; I place my hand on Jake's handsome but battered face and kiss him full on the lips. "So help me, Jake, if I ever see Rafaellus MacTire, he'll regret the day he ever set boot or paw in Riddle Hill."

Jake starts to laugh and then winces. "I believe you could give him a tongue lashing he would never forget." Jake runs his hand through my curls, twisting a long spiral around his finger. "Mona Lisa DeMaris," his voice is low, gravelly, "I'm a foolish man."

"You don't need to tell me that twice."

Jake grins and then rasps, "I'm a fool for arguing with

you; I'm a fool for letting you leave without saying I'm sorry, and I'm a fool for not telling you how much I love you."

"Oh my foolish, foolhardy, furry man... I adore you." I kiss his cheek. "Now get some sleep."

"Promise you're not going anywhere."

"I'm not going anywhere," I whisper, echoing Jake's words to me at the lighthouse. But even as I say them, I know they're not true. The departure date on my plane ticket tells a different story. I have a contract to fulfill, and a ship to board.

Squeezing my eyes shut to keep the tears from spilling over, I count the days until I need to leave Jake.

Six.

CHAPTER 37

BEWITCHED

JAKE

Friday, February 1

I wake up, every muscle screaming with pain, my throat so raw I can barely speak, but Mona's heady scent fills my nostrils... and nothing else matters.

She's here! She stayed with me all through the night.

I open my eyes and smile, carefully brushing her dark curls from her face. She stirs but doesn't awaken, and I'm grateful to simply be here beside her, watching her sleep. Waking up beside Mona is the sweetest dream of all, one I've fantasized about for years, and it's finally come true. I want to repeat this moment—minus the hospital bed, painful injuries, and IV drip—every morning for the rest of my life.

How am I going to live without my beautiful, bewitching mermaid for the next eight months? Acid forms in the back of my throat. As I swallow it down, I

305

wince at the aching rawness, not all of it caused by Rafe's teeth and claws.

I realize, with all the clarity of hindsight, I waited too long to tell Mona I love her. I was so worried about her rejection and her father's wrath that I kept my mouth shut when I should've spoken up. If I'd been forthright with Mona from the start, perhaps she would've looked for a cruise director job closer to home; perhaps she would've decided the chilly waters of Lake Michigan and Green Bay were enough.

But she's leaving again and all too soon. She hasn't said when, probably because she knows I'll react poorly. I can't help myself. Riddle Hill without Mona will be... uninhabitable.

MONA'S FATHER dropped off an overnight bag for her half an hour ago. She returned to my room with her duffle slung over one shoulder and carrying a large vase filled with roses, gardenias, carnations, and gerbera daisies in a riot of colors—hand selected and sprinkled with faerie dust by Rick DeMaris himself.

Rick also gave Mona a cryptic message for me, which she repeated word for word, confusion written across her face. "Tell Jake to get well, and the alternator is on back order."

I burst out laughing and immediately stopped, grimacing in pain. Mona demanded an explanation, and when I told her I'd promised to help Rick rebuild the hearse, her face softened. When she realized I'd made that promise while she was on her date with Captain Emilio, she started to cry.

Mona is sitting beside me now in one of the plastic chairs, her hair still damp from the shower. She's changed into fresh jeans and a sweater the color of the bay in summer, reminding me yet again of her affinity for the sea.

There's a soft knock on the door, and in walks Aunt Phoebe and Uncle Nash, tanned and rested from their vacation. Phoebe rushes to the bed, throws her arms around my neck, and smothers my brow with motherly kisses. When she finally pulls away, I see tears glistening on her cheeks. Nash, standing next to her, grips one of my bandaged hands and blinks a few times, sniffling like he's got a cold. He's obviously trying to maintain his composure, and I love this big, baldheaded kitchen faerie all the more for it.

Phoebe finally registers Mona sitting on the other side of the bed, and she smiles. "Then it's true."

"What's true?" Mona tilts her head to the side, her damp locks tumbling down her shoulder in the most fetching way possible, clearly unaware of the effect even that simple gesture has on me. The stupid heart monitor starts to beep faster, and I take a few steadying breaths so the stern faerie nurse with the bright blue wings doesn't storm in here, looking for the culprit.

"I've had text messages from Sophie, Cassia, and even Malaki, all telling me you're Jake's mate."

Mona gives Phoebe a shy smile, and I reach my free hand toward Mona, who takes it. "It's true," I rasp, unable to speak any louder than a hoarse whisper. "She's my mate... and it seems I've known it most of my life."

Nash nods. "Malaki called us when we were driving back from the airport and told us about Zeke's spell; what a remarkable piece of magic."

"I only wish we'd known sooner... you both might have been spared some pain," says Phoebe.

"Perhaps," I murmur. "But teenagers are bound to be angsty."

"I wasn't talking about your teen years," replies Phoebe, arching her tipped-up eyebrows. Then my aunt smiles at Mona and spreads open her glorious black-and-gold wings, engulfing all four of us in her feathery faerie embrace. "We couldn't be happier to welcome you into the Spellman-Brownlee clan, Mona dearest."

Mona bites her bottom lip and murmurs, "I couldn't be happier anywhere else."

A steady stream of hospital staff—interspersed with visits from Cassia, Will, and Olivia, plus Sophie, Teddy, Malaki, Granny Catbeam, and my entire pack—precludes any more private time with Mona until after ten p.m., when visiting hours officially end. The duty nurse informs Mona she can stay until midnight, when Doc's twenty-four-hour order expires.

"I think it's time we talk about the future... our future," I murmur, my pulse throttling into overdrive. I take a stabilizing breath, and then another. I've imagined this conversation countless times, and I always figured I'd have it on the beach, or in a fancy restaurant, or even in Malaki's lighthouse again.

I never thought I'd propose to Mona while propped

up in a hospital bed, barely able to speak above a whisper.

I reach out my hand toward her, and she moves over to the bed, but rather than nestling in my arms, she sits and turns toward me. Maybe this is better; at least I can see her beautiful face, each feature so precious to me. "I love you, Mona Lisa DeMaris. It seems I've always known that, although the truth was hidden from me for a long time. You are the only woman for me, my one true love. I need you as much as I need the air in my lungs and the sun on my face." I hesitate, and Mona picks up my hand, gripping it in both of hers.

"Life without you is nothing but dust and shadows," I confess hoarsely. "Please tell me you will be my mate for life. Please marry me, Mona."

There, I've said it. My heart's thundering so hard I've set off the stupid alarm. The duty nurse, a tall vampire with exceptionally long fangs, rushes into the room. Mona moves back to the chair as the nurse checks my pulse, takes my temperature, resets something on the equipment, and gives my pretty mermaid a hard glare. "He needs to rest. No more kissing!"

After the nurse stomps out of the room we both begin to titter. Mona's eyes are twinkling with mirth, and I'm dying to know her answer to my all-important question. "Did you ever read the text message I sent you before your pack meet?"

That's not exactly what I was hoping to hear. I shake my head, apprehension and curiosity warring within me. "Malaki pocketed my phone right after you left the fire station, and told me he'd return it after the meet—

doctor's orders. I guess Doc Demetrius told Malaki I needed to prepare for the pack meet as if it were a football game; one hundred percent mental and physical focus on the challenge and zero distractions." I chuckle softly. "And my dear mermaid, you are a major distraction."

Mona winks at me, my heart starts thrumming again, and I take a few fortifying breaths. She opens the top drawer of the bedside table, withdraws my phone, and hands it to me before sitting back down on the bed.

I turn on the phone and wrinkle my brow at the number of unanswered texts and voicemails. I'll go through them tomorrow. Right now, there's only one text I'm scrolling to find. Before I tap on it, I glance up at Mona. "Is this where you decide to break my heart? Because I need to prepare myself."

Mona rolls her eyes. "Just read it."

I tap my phone and read Mona's text, which she sent me a couple hours before the pack meet. "Jake, I have so much to say to you that I've been struggling for hours to compose my thoughts. But the pack meet starts soon, and I want you to know this before you face any challengers. You are an infuriating, stubborn, overachieving fusspot."

I glance up at her. "Wow. A fusspot? Gee thanks."

She flaps her hand. "Keep reading."

I draw my brows together and brace myself for more insults… but by the time I'm done reading Mona's message, I'm grinning from ear to ear. "You are also kind, caring, generous, and forgiving. You are the only man I have ever loved and ever will love. Past, present, and future—my heart is yours. And now go out there and wallop any challengers so you can come back and give me a victory kiss, my gorgeous, growly werewolf."

I ignore the moisture gathering in the corners of my eyes, reach my arms toward Mona, and murmur in my low, throaty voice, "So I take it that's a yes?"

Mona scoots up the bed toward the pillow, takes my battered face in both her hands, and plants kisses on every bruise, stitch, and scar. Then she fits her lush lips over mine, kisses me until the beeping starts up again, and whispers, "Yes, yes… yes!"

CHAPTER 38

A SIGN COMES DOWN

JAKE

MONDAY, FEBRUARY 4

I'm sitting across from my stunning fiancé in one of the booths in Aunt Phoebe's café, chowing down on my uncle's Nash's spicy Tex-Mex chicken wrap, and laughing at the gargoyles beneath the stone counter. They're blowing kisses at us and fluttering their hands over their hearts. Even Cassia, who's often fed up with their antics, chortles as she tops up our coffee.

"Those little stone fiends have finally moved on!" smirks Cassia.

"What do you mean?" asks Mona, still chuckling at them.

"They spent weeks poking fun at Will and me... now it's your turn to deal with all their sauciness!" Cassia winks before heading over to the next booth.

I peer into my mermaid's eyes, sparkling with humor, and give her a wicked grin. "Maybe we should give those gargoyles something to really wet their stony whistles."

"What do you have in mind?"

I pat the seat next to me. "Come join me over here so we can snuggle."

"But you're still eating."

I arch my eyebrow, the one that's not still puffy and painful. "Snuggles and snacks are a scintillating combination."

Mona rolls her eyes but slides into the bench seat next to me. A contented sigh escapes from me as I drape one arm around Mona and use my free hand to finish my lunch. One of Nash's faerie cousins—Wick or Vick, I'm not sure—clears away our plates and wipes off the crumbs. I notice they've become more efficient; perhaps they'll be suitable successors to my sister after all.

While Cassia still plans to work a couple days a week at the Sit for a Spell Café, her wedding planning business is booming, and she and Will are also refurbishing Gold-meadow, an old barn with an auditorium and sound stage that will soon become Door County's newest concert venue. My heart is overflowing with happiness for my sister and Will, and for Mona and me. The only cloud on the horizon is the fact I need to kiss Mona goodbye in three days.

Aargh! How am I going to survive the next eight months without Mona, except for one all-too-short week in the middle? We've asked Cassia to help us plan our destination wedding in Italy, where Mona and I will be married during her shore leave in June. We'll get to spend seven days together before she has to return to her ship, and I have to fly home. It's going to be sheer torture for me to be separated from Mona for so long.

Mona leans over and kisses my stubbly face. That's another thing I miss: my beard, which I'll grow out as soon as possible. The winters in Wisconsin are cold, and now so is my face.

"Stop brooding," she admonishes me.

I snort. "Goes with the territory. I'm a growly werewolf, remember? Although I believe you also said I was kind, caring, generous, forgiving and um... let me see... ah yes, gorgeous."

Mona pinches my arm, accidently pressing one of my wounds, and I yelp.

"I'm so sorry, Jake!" She throws her arms around my neck, which is still stitched and sore, and plants feather-soft kisses all along my jawline.

Sweet moonglow! This woman just might kill me after all. My bones are melting, my pulse is speed racing, and my heart is hammering so hard my hands are shaking. I clear my throat. "Mona dearest..."

"Hmm?"

"You're going to have to be strong for both of us."

Mona stops kissing me long enough to ask, "What do you mean?"

"We need to pace ourselves. Otherwise I'm going to die from unrequited desire. Four months until our wedding night is a long time, sweetheart."

Mona gives me a saucy grin. "A little anticipation never hurt anyone."

Chuckling, I draw her close and nuzzle her hair. Her phone buzzes on the table, and we both glance down. It's

Rick. She answers and listens. "That's great news, Dad... Sounds good... Yeah, I'll tell him."

"Well?" I ask, but I can already guess the answer.

She smiles. "The chapel passed inspection! Teddy pulled down that ugly red *Closed* sign. We're open for business!"

I squeeze her hand in mine. "I had no doubt the chapel would pass this time. Everyone worked so hard to make this happen."

"But how about you? It must feel a little strange for Teddy to be handling the inspection in your place."

"Actually, it feels pretty good. I think I could get used to delegating."

Mona raises both her eyebrows. "Really?"

"Why? Don't you think I can learn to delegate?"

"A triple-threat overachiever like you? No way."

I start to laugh. "Well, missy, you're going to have to come up with some new insults, because I'm no longer a triple threat."

"How do you figure that?"

I raise one of her hands to my lips, turn her wrist over, and plant a row of kisses from her palm all the way to her elbow. I feel her trembling next to me, and my mouth turns up in a self-satisfied smile.

"Jake," she says, her voice sounding breathless and wispy. "I can't be strong for both of us if you're going to get all swoony on me. Now stop kissing me long enough to explain why you're no longer a triple threat."

"I resigned my post as fire chief."

Mona pulls her arm away. "What? Why? Is something wrong you're not telling me?"

"Nothing's wrong. You were right when you called me a workaholic, and I've decided it's time to make a change." Mona looks so worried that I lean over to kiss the tip of her nose. "Being pack alpha and mayor of Riddle Hill is more than enough leadership responsibility for any man. I'm still a firefighter—it's part of my identity—but I'll be strictly volunteer going forward. I don't want to be on call twenty-four/seven anymore."

Mona cocks her head to the side. "You're sure you're not going to miss the adrenaline rush of being fire chief?"

"Not with you in my life." I smirk. "That's more than enough adrenaline for any man."

Mona starts to pinch my arm but thinks better of it. Then I point to the gargoyles, and we both laugh. Each little stone monster is making loud, smoochy noises as they smother their wrists with kisses.

CHAPTER 39
LITTLE GREEN-EYED MONSTER

MONA

Wednesday, February 6

It's after four, and Phoebe, Cassia, and I are sitting in the inn's lobby, having tea and chatting with Auntie Imogen whenever she stirs from her afternoon nap. We're finalizing the details for Cassia and Will's Valentine's Day wedding, which I'm sorry to be missing, but Dad is feeling much better, and Twila is ready for the additional responsibility. I have no doubt Cassia and Will's wedding will go off without a hitch.

"Hello, ladies," says a gravelly voice behind me, and my heart leaps like a school of porpoises riding sun-kissed waves.

Then I feel Jake's hand on my shoulder, and I turn my face upward, smiling at my handsome yet wounded werewolf. His throat and one eye are still bandaged, and he's covered with bruises and bitemarks. Sometimes my eyes fill with tears just gazing at him, which Jake brushes away with petal-soft kisses that make me cry all the harder.

I'm so crazy in love with this man that I've contemplated breaching my contract and not returning to my ship... but I'd lose too much financially. Jake agrees I need to fulfill my obligation, despite how much we're going to miss each other.

"Come have a seat. I'll get you some tea." I start to rise, but Jake waves me back down.

"No thanks. Malaki just plied Nash, Will, and me with his newest recipe, a tart cherry juice cocktail laced with cream sherry."

"Yuck." Phoebe wrinkles her nose.

"Exactly. Nash suddenly remembered he's allergic to cream sherry, and Will's face took on a greenish pallor. But we did manage to complete the final fittings for our suits before Will got sick."

"Oh no!" Cassia jumps up from her chair. "I'd better go check on Will. There's something about Malaki's concoctions that always makes him nauseous."

"I'd better be leaving too." Phoebe waves goodbye to me, Jake, and Auntie, who wakes up long enough to mumble something about tea with the queen.

The lobby is quiet, peaceful; even Imogen has stopped snoring. Jake joins me on the sofa facing the fireplace and draws me into his arms. I nestle against his chest with a contented sigh, dreading our pending separation.

We both hear the cheery notes of Under the Sea coming from the coffee table, where I left my phone. Good grief, that's Em calling. I tense and I think Jake senses it. "Let me guess," his grumbles. "That's got to be Captain Emilio."

I let the call go to voicemail, but Jake furrows his brow. "You may as well listen to the message. You're not the only one who's wondering why he's calling."

Something tells me I might want to listen to Em's message in private first, but I don't want to do anything to spark Jake's jealous streak, so instead I pick up the phone and tap speaker mode. This is a good way to demonstrate there are no secrets between us, especially when it comes to Em.

"My darling Mona," begins Em. "I miss you. I hope you don't mind me saying that."

Barnacles! I definitely should've screened the call and given the pertinent highlights to Jake. He's gone suddenly rigid, drawing me more closely against his hard, muscular frame.

"I have some surprising news for you. My new ship is still in dry dock for various reasons, and I've been laid off. So I reapplied for any open captain's role—and can you believe it? I'm back on our old ship. We'll be working together again!"

I tap the phone to pause the replay. "Why'd you stop it?" Jake growls. "He clearly has more to say."

"I stopped it because your claws are digging into my side, and your hands are getting furry. You're wolfing out, and I have a non-super family who'll be checking in soon." I don't add that I'm getting really nervous about whatever else Em is about to say.

Jake withdraws his arm from my side and slides a foot away from me on the sofa. I immediately miss the warmth of his body pressed against mine. "Sorry," he rasps. "I'll get my wolf under control."

I give him a curt nod, but all I really want is to throw my arms around this precious man and reassure him with my kisses. I tap my phone, and Em's voice resumes.

"I know what you said, about us not being able to work together again. But I've learned my lesson, Mona. I hope you've forgiven me for breaching your trust. And I hope you will see this as an opportunity for us to still be friends. Take care, and call me if you want to talk."

Jake jumps up from the sofa and starts pacing in front of the fireplace. "I don't believe this guy!" he mutters gruffly. "He wants to pick up right where he left off! And what's he talking about—breaching your trust? You told me he slipped in a kiss you weren't expecting. He sounds like it was much more than that." Jake turns and folds his thick arms across his chest. He trains his amber eyes on me, the gold in the center of his irises widening. Jake's wolf is just beneath the surface, but true to his word, his hands have returned to normal.

I drop my head and stare at the coffee table. It's easier for me to tell Jake what happened if I'm not looking directly at him. "Do you know what water tremors are?"

My voice catches, which Jake must hear, because his voice is gentle as he whispers, "No, I don't. Please tell me."

I detect some movement in Auntie Imogen's portrait, which I choose to ignore. If my mostly ghostly faerie auntie wants to eavesdrop, there's not much I can do about it.

I tell Jake about water tremors, and how important regular swimming is for all merfolk, and how I'd gone too long without a visit to the pool because of everything happening with Dad and the inn. Then I describe what Em did, and how upset and angry I was, and my tears start flowing all over again.

By now my big, burly fiancé is right next to me, engulfing me in his arms. I cry into Jake's shoulder, and he rubs circles into the small of my back. "Oh sweetheart, I'm so sorry that happened to you."

He hands me a tissue, which I use to dab my face. "I'm sorry too, because the last thing I want is for you to be worried about Em all over again when I go back to work."

Jake stops rubbing my back. "You're not seriously thinking of returning to that ship, are you?"

I ball up the tissue in my hands, scowling. "Of course I am. We've already discussed this. I'd lose all my benefits if I don't show up at my ship on time."

Jake clutches his hair. "Mona! This is insane! Can't you see this guy is going to try something again? He's obviously in love with you... and he won't give up until there's a ring on your finger and we've said our vows... which is four months away! Captain Handsy may be classier and smarter than Rafe, but he's just as much of a creep."

"Em got carried away... but he's not violent like Rafe. He wouldn't do anything to hurt me!"

"He's already hurt you," says Jake softly. Then he adds more firmly, "I don't want you anywhere near him." He gazes at me steadily, my protective alpha, and my heart fills to capacity for this man. So much love is coursing through me I'm like the Mighty Mississippi after the spring rains, flooding everything in its wake.

"I suppose I could request a transfer."

"How long before that would come through?"

I roll my lips together. "Months, if it comes through at all." Jake starts to object, but I raise my hand. "We've talked about me finding a U.S.-based job, which I will look for as soon as I finish this tour. But if I break my contract now I'll never find another job in the industry."

Jake tugs me up from the sofa. He tips my chin up and kisses me with such heat my stomach drops to my knees, and my toes curl inside my boots. "You can't go, Mona. You can't work on the same ship with that man."

"I have to go."

Jake's nostrils flare, and the gold in his irises deepens. But before he can growl anymore, we both hear a sudden flap of faerie wings as a dozen silvery feathers flutter to the rug.

"Oh, my heart!" cries Auntie Imogen, flapping again and sending more wing feathers tumbling to the ground. "These chest pains are going to kill me!"

Auntie Imogen's physical heart gave out decades ago. Nevertheless, something is clearly causing her discomfort, so I rush over to the portrait and call up to her. "Can I get you anything for the pain, Auntie?"

She clutches the pearls at her throat, which contrast nicely with her blue evening gown and snowy white velvet stole. If her wardrobe changes are any indication, Auntie Imogen appears as healthy as any other unalive faerie ancestor in Riddle Hill. She's certainly the most vocal. "Oh yes, child. Please go to the walk-in pantry in the kitchen and fetch my smelling salts."

My auntie keeps smelling salts in the kitchen? I suppose I shouldn't be too surprised; Cosmo and Elmo would procure whatever she needs. "Hurry!" she warbles, as if she's going to collapse at any moment.

"Be right back, Auntie!"

Jake starts to follow me, concern etched on his handsome features, but Auntie calls him back. "Yoohoo! Jake Spellman! Please don't leave me alone at a time like this!"

Jake gives me a little shrug as I turn and run down the corridor to the inn's kitchen. I search through every nook, cranny, and container in the walk-in pantry without finding anything resembling smelling salts. Then I move over to the spice racks to no avail, and finally start opening every wooden cabinet in the kitchen, fearing my auntie is going to have a conniption any minute if I don't produce her salts.

Jake finds me scouring the last of the kitchen shelves and takes my hand. "It's okay, honey. Imogen says she's feeling much better. You can stop searching now."

"Are you sure?" I give him a worried look.

Jake brushes back one of my curlicue locks and kisses my forehead. "I'm sure. She's resting comfortably again."

We return to the lobby, where Imogen gives me a beatific smile. "I'm sorry, dearie. I'm feeling much better."

"I guess it was a false alarm," murmurs Jake.

"Yes, a false alarm," repeats Auntie.

I'm relieved Auntie Imogen is better but a little

confused all the same. I take a seat on the sofa next to Jake, bracing myself for another round of arguments, but instead he pulls me against his chest again, cuddling me close. I inhale his wolfish, outdoorsy aroma of pine needles, tilled soil, and night air after a rainstorm. Even sandy shores, sea breezes, and salt water can't compare to Jake's earthy scent.

It's only much later, after I've checked in the non-super family and shown them to their suite, that I notice Jake and Auntie Imogen whispering and tittering together.

They're up to something... but so long as Auntie has found a way to help calm my werewolf... I don't need to know the details.

At least I hope not.

CHAPTER 40
MOONCREST, MONA, AND ME

JAKE

Thursday, February 14

I wipe my greasy hands on a shop rag and toss it onto the tool cabinet inside Rick's shed. "Try it again."

Rick turns the ignition, and the banged-up ancient hearse sputters, shudders... and finally... purrs! Rick shouts, "Woohoo! Rescued—once again—by Jake Spellman!"

Grinning, I lean down to the window so Rick can hear me over the engine. "Let's run her for a good thirty minutes, just to make sure the battery is fully charged."

Rick gives me a thumbs up and climbs out of the hearse, closing the door with all the gentleness of a father soothing a newborn. "You better get home and change. Your sister's getting married in a few hours."

"Yeah... and I still need to pack for the trip."

"Then get to it! I wouldn't want you to miss your plane. Mona would never forgive you."

"Mona has no idea I'm coming," I chuckle. "But don't worry. I'll be on that flight tomorrow morning no matter what."

Rick walks me to the parking lot and gives Granny's motorcycle a reverent pat. "Another classic." Then he tugs one of his pointy ears, which I've learned means he's got something on his mind. "I know you've been wondering about my plans to sell Mooncrest Inn. The truth is... I don't like any of the potential buyers."

"Why not?" I'm grateful Rick is beginning to open up more to me and curious about his plans for Mooncrest.

"They're all a bunch of real estate developers. There isn't a single one of them who wants to run an inn."

"What do they want?"

"Condos!" Rick throws his hands in the air in disgust. "They want to tear down Mooncrest and put up a bunch of condos! Can you believe it?"

I guess my face says it all, because Rick nods. "My thoughts exactly. I guess I don't get to retire after all. I'll just have to work until I'm ready to join Auntie and our other ancestors."

"Aw come on, Rick. There must be some other solution."

"Not really." He shrugs. "Unless..."

"Unless... what?" I prompt.

Rick tilts his head to the side just like Mona, and I find myself softening a little bit more toward my curmudgeonly future father-in-law. "Unless I sell the inn to you and Mona. You're going to need extra income since you gave up your fire chief job, and Mona is going to need to find something closer to home. What could be closer than Mooncrest Inn?"

"Hmm." I'm stupefied by Rick's suggestion, but in a good way. "Becoming an innkeeper isn't something I've ever considered... but if it would allow Mona and me to be together... it just might work. First we need to see what Mona thinks about this idea."

"Mona loves the idea!"

"Oh?" I arch my eyebrows at him. "Is that so?"

Rick gives me a sheepish grin. "Imogen and I called Mona last night and ran the idea past her. Mona says she's in... if you are."

"If my beautiful mermaid fiancé wants to run Mooncrest Inn, who am I to stop her?"

Rick claps me on the shoulder. "Alright, we'll draw up the paperwork after you're back from your trip. Now you better skedaddle—you have two weddings to get to —neither of which you can afford to miss!"

CASSIA'S WEDDING to her rock star husband is everything she hoped it would be—and everything I wanted for my kid sister. It's almost nine, and the reception is going strong in the inn's ballroom, which Mona decorated last week in Cassia's colors, bright pink, purple, and white. Twila has added fresh flowers in tall crystal vases, and scattered hearts and miniature guitar ornaments across every table. It's cheerful, kitschy, and perfectly suits my sister and her husband.

I wander over to the dessert table, which is laden

with slices of red velvet cake. I gulp and turn away, but not before Malaki snatches up two plates and shoves one in my hand. "Here, eet used to be yer favorite."

"I *never* liked red velvet cake."

"Of course you did... You loved eet." He leans over and whispers, "An' this eez my recipe, which I geeve to Sophie so she can make it at da bakeshop. I used to make this all da time when you ver little boy. Then one day, pouf, you stopped likin' eet."

Frowning, my hands shaking slightly, I accept the cake from Malaki and take a bite. Then another and another. "It's... fantastic. Absolutely delicious."

"I told you dat. Vhy you not believe me?"

"When was the last time you made this cake for me?"

Malaki shrugs. "I guess a long time. Mebbe... mebbe... ven you five years old."

"Around the time Dad cast the memory spell..." I pause, contemplating the kind of magic Zeke would have incanted to make me forget the love of my life. What if other random things got caught up in his spell? Like maybe I loved red velvet cake almost as much as I loved Mona when I was five. "I wonder..."

"You wonder if you associate dis cake vis Mona Lisa?"

"Maybe." I shrug. "All I know is I forgot I liked it for the longest time... and now I want that recipe."

Malaki chuckles. "Who knows? Mem'ry spells, they are a funny business." He pats my shoulder and tells me to enjoy my trip.

I'm about to go search for my sister when she sidles up next to me with her new husband. "I think it's time you hit the road, Jake."

I roll my eyes at Cassia's lame joke. "I guess I should get going. With any luck, I'll grab a few hours of shuteye before the flight."

Cassia stands on her tiptoes and kisses my cheek. "She's going to be so surprised!"

"You sure everything's set?"

Cassia nods. "It's all handled. You just need to be on that ship before it departs."

I give my sister a hug and turn to shake Will's hand. "Congratulations! You married an amazing woman."

Will grips my hand, giving me his high-wattage celebrity grin, the one that still makes grown women swoon. "I sure am one lucky fool," he drawls. "Now it's your turn, brother."

I clap him on the back, wave goodbye to our assorted relatives and friends, and dash out front to Granny's motorcycle. I layer up; it's going to be a mighty chilly ride to O'Hare Airport, but it's a clear moonlit night, and I'm ready—more than ready—for my next chapter.

CHAPTER 41
ALL ABOARD

MONA

Saturday, February 16

I'm standing with the other officers in the ship's crowded main atrium, welcoming guests as they board our vessel through the passenger terminal. A live band is playing music from the past few decades, servers are circulating with finger food and cocktails, and there's a magician performing tricks for the kids nearby. Guests and crew alike are laughing all around me, and my newly trained staff is stepping right up to answer questions and offer directions.

Meanwhile, I'm struggling to keep my fake smile plastered in place.

I miss Jake so much my stomach twists with loss every time I think of him; my yearning feels more like grieving. I know I'll be seeing him in four months, but right now that seems a lifetime away, and I don't know how I'm going to manage in the meantime.

Most of the guests have arrived, and my team is beginning to herd them toward the various dining areas. Standing in a crowded room, mourning the man I left behind, has left me breathless. As the atrium begins to thin out, I feel a little less claustrophobic and start to regain my composure.

Until I see a tall, broad-chested man with a week's worth of stubble coming down the passenger tunnel. He looks so much like Jake that I intake a sharp breath, pressing my hand against my heart. The man is wearing a light tan jacket, gray tee, and jeans. He pauses as he enters the ship and glances upward, smiling at the glass-enclosed levels soaring above us. I get the impression this is his first cruise.

Then he slowly scans the room as if he's searching for something... or someone. I take a step closer, drawn by his similarity to my fiancé, who's an ocean away. The man finally turns his head in my direction, and his handsome face, which has a pink scar above one eyebrow, breaks into a wide grin.

"Mona!" he says, his voice low and gravelly.

I bring a hand up to my mouth, so shocked I'm unable to speak. My eyes begin to water and soon they're gushing, tears streaming down both cheeks.

It's him, my handsome, scarred werewolf, the triple threat of Riddle Hill, the grown man who's never traveled more than three hundred miles from home. "Jake?" I murmur, my voice shaking.

One of my crew members, a young selkie named Selina, gives me a gentle nudge. "I think it's customary to greet your fiancé with a kiss."

Hmm... it seems my crew is in on this little secret.

I start to laugh through my tears as Jake strides over, picks me up by the waist, and spins me around. I throw my arms around his neck, giggling like a teenager. Everyone in the atrium—mostly strangers, but also my friends on the crew—begin to applaud and cheer. Someone starts a silly chant and soon everyone joins in. "Kiss! Kiss! Kiss!"

Jake sets me gently on my feet and winks. "Show time." Then he bends me back at the waist, fits his lips over mine, and gives me a kiss so swoonworthy I hear happy sighs from the older women in the crowd. I'm turning red from all the attention as well as the lack of proper crew member decorum I'm displaying, but my heart is so light I think it might sprout faerie wings and take flight.

When we finally come up for air, Jake whispers, "It's time for you to go get changed, sweetheart."

"Changed?"

Selina loops an arm through mine and gives Jake a friendly nod. "I've got this, Mister Spellman. Meanwhile, Fernando will show you to your cabin." She addresses another one of my teammates, a recent college grad from Nebraska who's never been on a boat before. "Meet you in the ship's library in an hour." Fernando nods, smiles at Jake, and leads him away.

Once we're in the elevator, I turn to Selina. "What's going on... other than the obvious... I'm absolutely shocked and thrilled Jake is here, but I get the feeling something more is happening."

Selina chuckles. "I'll say."

"Miss Mahoney, could you please explain to your boss—you know, the lady who writes your performance reviews—what in the seven seas is going on!"

Laughing, Selina says, "Okay boss! Mister Spellman has purchased the Shipboard Wedding Package."

"But I'm working."

Selina grins. "True, but the captain has granted you twenty-four hours' leave starting right now, so you can get married tonight, dance under the stars, and then... ahem... stay in your cabin and um—"

I hold up my hand to stop my overly helpful crew member. "Thanks. I can fill in the rest of the blanks on my own." Selina starts to titter, and I wind up chuckling along with her.

I arrive at my cabin door to find it covered with sparkly hearts, magic wands, faerie wings, and mermaid decorations. I duck under a large *Jake and Mona* sign dangling from the doorframe and step inside. Balloons dot the corners of my cabin, an enormous gift basket filled with gourmet snacks sits on the desk beside two dozen roses, and a bottle of champagne is chilling in an ice bucket.

But the best part is the large gift box on my bed. Removing the lid, I bring a hand to my mouth, speechless. My amazing Jake—and I suspect his equally remarkable sister—surprised me with a lovely sleeveless dress with a beaded bodice, *V* neckline, and short, flouncy skirt in my favorite shade of blue-green, the exact shade of Green Bay in the summer.

Tears prick my eyes as I turn to Selina. "I don't know how you and the staff pulled this off behind my back but thank you!" I give the young selkie a quick hug before she scoots out the door.

My stomach is fluttering as much as my pulse by the time I arrive at the library. I'm relieved to see Em will not be performing the ceremony; instead the ship's chaplain, a jolly white-haired man who I suspect has a bit of leprechaun in him greets me as I enter. Selina and Fernando will be witnessing the ceremony; they're standing just inside the door talking to Jake, who is so dashing my knees go all wobbly. I almost wish I could extend my tail fin for stability, but if Jake can keep his wolf in check, I can certainly manage my inner mermaid.

Jake's wearing a white suit with a blue-green tie the same shade as my dress. When he sees me his face splits into a broad smile. He steps toward me, gives me a small bow as if we're living inside a Regency novel, and then extends his elbow. "You look stunning," he whispers.

"So do you." We both chuckle as we turn toward the chaplain.

Before we know it, we're exchanging vows, and Jake is slipping a white gold ring encrusted with diamonds and sapphires on my finger. It's exquisite, but I don't have time to admire it now because the officiant is asking me to place a ring on Jake's finger.

I widen my eyes, about to confess I'm completely unprepared, when Jake reaches into his pocket and places a band in my hand. It's a more modest, masculine version of my ring, which I place on his finger. Then we're pronounced husband and wife, and Jake sweeps me into his arms for another kiss so filled with ardor and longing that I'm lightheaded when he finally breaks away.

"My turn." Smiling, I gingerly brush back the wayward lock of hair that's flopped over Jake's forehead, something I've been itching to do since high school. Then placing my hands on either side of my husband's stubbled jaw, I press my lips against his, pouring all my love and devotion into a single, searing kiss.

Eventually we stop necking long enough to catch our breath, sign the legal documents, and thank the crew for arranging everything. When we're finally alone inside my cabin, Jake pulls me close with a saucy smirk. He turns my hand over and proceeds to plant butterfly kisses on my palm, my wrist, and all along my arm, sending ripples of heat up and down my spine.

Placing my hand against his chest, I ask the question that's been on my mind since he boarded the ship. "How long have you been working on this utterly crazy and completely romantic surprise?"

"A little over a week, which was cutting it close by about four months." Jake grins. "All credit goes to Cassia for the planning and Imogen for the original idea."

My mouth gapes open. "I figured Cassia was involved, but I had no idea Auntie Imogen was so..." I narrow my eyes. "Sneaky! The smelling salts, right?"

Jake winks. "Worked like a charm." He draws me into his chest, his breath warm against my neck as he nuzzles my hair. "This is my dream come true."

I wrap my arms around my husband's muscled torso with a contented sigh. I'm living out my dream too, the one I had back in high school when I finally worked up enough nerve to invite the hot quarterback to my turn-about dance.

I'm married to Jake Grayclaw Spellman—pack alpha, mayor, firefighter, hero—and the only man on land or sea I've ever loved.

In a voice as low and sexy as my werewolf husband's, I whisper, "Mine too."

EPILOGUE - FAMILY REUNION

JAKE

One Year Later

"Found it!" cries Mona, sweeping into our blue-and-white kitchen. "You left it on the hickory shelf in the bathroom." She chuckles. "I think you're as fond of Mama's old tub as I am!"

I put away the last dish in the cupboard, turn toward my stunning wife with a teasing leer, and arch an eyebrow dramatically. "I've discovered the many healing qualities of mutual water therapy."

Mona snorts at my corniness and hands me the cell phone, her fingers brushing over mine. A familiar zing runs through my hand, up my arm, and encircles my heart with a sizzling jolt of heat. It's a strange reaction, one that still confuses and exhilarates me. Some supers, like Trixie and Doc, tell me it's the sign of perfectly attuned mates. Others, like Auntie Imogen and Granny Catbeam, smirk and tell me it's the magic of true love.

Whatever the reason, I'll never tire of the zaps from Mona's touch. Whether they occur when she tucks her hand inside mine, or seals her lips over mine, or presses her body against mine when we settle in at night... I'm entirely undone by her love.

Mona grins up at me, her chocolate-brown eyes twinkling, and I know she feels it too.

"Did you give our flight and hotel info to Twila?" I ask. As Mona nods, I continue down my mental checklist. "And Cassia and Will... and Phoebe and Nash... and—"

"I've told half the town by now!" Mona laughs. "You really are such a fusspot."

"But I'm also kind, caring, generous, forgiving and—"

"Gorgeous." Mona pats my thick beard, nips my lip, and winks. "But if you don't finish packing, my hunky werewolf, we're going to miss our flight."

"Oh, Mona," I groan, reaching for her waist.

But she deftly hops out of reach. "No more hugs until we're at the airport."

I growl playfully but don't argue with the CEO of Mooncrest Lodgings and Resort. After all, she's the boss.

"MONA LISA! JAKE! OVER HERE!" calls Rick DeMaris, rising from a table inside a small, crowded bistro in Rome.

Mona gives a little squeal and dashes over to her father, throwing her arms around him. A stunning woman bearing a striking resemblance to my wife rises from her chair, skirts around the table, and walks toward Mona. She gives me a shy smile and then waits as Mona unwinds herself from Rick's embrace.

"Mama," whispers Mona, her voice quaking. The two raven-haired beauties take a tentative step toward each other, and then suddenly they're hugging and crying and laughing all at once. I feel my own eyes watering at Mona and Karyn's reunion, and swallow against the tightness in my throat.

Rick sniffles a few times and murmurs, "I think they need a little time to themselves. Come on, there's something I want you to see."

I fall into step beside my father-in-law. We cross a couple of streets, avoid getting mowed down by a Fiat, and enter a palazzo. "How has retirement been treating you?" I already know the answer, because there's no doubt in my mind Mona's dad is happier than I've ever seen him.

Rick turns to me with a contented smile, nothing like his former Jack O' Lantern grimaces. "It's been good, Jake, really, really good."

As we meander through the square, Rick inquires about Mooncrest, the Peppertail elves, and Auntie Imogen, who's feisty as ever. We come to a stop in front of a tall, stone pedestal, and Rick points out the statue on top. "That's the Capitoline Wolf, suckling the twins, Romulus and Remus. According to legend, she saved the founders of ancient Rome. That wolf reminds me of you."

"Me? How so?" I ask, gazing up at the famous sculpture.

"You saved my old hearse from the junk heap, you

saved Mooncrest from fire and real estate developers—and most important of all—you saved my daughter's life. That makes you a hero in my book."

I continue peering at the statue, wondering whether the she-wolf is my progenitor, my first ancestor. Then I glance at Rick and shake my head. "Actually, it's the other way around. Sometimes it's the wolf that needs rescuing."

"Huh? I don't get it." Rick draws his eyebrows together, waiting for me to explain.

"Mona saved me."

Rick gives a small shrug, like he's not about to argue the point. Then he claps a hand on my shoulder and guides me back to the bistro, where my mate is waiting for me.

She knows as well as I do who really did the rescuing.

She knows the strength of her healing touch, the magic of our conjoined hearts.

Mona Lisa DeMaris freed Jake Grayclaw Spellman, the former triple threat, from his darkest nightmares and deepest fears.

The beautiful half mermaid of Mooncrest Inn saved the loneliest, neediest werewolf of all.

MALAKI ACHERON'S SPECIAL RECIPE

FORGET-ME-NOT RED VELVET CAKE

LIKE I TOLD JAKE, MEM'RY SPELLS ARE A FUNNY BUSINESS. When he vas a little boy, he loved this cake, den he forgot an' panicked whenever it vas on da menu. Weird, huh? All I can tell you ees this: it's da most popular cake at Sophie's shop. Now it's yer turn to try it out.

Cake ingredients and instructions:

1 ½ cups sugar

½ cup butter

3 eggs

2 ounces red food coloring

2 tablespoons cocoa

1 teaspoon salt

1 teaspoon vanilla

1 cup buttermilk

2 cups flour

1 ½ teaspoons baking soda

1 tablespoon white vinegar

Grease and line the bottom of two 9-inch layer cake pans. Cream butter for 1 to 2 minutes. Then add sugar and eggs, beating until combined. Next, add red food coloring and cocoa. Mix salt, vanilla, and buttermilk in a separate bowl; add to the mixture, alternating with the flour. Mix baking soda and vinegar in a separate bowl, and then fold it into the batter without beating. Immediately pour into layer pans and bake at 350 degrees for 30 minutes or until the cake springs back when lightly touched. Let it cool thoroughly before frosting.

Frosting ingredients and instructions:

5 tablespoons flour

1 cup milk

1 cup butter

1 cup sugar

1 teaspoon vanilla

Rainbow sprinkles

Boil flour and milk until smooth and thick, stirring constantly. Let stand at room temperature until cold. Beat butter, sugar, and vanilla until creamy. Add flour mixture and beat until fluffy. Frost the cake and dust with rainbow sprinkles.

Author's Note

Thanks so much for reading *Return to Mooncrest Inn*! I hope you enjoyed this sweet, closed-door paranormal romance about Jake, the triple-threat werewolf, and Mona, the sassy mermaid. Please consider taking a moment and leaving a review, even a sentence or two. Reader reviews help other readers discover new books—and they are vitally important for indie authors like me.

If you're new to the Faeries of Door County series, each novel is a standalone story focused on a different main character from the Spellman family. Chronologically speaking, *Rhyme, Riddle, and Romance* occurs the summer before the events in *Half a Faerie* and *Return to Mooncrest Inn*, however, the books can be read and enjoyed in any order.

Producing a book is a collaborative process, and this one is no exception. Many people helped to shape this story, including friends, family, and my husband Steve, who read and commented on early drafts, Martha Reineke of MK Editing who provided invaluable feedback, Diogo Leite of Book Design Company who designed the cover, and my amazing ARC team of readers and reviewers. I adore you all—thank you!

Lastly and most importantly, I give thanks to my

Heavenly Father, the Author of the greatest story ever told. All other love stories pale in comparison to His.

Toni Cabell

John 1:1

BOOKS BY TONI CABELL

If you're looking for sweet, slow-burn romance with swoony kisses, second chances, and funny, heartwarming characters, don't miss the complete **Faeries of Door County** series. Winner of Best Paranormal Romance, each novel is a standalone story set in the same cozy small town:

- *Rhyme, Riddle, and Romance*
- *Half a Faerie*
- *Return to Mooncrest Inn*

A fast-paced adventure full of magic, romance, humor, sword fighting, dangerous creatures, and the power of light versus darkness, **Serving Magic** is a YA Epic Fantasy series with Steampunk and Regency vibes. Winner of The Wishing Shelf Book Awards and recognized by Indies Today as a Top 5 YA Fantasy series by an indie author:

- *Lady Apprentice, Book 1*
- *Lady Mage, Book 2*
- *Lady Liege, Book 3*
- *Lady Spy, Book 4*
- *Lady Reaper, Book 5*

In the arid hills of Toresz, there's one thing more dangerous than divining for water... falling in love with the enemy. **Water Witch** is YA Romantasy duology packed with action, danger, intrigue, royal politics, and romance. Winner of The Wishing Shelf Book Awards:

- *The Lightness of Water, Book 1*
- *The Way of Water, Book 2*

Find all Toni's available books and upcoming new releases on tonicabell.com and Amazon. All her novels are also available in audiobook format on Audible and Apple Books.

About the Author

Toni Cabell is a closed-door fantasy romance author whose books reflect her Christian values, which means you'll find no swearing, no excess violence, and no spice. Here's what you *will* find...

- Clean fantasy | magical worlds
- Wholesome romance | just kisses
- Deep friendships | quirky families
- Sassy and strong gals | swoony and protective guys
- (YA books) Swords and battles | no gory descriptions

Her novels have won Silver and Bronze Medals in The Wishing Shelf Book Awards, two Gold Medals in the Global Book Awards, multiple B.R.A.G. Medallions, and awards for writing Clean YA Fantasy from Incipere Awards.

Toni lives with her handsome husband in a small village along the shores of Lake Michigan, where she's able to walk to the bookstore, library, coffee shop, and bakery (although not always in that order). She's happy to report her adult children reside nearby and provide her with a steady supply of affection, amusement, and just the right smattering of chaos.

Toni loves to stay in touch with her readers. Please sign up for her newsletter at tonicabell.com, where you can download two free novellas:

Toni posts regularly about her indie author journey, life lessons, what inspires her, and her books on Instagram and Facebook. Also consider joining her Reader Group on Facebook, @onceuponaswoon, where she hangs out with some of her closed-door author friends and readers like you.